AROUND THE
RIVER'S BEND

★ ★ ★

BOOKS BY GILBERT MORRIS

Through a Glass Darkly

THE HOUSE OF WINSLOW SERIES

1. *The Honorable Imposter*
2. *The Captive Bride*
3. *The Indentured Heart*
4. *The Gentle Rebel*
5. *The Saintly Buccaneer*
6. *The Holy Warrior*
7. *The Reluctant Bridegroom*
8. *The Last Confederate*
9. *The Dixie Widow*
10. *The Wounded Yankee*
11. *The Union Belle*
12. *The Final Adversary*
13. *The Crossed Sabres*
14. *The Valiant Gunman*
15. *The Gallant Outlaw*
16. *The Jeweled Spur*
17. *The Yukon Queen*
18. *The Rough Rider*
19. *The Iron Lady*
20. *The Silver Star*
21. *The Shadow Portrait*
22. *The White Hunter*
23. *The Flying Cavalier*
24. *The Glorious Prodigal*
25. *The Amazon Quest*
26. *The Golden Angel*
27. *The Heavenly Fugitive*
28. *The Fiery Ring*

THE LIBERTY BELL

1. *Sound the Trumpet*
2. *Song in a Strange Land*
3. *Tread Upon the Lion*
4. *Arrow of the Almighty*
5. *Wind From the Wilderness*
6. *The Right Hand of God*
7. *Command the Sun*

CHENEY DUVALL, M.D.[1]

1. *The Stars for a Light*
2. *Shadow of the Mountains*
3. *A City Not Forsaken*
4. *Toward the Sunrising*
5. *Secret Place of Thunder*
6. *In the Twilight, in the Evening*
7. *Island of the Innocent*
8. *Driven With the Wind*

CHENEY AND SHILOH: THE INHERITANCE[1]

1. *Where Two Seas Met*

THE SPIRIT OF APPALACHIA[2]

1. *Over the Misty Mountains*
2. *Beyond the Quiet Hills*
3. *Among the King's Soldiers*
4. *Beneath the Mockingbird's Wings*
5. *Around the River's Bend*

LIONS OF JUDAH

1. *Heart of a Lion*

[1]with Lynn Morris   [2]with Aaron McCarver

02C

AROUND THE RIVER'S BEND

★ ★ ★

GILBERT MORRIS & AARON McCARVER

BETHANY HOUSE PUBLISHERS
MINNEAPOLIS, MINNESOTA 55438

Published by Bethany House Publishers
A Ministry of Bethany Fellowship International
11400 Hampshire Avenue South
Bloomington, Minnesota 55438
www.bethanyhouse.com

Printed in the United States of America by
Bethany Press International, Bloomington, Minnesota 55438

Library of Congress Cataloging-in-Publication Data

Morris, Gilbert.
    Around the river's bend / by Gilbert Morris & Aaron McCarver.
        p.   cm. — (The spirit of Appalachia ; 5)
      ISBN 1-55661-889-1 (pbk.)
      1. Frontier and pioneer life—Fiction. 2. Appalachian Region—Fiction. I. McCarver, Aaron. II. Title.
      PS3563.O8742 A88   2002
      813'.54—dc21   2002011111

Dedication

To my friend Aaron McCarver—

a friend that sticketh

closer than a brother!

GILBERT MORRIS spent ten years as a pastor before becoming Professor of English at Ouachita Baptist University of Arkansas. During the summers of 1984 and 1985, he did postgraduate work at the University of London. A prolific writer, he has had over twenty-five scholarly articles and two hundred poems published in various periodicals. He and his wife live on the Gulf Coast of Alabama.

AARON McCARVER teaches drama and Christian literature at Wesley College in Florence, Mississippi. His deep interest in Christian fiction and broad knowledge of the CBA market have given him the background for editorial consultation with all the "writing Morrises" as well as other novelists. It was through his editorial relationship with Gilbert that this book series came to life.

Contents

PART V: The Captives

Character List

After Sabrina Fairfax's father dies, Sabrina comes upon a deed to a piece of land in the New World. The description of her property is vague, and she doesn't even know if the deed is legal, but since she has nothing to lose, she decides to set off across the sea. She struggles with the unidentified emptiness she feels inside her while at the same time trying to adjust to this strange new land, where log cabins with dirt floors replace the finer things she was accustomed to back in England. Endless suitors make their way to her doorstep, while the man who can truly make her happy watches patiently as her servant.

Sabrina Fairfax—When Sabrina's father dies, she is forced to leave the life of luxury that she has always known and make her way to America to claim a wild tract of land her father had purchased. She struggles with an emptiness that she can't identify.

Sion Kenyon—He grew up poor in Wales and worked as a farmer and a miner before being jailed for a crime he didn't commit. Sabrina agrees to take him to America as her indentured servant. There he learns to hunt, fish, and live off the land.

Rees Gruffyd—Sion saves Rees's life when Rees is injured in a mining accident. Sion feels indebted to Rees for taking him in when he had no job and no place to live.

Hannah Spencer—She is a friend to Sabrina as she learns the ways of the frontier. She finds herself attracted to a handsome newcomer, even though she is promised to Fox.

Fox—He thought his relationship with Hannah was secure until a stranger from the Old World threatens to take his place in Hannah's life.

Josh Spencer—Hannah's brother is determined to help Hannah get her land free and clear with the help of his boss, Andrew Jackson.

Hawk and Elizabeth Spencer—Hannah and Josh's parents struggle to stay out of their children's lives as the children learn to make good decisions.

Around the River's Bend

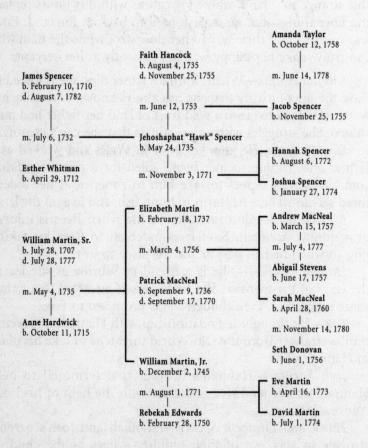

James Spencer
b. February 10, 1710
d. August 7, 1782

m. July 6, 1732

Esther Whitman
b. April 29, 1712

Faith Hancock
b. August 4, 1735
d. November 25, 1755

m. June 12, 1753

Jehoshaphat "Hawk" Spencer
b. May 24, 1735

m. November 3, 1771

Amanda Taylor
b. October 12, 1758

m. June 14, 1778

Jacob Spencer
b. November 25, 1755

Hannah Spencer
b. August 6, 1772

Joshua Spencer
b. January 27, 1774

William Martin, Sr.
b. July 28, 1707
d. July 28, 1777

m. May 4, 1735

Anne Hardwick
b. October 11, 1715

Elizabeth Martin
b. February 18, 1737

m. March 4, 1756

Patrick MacNeal
b. September 9, 1736
d. September 17, 1770

Andrew MacNeal
b. March 15, 1757

m. July 4, 1777

Abigail Stevens
b. June 17, 1757

Sarah MacNeal
b. April 28, 1760

m. November 14, 1780

Seth Donovan
b. June 1, 1756

William Martin, Jr.
b. December 2, 1745

m. August 1, 1771

Rebekah Edwards
b. February 28, 1750

Eve Martin
b. April 16, 1773

David Martin
b. July 1, 1774

PART I

Sabrina

December 1791 – March 1792

A New Kind of Woman

One

*L*ong slanting beams of pale sunlight illuminated the dusky shadows in the room where Sabrina Fairfax lay soaking in a copper tub filled with soapy water. The bars of light swarmed with tiny motes of dust that rose from the multicolored carpet, and for one moment Sabrina opened her eyes and watched them sleepily. "They dance like tiny butterflies," she murmured, then smiled and sank her body lower into the warm water. "I'm starting to talk to myself—the first sign of losing my mind. I'll wind up in Bedlam if I keep on doing that!"

The renovated bathroom had once been one of the smaller bedrooms on the upper floor. It was large with a high ceiling of copper tiles inlaid with intricate designs of shells and ivy. The twin floor-length windows were decorated with light blue damask draperies now pulled back to let the light in, and the dark wooden floor had a large and colorful Wilton-type carpet in the center.

The room had been painted white with accents of gold around the door, windows, and dado. An assortment of framed pictures of outdoor scenery, all with horses in them, covered the walls in all shapes and sizes. The pictures had been chosen by Sabrina, and while some were very expensive paintings, others were simple sketches that she had bought simply because they appealed to her. She was a young woman who lived by whim, and since she was the daughter of Sir Roger Fairfax—his only child, in fact—she could afford to indulge most of her desires. Several of the pictures featured horses jumping over fences. One was a painting of a fox chase with a young woman leading the riders, and since the woman was Sabrina herself, she favored it. She had hired Sir Charles Patton, one of England's foremost artists, to do the painting, and despite his protests she had dictated every item of the painting—even insisted that the dog be true to life. Sabrina let her gaze rest on the hound that led the pack. "Good old Thor," she murmured. "Next Thursday's the hunt. I'll have to remember that. I haven't been out in two weeks now."

It had been a pleasant fall, but now that they were in December the weather had turned chilly. Individuals like Sabrina Fairfax could insulate themselves against the biting, icy winds and the freezing snows with money. Money would buy warm fur coats. Money would buy warm underwear and thick socks and tight boots. Money would buy endless logs to burn in the huge fireplaces, driving away the chills and protecting the wealthy. The poor, of course, shivered and hugged their thin clothing about them and nurtured the few coals that they could afford. Sabrina Fairfax knew little of this, for she had scarce contact with any world save that of the wealthy who inhabited London's environs.

A faint sound caught Sabrina's attention, and she twisted her head around until she could see the far side of the room. A very large multicolored cat had gotten up from the red plush chair and was stretching mightily. The cat yawned, exposing an enormous red mouth, then jumped out of the chair and came across the room, regarding Sabrina with round green eyes. The tortoise-shell cat with a beautiful coat reared up on his hind legs, placing his front paws on the edge of the copper tub. Sabrina laughed as she stroked his fur. "Why don't you jump in, Ulysses? You could use a bath, too."

The cat stared at his mistress for a time as if waiting for her to say more, then turned and went back to his chair. He curled up and went back to sleep at once.

"You're the laziest cat I've ever seen, Ulysses. You don't do anything except catch a few mice. I should rent you out as a mouser."

Sabrina took her eyes off the cat and idly lay luxuriating in the warm water. She loved baths and scandalized the whole household by insisting on at least one every day. Paul, one of the servants, was kept busy hauling gallon after gallon of hot water up the stairs and then emptying it later. Sabrina had heard him once whisper to her maid, Cecily, "Gor! She don't do nothin' but lay around in that hot water. It's a blazin' wonder she ain't puckered from head to foot! Maybe she is, hey?"

Sabrina glanced down at her soapy form to assure herself that she was not puckered yet. The sight assured her, for at the age of twenty there was not a sign of a pucker. She was a tall young woman with long blond hair now tied up to keep it dry and a pair of astonishingly large and brilliant green eyes. She didn't think of herself, however, as a true beauty. She felt that her face was too broad, her cheekbones too prominent. Still, men didn't seem to notice her imperfections. They were dazzled by the directness of her glance, the creamy texture of her skin, and her tall, erect carriage. She was a full-bodied young woman aware of her own charms and not in the least averse to using them to tease the men that came flocking around her.

Finally Sabrina sat up and called out loudly, "Cecily— Cecily, where are you? Come here at once!"

The door opened, and a diminutive young woman with thick white towels over her arm came sailing in. She was no more than eighteen and was as small and thin as her mistress was tall and statuesque. "I 'ad to get the fresh towels, didn' I, miss," she protested. "I can't do everything!"

Sabrina laughed. "No, you can't. Here, I think I've had enough of this." She stood up carefully and stepped out onto the thick crimson rug that had been placed to catch the water. She stood as Cecily industriously dried her off. Finally she said, "Here, that's good enough. Now the powder."

As Cecily fussed over Sabrina, powdering her and helping her into a thick, fluffy robe, it never occurred to Sabrina Fairfax that most young women never got this sort of care. She had been accustomed to it from the time she was a child, and now it was the way the world operated as far as she was concerned.

Leaving the room, she walked down the hall barefooted, turned into a huge walnut door that swung silently as she entered, and moved across the room to stand before a dressing table. Her clothes were laid out on the bed, and she snapped,

"Hurry up! It's cold in this room. You let the fire go down."

"Well, that's Paul's job, ain't it, now?" Cecily protested. She went over and poked the fire up quickly, then was back and helped Sabrina dress. First a fine white linen chemise and then a pair of white silk pantalettes ending just below the knee. Next came the fine silk corset with whalebone stiffening at the ribcage and sides that Cecily fastened tightly in back, pulling and tugging until it met her satisfaction. Cecily then helped her into a pair of fine silk stockings, and Sabrina stepped into a three-tiered panier that was arranged at her waist. Finally, Cecily slipped a dress of light green silk over Sabrina's head and fastened it.

Finally Sabrina sat down and said, "Now see what you can do with my hair. It's a mess! I should have washed it."

"Oh, miss, it would 'ave taken forever to dry! We'll do that later in the day."

"I'm going riding today. We'll have to do it tomorrow." Sabrina pulled several pins out of her hair and let it fall over her shoulders. The long blond tresses were thick and lustrous and took considerable care—which she herself never gave it. She had been glad to find Cecily, who had been with her for two years now, and was better at fixing hair than anyone Sabrina had found in all of London. Cecily was a rather flighty young woman, nervous and prone to crying jags at times when things did not go right. Nevertheless, she was a marvelous hairdresser, and now with skilled fingers she gathered Sabrina's hair back off her forehead and then proceeded to make ringlets around the sides and back, curled the ends under, and then tied the back up with a dark green ribbon.

"You're going riding with Sir Charles?"

"Yes, but it won't be a long ride. He tires so easily."

"*You* never tire!" Cecily said firmly. "I don't see 'ow you do it, miss."

"How I do what?"

"How you sit sideways on a 'orse. Wot keeps you from falling off backward? I can't tell for the life of me."

"There's a horn that goes to the side. I keep my right leg hooked around it."

"It don't seem natural, though, sitting *sideways* on a horse.

None of the riders at the races do."

"The jockeys? Well, of course not! They're all men." A rebellious streak surfaced then in Sabrina, and she muttered, "Men have all the best of it."

"Well, don't you worry none about it. I'll bet you do just as well as they do, even if you do 'ave to ride a horse funny."

Sabrina did not answer for a moment, but a light of mischief danced in her eyes. She thought hard, sitting still as Cecily finished her grooming, and then suddenly she laughed aloud. She had a round, full laugh—like a man's, in a way. When Cecily asked her what she was laughing at, she replied, "Oh, I'm just planning a surprise for Charles."

"Wot is it, miss?"

"He's so stuffy. I like to shake him up now and then."

"But he's dreadful rich, miss!"

"Yes," Sabrina shrugged. "And I've often thought if he didn't have thirty thousand pounds a year, what a dull man he would be." She got up and examined herself in the mirror. She laughed again. "Well, Sir Charles Stratton, you'll get quite a surprise when we have our riding date this afternoon!"

"Don't do nuffin' to run 'im off, miss. You done run off most every man that's ever come courtin' you."

"I don't think I could run Charles off with a broadax."

"He's fair in love with you, ain't he, now?"

"I don't know that for sure, though, do I?"

Cecily looked up, surprised at her mistress. "Why, what ever do you mean, miss?"

"I mean I can never tell whether a man loves me or my father's money."

"Why, Sir Charles 'as a pile of money of his own."

"Not as much as Father has—and even if he does, he always wants more. He's a greedy beast where money's concerned."

"Why, you mustn't talk that way about your intended!"

"I suppose not." Sabrina reached out and put her hand on Cecily's cheek. "You're a sweet thing. It's too bad Sir Charles isn't in love with you. You'd make him a beautiful wife. Always submissive to everything he would suggest."

"Me, miss? Lor!"

"*Lor,* indeed!" Sabrina smiled. She examined herself once more in the mirror. "No, I'll never know if a man loves me or if he loves my father's money." The thought troubled her, and as she turned, it would not leave. For most of the morning, in one form or another, she thought about what it would be like to be loved completely for herself alone with no attention to that awful thing called money.

Sir Charles Stratton was not a tall man. Indeed, he was just an inch taller than Sabrina's five feet seven inches. As he came down the steps, Sabrina noticed that Charles was dressed, as always, at the height of fashion. He was overweight, and his face had an unhealthy, rather pasty look, but his clothes were always exactly right. He wore a cap-length redingote without a side seam and a narrow neckband hidden by a large bow. Over tight-fitting knee britches he wore high, soft leather boots, and he had swept off his beaver hat. He was smiling nervously, for something about Sabrina Fairfax always made him slightly edgy. Most women would gladly adapt themselves to his ways, but somehow he had never been able to find the proper submission in Sabrina Fairfax.

"Good morning, my dear Sabrina. A fine day for a ride."

"Indeed it is. I hope the horses are spirited. Perhaps we can have a race."

"You always want to ride full-speed ahead," Charles complained. He shook his head as he surveyed Sabrina's costume. She was wearing a full-length coat that covered her down to her boot tops. "Come on," he said. "I've got a full day planned. We'll be going over to have tea this afternoon with Sir Lawrence and his family."

"Oh, Charles, they bore me stiff!"

Charles stared at Sabrina. "But—they're such *important* people!"

"Does that make them less boring?"

Stratton slapped the side of his boots with the riding crop he carried. "I say, Sabrina, I'll never in this world understand you!"

"You'll just have to try harder, Charles. After all, a woman must have her mystery." Her eyes sparkled, and she said, "Come along. I'm anxious for the ride."

Charles nodded and stroked his luxurious muttonchop whiskers. He seemed to be in love with them, for he could not keep his hands off of them nor the bushy mustache that covered his upper lip. Sabrina had once told Cecily that Charles looked like he was eating a muskrat with that horrible mustache. "You go right ahead. I have to give some instructions to the manager."

"All right, Charles, but hurry."

"I shan't be long."

Sabrina gave scarcely a glance to the magnificent mansion that Charles called home. It was a large stone affair two stories high with a double set of stone steps leading to the entrance. The front had a doorway graced with pilasters and pediments, and the massive wooden door was flanked by large floor-length windows. When she reached the stable, she greeted the gnomish man that came forward knuckling his forehead and smiling at her.

"Good morning, Billy."

"Good mornin', Miss Fairfax. Reckon I can guess which horse you want."

"I'll bet you can. The liveliest one you've got."

"That'll be Betty. She's got a mighty tame name, but she's got spirit—just like you, miss. I've already got her saddled up for you."

Sabrina had a real affection for the groom. She usually paid no attention to underlings, but Billy had been a jockey and had traveled the world. He was far more interesting than his master. "I think Betty will do fine." The two walked over to where the horses were tied just outside the stable, and Sabrina studied the sidesaddle on the mare. A smile turned the corners of her lips upward, and she said, "Billy, take that saddle off."

"Miss?"

"Take that saddle off. Put a man's saddle on her."

"But, miss—!"

"Quickly! Do what I tell you."

Billy had learned long ago the futility of arguing with Sabrina Fairfax. He swallowed hard, then shrugged. "You'll 'ave to tell Sir Charles it weren't my idea."

"I'll take care of that. Quickly now, before he gets back."

It only took Billy a few moments until the horse was wearing the man's saddle. Billy had just finished tightening the cinches when Sir Charles came puffing down the pathway. "Well, are we all ready?"

"Oh yes, I'm ready."

Sir Charles was about to say more when his eyes fell on the saddle. Instantly he grew angry, and his face turned red. "Blast your eyes, Billy, what were you thinking of? Where's Miss Fairfax's sidesaddle?"

"It weren't my fault!" Billy said indignantly. "She made me do it!"

Turning to Sabrina, Charles said, "What in the world—" His words were cut off, for Sabrina had been unbuttoning her long coat. She shrugged it off and then turned to give Charles a brilliant smile. The smile had no effect, but her costume did. Charles blinked and shook his head and then stood absolutely still, as if smitten.

"Don't you like my outfit, Charlie?"

"It's—it's—" Stratton could not think of a reply, for Sabrina's riding costume had robbed him of all words. Sabrina was wearing a pair of fawn-colored men's britches, tight-fitting and clinging to the curves of her legs, and a maroon coat that came down to her fingertips and was buttoned at her waist with one button. The curves of her figure filled the white silk shirt that she wore, and a man's black bow tie was fitted around her neck.

Sabrina could not keep from smiling as Charles stared at her in absolute shock. She saw that he was looking at her legs, and she laughed aloud. "Didn't you know I had legs, Charles, under those long skirts?"

"Sabrina, I'm surprised at you!"

"Women *do* have legs, you know, even though we try to disguise them. Come along. I'm ready for a ride.

"Give me a leg up, Billy." She put her foot in Billy's ready hands and sprang up and threw her leg over. She fitted her feet into the stirrups and laughed again. "Now, *this* is the way to ride a horse!"

Charles Stratton sputtered, "But-but-you can't—"

"Of course I can, Charles. Now get on your horse."

Charles Stratton knew it was useless to argue with this woman. "I'm glad nobody's here to see you in that outlandish outfit!" He labored to get on his horse and then kicked it into motion.

Sabrina spoke to Betty, then turned back and winked at Billy. "Thank you, Billy. You think I look nice, don't you?"

Billy glanced furtively at his master, then winked back. "Yes, ma'am! Top rate!"

"You see, Charles, Billy thinks I look nice."

It took Charles Stratton a hundred yards before he could gain his voice. "People will talk if they see you like this, Sabrina."

"Have you ever thought, Charles, how hard it is to ride sidesaddle? Did you ever try it?"

"Of course not!"

"Try it sometime. Now this is the way to ride a horse! I'm never going to ride that awful sidesaddle again."

"But think of what people will say."

"No, *you* think of it. I've decided to become a new kind of woman, Charles, and this is the first shot in my war."

She touched Betty with her heels, and the mare shot forward. Charles kicked his stallion into motion, but he could not catch the fleet mare. He was not a good rider, and it was fifteen minutes later before Sabrina pulled up and waited for him. "You're going to break your neck riding like that—and you must not wear that outfit in public!"

Sabrina's face was full of color. The exercise had brightened her cheeks, and the thrill of riding astride had given her a new freedom. "Charlie, don't you ever want to break the rules?"

"Break the rules! Why, of course not! Rules aren't made to be broken."

"Why are they made?"

"Why, because they are necessary."

"I think most rules are foolish," Sabrina said. She tried to explain the part of her that rebelled against the foolish rules she saw all about her, but she could not put her thoughts into words that Sir Charles Stratton would understand. He was a young man, only two years older than she, but his character had been molded by his position in life and by a rigid set of English rules. He had a typical Englishman's mentality, and finally Sabrina saw the uselessness of it. "Where are you going tomorrow?"

"To see a boxing match."

"Where is it, Charlie?"

"They're holding this one down on the wharf on a barge."

Sabrina turned and said, "Take me with you, Charlie."

"Are you insane, Sabrina? Women don't go to boxing matches."

"Why not?"

"Because they're—well, they're not suitable for women."

"What's unsuitable about them?"

"Well, the language, for one thing."

"I doubt if I'd hear anything I haven't heard before."

"I certainly hope that's not true! You can't imagine how rough the talk is. Besides that, they're brutal, bloody things."

"Then why do you go?"

"Why, it's sport, don't you see?"

That seemed to settle everything for Sir Charles Stratton. If it was sport, it was acceptable, and he could attend things as cruel as bearbaiting, cockfighting, dogfighting, or men battering each other into insensibility with a clear conscience. He liked his answer so well he said again, "It's sport. That makes it fine."

"Why don't you try it yourself?"

"Me? Why, that's for another kind of man. The boxers are not really human, Sabrina. They're brutal beasts. Nothing but muscles. No mind at all."

"I wouldn't think it would be very much fun."

Charles spent some time explaining to Sabrina the attractions of the bareknuckled art of self-defense, but he was adamant when he said, "No, you absolutely must *not* go to a boxing match."

Sabrina stared at him. The words *you absolutely must not* had always been a challenge for her, and although she said no more about it, her thoughts were on the event. She smiled to herself as she began to create a plan in which she could manifest the fact that she was a new kind of woman.

Sir Roger Fairfax had the same blond hair as Sabrina and big blue eyes. He was a busy man, always in motion, quick to make decisions, and often quick to rue those hasty decisions. He looked across the table now at Sabrina and said, "What are you doing up so early?"

"Oh, I just couldn't sleep."

"You look very well this morning, Sabrina." He noted that her green dress picked up the color of her eyes and felt a moment's pride at this beautiful young woman that was his daughter. He had longed for a son but had never had one. Instead, he had made Sabrina the pride of his life. The loss of his wife five years earlier had been a blow, but he had filled his loneliness by staying busy with his many interests. He enjoyed hunting of all sorts and sports, and he had even served a term in the House of Commons. He did not like the bondage of politics, however, for they seemed to interfere with the things he found much more exciting.

"How are things at the office?"

Sir Roger had been eating the kidney pie that the maid had set before him, and now he put his fork down abruptly and took a long pull of ale from the silver goblet. "Not very well, I'm afraid."

Sir Fairfax had inherited a stockbrokerage from his father, who had made a rather large fortune in it. It was exactly the kind of activity that Fairfax loved because it involved taking risks. He had often said, "Let others take the short money and the low interest. I'd rather make a big killing. It's more exciting that way."

Now, however, Sabrina's father looked troubled. "I must confess I've made a few bad decisions, Sabrina."

"Are you in serious trouble?" Sabrina could not imagine a life that was different from the one she had. Money had never been a concern for her, because whatever she wanted or needed was always there. Her father looked worried now, and she asked, "How bad is it?"

"Oh, you know how it is when dealing with stocks. You lose on five deals and then on one you get it all back plus a lot more."

Sabrina knew her father was an inveterate gambler. The stakes seemed not to be important. He enjoyed the risk. She had known him to come home rejoicing after having won five thousand pounds on a single race—and she had known him to lose an equal amount on another race. Now, for the first time in her life, a twinge of something close to apprehension, almost fear, touched her. For one brief moment she considered what a moneyless future would be like, and she didn't enjoy the picture she envisioned. "Maybe you ought to cut back on risky ventures."

"You may be right about that, Sabrina. But I have one thing in the fire that is going to save us."

"What is it? Buying more stock?"

"No. A different sort of thing altogether. There's big money to be made in black ivory."

"Black ivory? I thought ivory was white."

Sir Roger laughed. "This is a different kind of ivory. It's what they call the black Africans, the ones that become slaves."

"What an odd thing to call them."

"Well, it is, I suppose, but there's big money in slavery. One good voyage under a good man, and a fortune is there. As a matter of fact, I've decided to get out of the stockbroking business and go into the black ivory business."

"But what about a ship?"

"That's what I was going to tell you, my dear. I've pretty well liquidated all of our holdings, including this house, up for mortgage, that is, and I bought a ship."

"But you don't know anything about ships!"

"I won't be sailing it, so I don't have to know. But I bought this ship and renamed it." He reached over and took her hand in his. "Guess what the name is."

"Why, I have no idea."

"How does the *Sabrina* sound to you?"

"Why, Father, how touching!" Sabrina's cheeks glowed with pleasure. "The *Sabrina*. Do you suppose I could go on one of the cruises?"

"You wouldn't like it, my dear. It smells rather bad, I understand, and it can be dangerous. There's always the danger of a slave uprising and a mutiny, you know."

Sabrina listened as her father described his new venture with great pleasure. It involved sending the ship to Africa and making contacts with the Arab slavers there, then transporting the slaves to places where they could be sold for a profit. "The Colonies are a good destination. We can sell them the slaves and buy molasses and bring it back to England. Good profit there, too. It's going to be much more exciting than dealing in stocks."

"But it's dangerous, isn't it? I mean, ships can sink."

"Well, of course, anything's dangerous. But I'll tell you, Sabrina, just one successful voyage will pay off all of our debts and put this house in the clear. And I intend to see more than one successful voyage."

Sabrina was wary of this new idea. *I've seen him like this before,* she thought, *always with some scheme that's going to make us immensely rich.* She considered trying to talk him out of it, but she knew that was useless. Her father had a stubborn streak, which Sabrina knew she had inherited, and he was past the point of changing his mind. She finally turned her attention to listening as he spoke with pleasure of what they would be able to do when the *Sabrina* had earned a large fortune for them.

Finally Fairfax rose, and Sabrina said, "What are you doing today, Father?"

"Didn't Charles tell you? He and I are going to a boxing match."

"Yes, he did tell me. I asked him to take me."

"Well, I'm sure he refused!"

"Yes, he did!"

"Well, I should hope so! It's not for ladies." He circled the table and leaned over to kiss her. "Why don't you do some embroidery?"

"All right, Father, I will."

"There's my good girl." Fairfax kissed his daughter again, patted her hand, and left the room.

Sabrina sat there and felt the rebellion growing in her. *"You absolutely must not go."* That's what Charles had said. *What should I do? Stay and do some embroidery?* The rebellion that lay not too deeply in her spirit began to smolder. "We'll just see about that!"

Big Ben

Two

A sudden pull at Sabrina's arm made her gasp, and she looked up to see a coach-and-four driven by a haughty driver in livery fly by, rattling over the cobblestones. She turned to see a big bluff man dressed in a snuff-colored suit looking down at her. "I'd be careful if I was you."

"Thank you very much," Sabrina said breathlessly. "I believe you saved me from a rather severe accident."

"These streets in London! The drivers pay little attention. They expect everyone to get out of their way. Will you be all right now?"

"Yes, sir. Thank you very much, indeed."

Sabrina smiled and turned away from her rescuer. She began threading her way down the streets of Cheapside between vehicles and pedestrians. It was the first time she had ever been afoot in this section of London, and she was frightened for a moment. But her courage always rose to a challenge, and lifting her head, she made her way along the street. Carts and coaches made such a thundering it seemed that the whole world traveled on wheels. At every corner she encountered men and women and children—some in the sooty rags of the chimney sweeps, others arrayed in their gold and gaudy satin of the aristocracy, gazing languidly out of sedans borne by lackeys with thick legs. Porters sweated under their burdens, chapmen darted from shop to shop, and tradesmen scurried around like ants. Tradesmen and vendors shouted their wares, many of them shoving things in Sabrina's face. She was aware also that there was a danger of slops being thrown out of the upper windows. She noticed with interest the drain in the middle of the street. She had read an article that described how the ditch, a foot wide and six inches deep, would carry all the slops and garbage away. The writer had been most proud of it, stating, "Most cities just let the slops and garbage pile up, but not London. We are certainly leaders in the world today."

Finally Sabrina saw what she was looking for—the wharf on the River Thames where the fight was to be held. She glanced around and saw a sign with a red lion, rather faded but recognizable, and assumed this was an inn. She went inside and found the low-ceilinged timbers stained with age and smoke. Three men were sitting at a table playing cards, and all three looked up at her. One leaned over and said something to another that she did not catch, and all three men laughed.

"May I help you, miss?"

Sabrina turned to the tall, thin man with white hair and sharp blue eyes. "Yes, I'd like a room if you have one available."

"Of course, miss. Come along. I'll show it to you."

Sabrina followed him up the narrow stairs to the second floor, and when he opened the door and stepped inside, she nodded. "This will do very nicely." Actually, it was not an ornate room, but for her purpose it would do fine.

"Will you be staying long, miss?"

"No, just the one day. How much is it?"

After she had paid for the room, Sabrina walked downstairs and left the inn. She walked the streets until she found what appeared to be a general store. When she stepped inside, a large woman greeted her, saying, "Yes, miss, 'ow can I serve you?"

"I need to buy some clothes for a servant. A man," she added quickly.

"We 'ave a fine selection, miss, if you'll step this way."

Sabrina followed the woman, who began pulling out various items of clothing.

"And whot would you be needing exactly?"

"Oh, just one full outfit please."

"Small clothes, too?"

"Why, yes, if you please."

"And how big would this person be?"

"Oh, about my height and somewhat heavier."

Sabrina left the store ten minutes later with the garments wrapped in coarse paper. It was after noon now, and she knew that the boxing match was to take place sometime after dark. She had asked her father particularly, and he had shrugged, saying, "Well, these things are never very punctual. The word is about six, but it could be later. I may be home rather late. Don't worry about me."

Sabrina made her way back to the Red Lion and ignored the whispers and the bold glances that followed her. Going up the stairs, she entered the room, shut the door, and locked it. She unwrapped the clothing and laid everything out on the bed. For a moment she wondered if she had lost her mind, but she put this thought aside. She still remembered Charles's words telling her that she must not go to the boxing match. Indeed!

She took off her feminine clothing and began putting on the men's clothes. It was something new, different, and daring—just the sort of thing that Sabrina Fairfax loved to do! The clothes were rough, suitable for a man of the poorer classes, and they felt out of place on her pampered skin. She pulled on the white stockings and then the knee britches, which fit her rather loosely, put on the white shirt and the waistcoat, added the tie, and then slipped into the roughly made black shoes, which were somewhat too large for her. Topping it off, she put on the coat, which came down to her knees, and buttoned it across the front. She had no mirror, but she could see that the clothing covered the curves of her body well enough.

To complete the boyish look, she began to pin her hair up, and when she had fastened it as tightly as she could, she tied it up with a silk scarf so it would not come loose. She put on the large hat with the floppy brim, and was relieved to find that it fit nicely over all the hair piled on her head. The last step was to scrub at her face until all traces of powder and rouge were gone, and then she brushed her hand across the floor and picked up enough dust to scour her face with it.

Finally she stowed the money she had brought in an inner pocket of the coat and stared out the window at the overcast afternoon. She was impatient for darkness to arrive. As she watched the crowd, everyone seemed to be headed down toward the wharf. She could hear two men who had passed beneath her window, one of them saying, "It won't be much of a match."

"You don' think so, Henry? Who is this fellow they found to fight the champ?"

"Never 'eard of him, but 'e won't be no match for Big Ben. . . ."

Their voices faded as they headed down the street. Taking a deep breath, Sabrina left her room and found she could walk through the lobby with no one paying any particular attention to her. She held her breath as she stepped out onto the street, wondering if she really looked like a man. She ignored the vendors she passed who begged her to buy their wares.

"Buy a 'andkerchief, mister?" A young woman held up a handkerchief, and Sabrina was pleased that the woman thought she was a man.

She pulled a coin from her pocket and, making her voice as deep as she could, said, "That's a nice kerchief."

"Oh, thank you, sir!" The young woman took the coin, her eyes bright.

The crowd all seemed to be going the same way, and most of the talk that Sabrina was able to pick up was of the match that was to come. She listened carefully, moving slowly, until finally a woman stepped out of the shadows of an alley and took her by the arm. She was a rather chubby woman with a heavily painted face, and she said impudently, "Come along, husband. I'll show yer a good time."

Sabrina was shocked. She knew prostitutes inhabited London but had never seen one—at least not this close. The woman's face was pitted, and her face was so covered with paint it was difficult to tell her age. Sabrina shook her head and muttered no and took the woman's curse as she went on down the street.

Finally she reached the wharf and found herself in the middle of the milling crowd. Drawn up close to the shore was a barge. Sabrina could see that a square had been marked off in the middle of the barge with four posts marking the corners and ropes running about the square. Two men were cleaning the surface of the ring, and crowds of men were jostling for good seats around it.

She edged in toward the gangway until she was stopped by a man who said, "Half a crown admission." He held his hand out and waited until Sabrina had fished the coin out of her pocket. She made her way onto the wharf and determined where she could get a good view of the action. Vendors selling beer and gin moved among the crowd, shouting the virtues of their wares. Every spectator, it seemed, was smoking. Sabrina pulled out one of the cigars she had purchased but realized she had no match.

" 'Ere, you need a light?"

Sabrina turned to her right, where a tall, lean man held his own cigar out. Putting the cigar in her mouth, she touched the other end to the glowing tip of the man's cigar. She had never smoked in her life, but she had seen enough men doing it. She got the cigar going, but then suddenly her throat was full of smoke. She began to cough, and the tall man beside her patted her on the back. "Come now, lad, none of that!"

Sabrina quickly drew back. "I'm all right," she said huskily.

"You come to many bouts?"

"No. As a matter of fact, this is my first."

"You tell me that! Well, let me explain the rules to you. . . ."

Sabrina was content to listen to her neighbor. He evidently loved the sound of his own voice, and it was, indeed, a pleasant voice. In fact, it was the best thing about the man, apparently. "It's like this, you see. When a man gets knocked down or thrown down, he's got thirty seconds to come to scratch."

" 'Come to scratch'? What's that?"

"Until he can come back to the middle of the ring and start fighting again. There ain't no hittin' below the belt allowed, and no strikin' a man that's fallen, don't you see."

"How long does the fight last?"

"How long? Well, you *are* a chicken, ain't you? It lasts until one of the men ain't able to come to scratch. Every time a man goes down, that's one round. I seen one bout once where there was a hundred twenty-seven rounds."

"I see." Sabrina listened as her neighbor continued his speech, like a river going on and on and on. She noticed that the noisy crowd around her was full of gamblers. Most of the men appeared to be from the lower class. She saw the tavern keeper from the Red Lion, and she even saw chimney sweeps dressed in the top hat of their trade. There were all sorts of young dandies out for a grand time. The only women there were prostitutes, and there were few of these.

But the upper classes were represented, also. As she turned to scan the crowd, she saw her father and Charles Stratton up at the very edge of the ring in the best seats. They were smoking cigars and talking and laughing, and for an instant Sabrina had an impulse to go down and join them. This, however, would be far too risky, so she simply stood listening as the tall man continued to tell her about the match.

"This won't be much of a bout," he said, waving his hand in a disparaging fashion.

"Why not?"

"Because, don't you see, it's Big Ben who's fightin'."

"Who is he?"

"Why, he's the *champion*. Benjamin Brain. You ain't never 'eard of Benjamin Brain?"

"No, but as I say, this is my first visit."

The tall man stared at her in amazement. "Well, I thought everybody in England knew Big Ben. He ain't never been beat, not 'im! I seen him take out four men one right after the other once over in Brighton. He can't be beat!"

"Who is his opponent?"

"The pug he's fightin'? Ah, he ain't nobody."

"What's his name?"

"Got a crazy name. Zion Kenyon. Somethin' like that. Ain't that a foolish name, now?"

"Have you ever seen him fight?"

"Not me. But my mate, he's seen 'im. He says he's fast, but that won't help 'im. He can run, but he can't hide! Big Ben will butcher 'im!"

The sky was growing darker now, and large lanterns had been lit on the tall pilings around the barge. The crowd continued to grow until finally there was standing room only.

"There 'e is—there's Big Ben!"

Sabrina put her eyes on the bulky man stepping into the

ring. He threw off the coat he had worn about his shoulders to reveal his muscular form. He was a broad man in every respect, at least six feet tall with swelling muscles. He slammed one fist into the palm of his other hand and said something to the two men beside him, evidently his handlers.

"Ain't 'e a daisy?"

"He looks very strong."

"Strong ain't all. That poor Kenyon fellow, he's in for a poundin'! Look, I reckon that's him there."

A handsome young man was stepping over the rope, accompanied by another man. The fighter glanced at the champion, who laughed at him and said something Sabrina couldn't make out. She heard the other men laugh.

"Blimey! Like a sheep to the slaughter," the tall man sneered.

Sabrina took a good look at the man who was, apparently, supposed to lose this fight. His long, dark blond hair was tied into a ponytail in the back, and he looked short compared to the other fighter.

"He looks so small."

"I reckon 'e is compared to Big Ben. I doubt if he weighs more than thirteen stone. The champ there, 'e weighs over fourteen. He's all muscle!"

Sabrina watched, and the proceedings took some time, but finally the two men came out to meet each other. The fighter called Sion Kenyon wore a pair of full-length blue trunks tied by a blue sash and a pair of black shoes. He was smoothly muscled and seemed to move very easily as he gave way to the advance of the champion.

Big Ben was a frightening sight. Even at this distance Sabrina could see that his face had been scarred by innumerable conflicts. He held his left hand out straight, and he held his right cocked. As she watched, he suddenly threw a tremendous blow, but the challenger simply stepped under it. The challenger responded with a solid blow to the side of the head as the powerful champion moved by. It had no effect on Big Ben, however, who whirled, and Sabrina could see the paleness of his eyes. He was a frightening sight indeed! A broad, brutalized face, little evidence of a neck, and not an ounce of fat on him.

The crowd yelled at each blow, and for a time it appeared that the younger man was making headway. He was very fast and seemed to be able to hit the champion easily, but most of the blows were caught on Ben's forearm. Finally Big Ben thrust his arms around the younger man and simply threw him down.

"Why, he didn't hit him, he just wrestled him!"

"That's fair. Any way you can get a man down. I'll tell you, it takes something out of a man to get thrown down like that and then 'ave to crawl to 'is feet." The tall stranger shook his head. "That young fellow's got more courage than 'e has sense. Why, 'e shouldn't be in the ring with the champ!"

As the bout progressed, time after time Big Ben either struck the young man in the head and drove him backward or else he simply grabbed him and threw him down.

Sabrina was appalled. The younger fighter's face was bloody, but he continued to get up. Looking around at the crowd, Sabrina saw no trace of sympathy for Kenyon's plight. The men were yelling and screaming, their faces red. The sight of blood seemed to inflame them. Sabrina had heard prize-fighters described as beasts, but she thought grimly, *This crowd is the beast—not those two men out there. They wouldn't be fighting at all if these men hadn't come and paid their money.*

The fight went on interminably. Sabrina saw the young man systematically beaten to the floor of the ring again and again, and she wished she could leave. She could not see the attraction it had for these men. Finally the young man struck his head as he went down, and though he tried, he could not get to his feet within the thirty seconds.

"Well, that's it. Weren't much, were 'e? Didn't 'ave no business fightin' Big Ben. It looks like they could find a better opponent."

Sabrina stood as the crowd began to fade away. She was watching the young man, who was still lying on his back. The champion gave him a contemptuous look as he passed him on his way out of the ring. Sabrina saw the man who had accompanied Kenyon and attended him during the fight, but he did not go to the fallen man. Instead, he left the barge and was standing on the wharf. He had taken his hat off and was talking to the spectators. Sabrina worked her way off the barge and as she passed the man, he said, "A bit for the loser, sir?"

She reached into her inner pocket and came out with a ten-pound note for the man. The man's eyes brightened, and he said, "Thank you, sir. You're a real gent!"

Sabrina nodded and then spotted her father and Charlie leaving. She turned back to see if someone was going to help the fighter, who was now beginning to stir. He came up on his hands and knees, and his face was a bloody mass. Slowly he rose and swayed.

Compassion came over Sabrina Fairfax then, a very rare thing for her. She watched the young man as he staggered toward the ropes and draped his body over them, apparently unable to go farther. Unable to watch, Sabrina turned. She had seen enough of bareknuckled prizefighting to last her a lifetime. She had to hurry now to get back to the inn, change into her own clothes, and get back home before her father did.

Sabrina was sickened by the spectacle and fled as quickly as she could. One thing she well knew, she would *never* go to another prizefight as long as she lived!

The World Turns Upside Down

Three

*Y*ou'll notice that the craftsmanship is the very finest, Miss Fairfax."

Sabrina had been walking slowly around the small vehicle, and she ran her hand along the polished shaft that extended forward. "It does seem very nice," she admitted. "I'd like to try it out, I think."

The carriage maker, a big burly man with bushy whiskers and shoulders like mountains, nodded eagerly. "Of course. I have a fine mare. I am sure you'll be able to handle her. Everyone knows what a fine hand you have with horses, Miss Fairfax."

Fifteen minutes later Sabrina was seated in the cabriolet and delighted with the mare and the feel of the small vehicle. The sun was still high in the sky, and a crisp breeze ruffled her hair where it had come loose from the pins. She leaned forward, urging the mare on to more speed, and at the same time was conscious that the small carriage offered a very fine ride indeed.

Finally she turned the mare around and drove back to the carriage shop. Crawford was the carriage maker's name, and he was there at once to hold the horse while Sabrina leaped to the ground without help. "I like it very much, Mr. Crawford."

"It's a beautiful piece of work. The very finest materials."

Sabrina laughed. "You don't have to sell me. I've been looking for a cabriolet for some time, and I like this as well as any I've seen. Even better. How much is it?"

Crawford's brow furrowed, and he shook his head as he said, "Well, I'm afraid I'm going to have to have a hundred and ten pounds for it, Miss Fairfax. The materials were very expensive, and as you know, I used only the best. I know it sounds high, but—"

"It sounds like a fair enough price. I'll take it. I'll come for it tomorrow and bring the money."

"Thank you very much, Miss Fairfax. I'm sure you'll be satisfied. If you ever have any problem, bring it back to me, and I'll make it right."

Sabrina smiled and turned to get back into her own carriage. It was a large affair requiring two horses, and she thought with pleasure how nice it would be to simply fly along behind in her new cabriolet. She spoke to the horses, and they leaned forward against their collars and broke into a trot.

Sabrina drove the horses hard, as she usually did, and when she finally pulled up in front of the house, Caesar was there at once. The tall black man with enormous hands apparently knew all there was to know about horses.

"I'll put your animal up, miss."

"Thank you, Caesar. Oh, and tomorrow I'll be bringing back a cabriolet. I think I'll ride Lady in, and then I won't have two horses to worry over."

"Yes, miss. I'll have her ready any time you say."

Sabrina went inside the house and went at once to her father's study. She found the door shut, which was rather unusual. She hesitated before knocking. "Father, are you there?"

"Come in, Sabrina."

Sabrina stepped inside and found her father seated at the desk. Before him was every sort of paper imaginable, and his eyes were troubled as he looked at her. He ran his hands through his hair and then suddenly slapped the desk. "I hate paper work!" he exclaimed.

"You always did." Sabrina kissed him and then indicated the mess of papers on the desk. "What are all these?"

"I'm trying to make sense out of the business, and I can't do it. I'll have to take all these blasted things down and let Smith put them in order." He rose and went to the window. He stood with his back to her, staring out for such a long time that Sabrina walked over to stand beside him.

Putting her hand on his arm, she turned him around and said, "You're worried about the business?"

"It's such a mess! Oh, what a tangled web the business world is."

"I don't see why Smith can't take care of it. That's what you pay him for."

"Well, to be truthful," Fairfax said, his mouth twisting in a cynical fashion, "he can't manufacture money. That's the problem."

"What do you mean, Father?"

"I mean we've been going downhill for some time now. Smith's been complaining about it. He's having to shift money from one account to another. Robbing Peter to pay Paul, as he put it. But he told me this morning that he had done all the arranging he could. Said we'd have to have fresh capital."

Sabrina stood there quietly. In fact, she understood little of business. She knew much more about balls and horses and dresses than she knew about the stock market. "Couldn't we sell something?" she asked timidly.

"I'd sell in a minute if I could."

"Well, this house must be worth a fortune. We could sell it and get a smaller place."

Fairfax shook his head. "We could if it weren't mortgaged already. As a matter of fact—" He walked to his desk and picked up a sheet of paper. "I have a letter here from the man who owns the mortgage. I've missed several payments, and he's threatening foreclosure."

A chill swept through Sabrina. "You mean we might lose this place?"

Fairfax looked up quickly and formed his lips into a smile, although the rest of his face didn't cooperate. Sabrina saw this, but he made the most of it. "I don't want you worrying about this. It's *my* problem. But I will ask you not to be spending any large sums of money until we get this straightened out."

Sabrina opened her lips to mention the cabriolet she had just agreed to buy but knew she could not worry her father when he was already burdened down. "Of course not, Father." She hugged him and said, "We'll get through this."

"Of course we will. When the *Sabrina* gets to America with

that load of slaves, we'll have cash in every pocket."

Sabrina was aware that her father was an optimistic man swayed by his moods. He could be as happy as a bird when things went well, but the next day he could be down deep in depression if he suffered a heavy loss at the gambling table. As she stood beside him, she realized suddenly that for all of his high family connections and the trappings of wealth he had inherited from his father, Roger Fairfax was a very unstable individual. He was basically a gambler at heart, not a business-man.

Now Sabrina pushed those thoughts out of her mind, not wanting to be disloyal to her father. She hugged him again and kissed his cheek. "The *Sabrina* will make us rich," she nodded with a laugh. "It can't miss with a name like that, can it?"

The sound of a carriage approaching startled Sabrina, who had been caught up in the novel she was reading about a man marooned on a desert island. The story intrigued her, for the man named Robinson Crusoe had to learn to do without the trappings of civilization, and lived by his wits and by the strength and skill of his hand. She found herself fascinated by the story, although she could not understand why. Certainly she herself had never had to live by her wits—nor by any sort of work at all.

She rose from her chair and put down her book. When she reached the window, she stared out and saw a carriage she didn't recognize. Caesar was holding the horse's head and speaking to the man who got out.

Sabrina watched as the man, a tall individual wearing a dark suit and tall black hat, ascended the stairs. She got one sight of his face and saw that he was a dark-complected, sober-looking individual, almost sour. "He doesn't look like one of Father's friends. He looks more like an undertaker than any-thing else."

Sabrina was accustomed to individuals coming to see her father and thought no more of it. She went back to her book, curled up on the couch, and soon was completely immersed in the adventures of Robinson Crusoe. She read for more than two hours, stopping once to send Cecily down to bring tea and crumpets up for a snack. Finally she grew sleepy and lay down on the couch, pulling a light coverlet over her. She dozed off almost at once but was soon awakened by an insistent knock on the doorframe. She sat up at once saying, "Come in, what is it?"

She expected Cecily to come in, but instead it was Randell, the butler. "Miss, you must come at once!"

Seeing the alarm on Randell's face, Sabrina stood up in one fluid movement. "What is it, Randell?"

"It's—it's your father, miss. Something's happened to him!"

Sabrina, with a start, saw that Randell was frightened. "Is he ill?"

"I think so, miss. Come quickly."

Sabrina flew out of the room and dashed down the stairs, followed by Randell. "He's in the study," Randell called out.

Sabrina turned into the study, but for a moment she did not see her father. Then she caught sight of him half hidden behind the massive rosewood desk that sat in the center of the room. "Father!" she cried and rushed over. Falling on her knees, she saw that his face was as pale as paste. His eyes were open, and he appeared to be trying to speak.

"What is it, Father? What happened?"

"Help me. . . !"

The words were faint, and Sabrina noticed that the left side of his mouth did not move—only the right. Fear touched her heart, and she cried, "Randell, help me get him into the chair."

The two of them managed to drag him to the overstuffed chair. She noticed that his right side seemed to work, but he had little control over his left side. She took his hand and began to chafe it. "What is it, Father? Did you fall?"

"Don't—know." The words came with great difficulty, and she saw the fear in his eyes.

"What happened? Can you tell me?"

"It's—can't seem to move my left arm. It's like it's gone to sleep."

Again Sabrina noticed that the left side of his mouth did not move.

"Can't talk!" he gasped.

"Randell, go for the doctor at once! Bring him no matter what he says."

"Yes, miss!"

Randell dashed out of the room, and Sabrina turned back to her father, holding his hand tightly. "It'll be all right. The doctor will be here soon. Are you in pain?"

"Not so much now." The words were faltering, almost inaudible. "I don't know . . . what's wrong with me. . . ."

Sabrina pulled up a chair and sat beside her father for some time. He was badly frightened, which brought fear to her own heart. She did not know what to do for him, for she had no experience with sickness. She knew, however, that something terrible had happened.

Finally Fairfax raised his head, and his mouth twitched with an effort to speak. "The *Sabrina*—she went down off the coast of Africa . . . with all hands."

"Oh no, Father!"

"We're ruined, Sabrina . . . we're ruined!"

The ship named after her was sinking half a world away, and she now understood, to some degree, the financial blow this meant to the Fairfax family. She saw the terror in her father's eyes and could only give part of her mind to that. Her father had spoiled her all of her life and had given her plenty of love, but now she felt a dire fear as she sat there holding his hand. He seemed to be looking to her for assurance—but Sabrina knew she had none to give.

"It's not good news, Miss Fairfax. I'm sorry I can't give you a better report." Dr. Blackman had spent over an hour with Sir Roger and now had come out, with Sabrina waiting for him in the parlor. He had been the Fairfax family physician for ten years and had been there for them when Sabrina's mother died, so Sabrina trusted him implicitly. "It looks like he had a stroke. You probably noticed that his left side isn't functioning, which is typical of a stroke."

"Yes, even the left side of his mouth wasn't moving."

"These things happen very suddenly," Dr. Blackman said.

"A man can look well, be as strong as a horse and never have an ill day of his life, then suddenly drop dead at the age of thirty."

Dr. Blackman's words put a chill on Sabrina, and she looked to him for assurance. "But you can do something, can't you? Surely there's medicine that will help?"

Dr. Blackman hesitated. Then, taking a deep breath, he said slowly, "We can always hope. I've had stroke patients who have lived for years."

Despite the doctor's encouraging words, Sabrina knew his eyes were sending a different message. "But—there's nothing you can do for him, then?"

Blackman shrugged. "See that he gets plenty of rest. Keep him from all kinds of stress. That's the most important thing. He doesn't need to be aggravated. It might well bring on another stroke."

Sabrina felt he was holding back worse news, but she didn't press him for more. The reality of the situation hit her even more severely than when her mother had died. At least then— then she still had a healthy father she could rely on for everything. Now she realized that if something happened to her father, too, she would truly be alone.

Dr. Blackman's words brought her out of her thoughts. "You must trust God in situations like this, I'm afraid."

The words gave cold comfort to Sabrina. She was a member of the Church of England, as was her father, but their religion was a mere formality. There was no reality in it—certainly nothing that would take the sting away from the doctor's plain meaning. She stood there mutely as the doctor gave instructions for her father's care.

"You may need to hire a man to help with your father. Or perhaps your butler can handle it. Sir Roger is going to need more physical care than you could give, Miss Fairfax."

"Randell is very good; he should be able to handle it. He's strong and he has a deep affection for my father."

"Yes. Well, I'll just go have a word with Randell, then, to give him some instructions. I'll call again tomorrow."

Dr. Blackman left the room, and Sabrina suddenly felt very weak. She sat down in a chair and clasped her trembling hands together. She shook her head and murmured, "You've got to be stronger than this, Sabrina. You're going to have to take care of things now. . . ."

Other than Sabrina, Elberta Symington was the sole living relative of Sir Roger Fairfax. She was a tall, thin woman with nervous mannerisms but at the same time gave the impression that she was always right about every issue. Elberta was the strong-willed widow of a businessman who had not prospered. During their whole married lives, Mrs. Symington's brother, Sir Roger, had helped Mr. and Mrs. Symington pay the bills. When Mr. Symington died, he left no more than a two-room cottage and a pitifully small allowance for his widow. Fortunately there had been no children for Elberta Symington to struggle with.

"I don't think my dear brother can live long."

Sabrina looked up and saw that her aunt had taken station in front of the desk in her father's study. She had a wraith-like appearance and still wore her widow's weeds of black even though her husband had died more than four years earlier. "It would be God's mercy if he were taken now."

"Don't talk like that, Aunt Elberta!" Sabrina said more sharply than she had intended. She had been struggling with Mr. Smith, the manager of her father's firm, for over a week, and things looked absolutely hopeless. "Father's going to be all right. He ate a great deal more this morning than usual."

"Well, I suppose it's best to look on the bright side, but we must face reality."

Sabrina had faced nothing *but* reality for the past week. Her head was aching from attempts to find some way out of the morass that the business had become. She had been totally unaware of how bad off financially her father was, but Smith had made it plain that the situation was grim indeed. The loss of the *Sabrina* had sunk the manager's hope, and he had told Sabrina that there seemed to be no way out, especially with Sir Roger helpless.

The two women were interrupted as Randell came to the door. "It's Mr. Franks to see you."

"Show him in, Randell," Sabrina instructed.

"Yes, miss."

"Would you excuse me, please, Aunt Elberta? I need to talk with the solicitor."

"I'll be glad to stay, but I'm sure he has nothing good to say."

"Thank you, Aunt Elberta. That won't be necessary."

Huffily Elberta rose and left, passing by a rather short man with sandy hair on her way out.

"Good afternoon, Miss Fairfax."

"Mr. Franks. Good of you to call. Will you have a seat?"

Franks looked around and then settled himself in the chair that Elberta had vacated. He had a case in his hand and balanced it on his lap, seemingly looking for words to say.

"I'm afraid you can't have very good news, Mr. Franks."

"I wish I had better." Franks shook his head. "I've done everything I could. Mr. Smith and I have been going over the accounts, and—"

Sabrina's heart sank. She had had some hope that Mr. Franks, who had been a good friend of her father as well as his solicitor, had found some solution, but she found no hope on his face. "You may as well tell me the worst. I'll have to hear it sooner or later."

"I'm afraid that's true—and I'm afraid it will be sooner."

"Is it really so terrible?"

"It couldn't be worse, frankly." He opened his briefcase and pulled out several sheets of paper. "Word has gotten out of the failure of your father's affairs, and several creditors have appeared. Your father made these loans but neglected to mention them to Mr. Smith." He passed the papers over and sat silently while Sabrina stared at them. They amounted to a great deal of money.

She handed them back, saying, "What's to be done?"

Mr. Franks shifted uneasily in his chair. He ran his fingers over the case, obviously embarrassed. "Things are very bad, Miss Fairfax. When something like this happens, creditors all converge. They all want their money, of course, and there is no money."

"We'll have to sell the estate, then?"

"That is not possible. It's already mortgaged. There's a second mortgage, as well. I'm afraid there will be a terrible lawsuit between the two mortgage holders." Franks went on speaking of the various loans that were out, and each one seemed to drive a nail into Sabrina's spirit. She finally interrupted him and said, "Give me the worst. What's going to happen?"

"I'm going to try to salvage a little something so you'll have a small income, but your father was a gambling man. That doesn't come as a surprise to you, I'm sure, but you're going to lose this house. There's no getting around that, and that includes the furnishings. And I'm afraid most of the personal property, as well."

Sabrina felt as if she had heard a door close, locking her in a dark, terrifying place. She had known little fear up to this time, but she was learning it now in a most terrible way.

———

For two weeks Sabrina had met almost daily with Mr. Franks or Mr. Smith. She did not tell her father the worst of it, but neither could she deceive him. He grew even paler and seemed to fall into a deep depression. Sabrina slept very little these days as she alternated between worrying about their financial lives and her father's precarious health. She was able to do little.

Sir Charles Stratton visited her once each week, offering his condolences, but Sabrina was aware that their relationship had changed. It was not so much what Stratton said as his attitude. *When I was a wealthy woman, you were interested in me, Charlie,* she thought as he left after his second visit. *Now I'm a poor woman, and you've lost interest.* As much as she had enjoyed Charles's company, the thought of losing him did not trouble Sabrina, for she could not picture a life with him.

One afternoon Mr. Franks came for one of his frequent visits. He fidgeted and spoke of the weather until finally Sabrina said, "What is it? More bad news, I suppose."

"I—I'm afraid you and your father are going to have to vacate the house this week, Miss Fairfax. The creditors have taken action, and they have the necessary papers."

"But where will we go?" Sabrina hated herself as soon as

she spoke these words. She was not used to looking for pity and knew that Mr. Franks had no answer for her.

"I understand that your aunt has offered to take you in."

"We can't live with her. She's so gloomy."

Mr. Franks looked down at his feet for a moment before lifting his face. "I'm afraid you have little choice, Miss Fairfax. We all have to do things we don't want to do."

The words struck Sabrina like a sharp blow. She realized that all of her life she had been protected from the harsh realities of life, but now there was no more hiding.

"Very well," she said wearily. "This week, did you say?"

"As soon as possible, I'm afraid."

Sabrina spent five days frantically trying to get ready to move. Aunt Elberta had been there to help but had warned Sabrina, "I have a very small house, you realize. You can't bring much."

"You don't have to worry. None of the furnishings are ours. They all go to the bank."

Sabrina had been told that her jewelry would have to be turned over to the court, but she had taken two pieces. One was a diamond necklace that had belonged to Sir Roger's mother, who had given it to Sabrina on her sixteenth birthday. She knew it was valuable and wondered if she would be prosecuted for keeping it. As far as she knew, there was no written record of the necklace. She also kept a large ruby ring that her own mother had given her when she was fourteen. It was a family heirloom that had belonged to Sabrina's great-great-grandmother. She kept these two pieces but nothing else.

The biggest problem, of course, was taking care of her father. There was only one bedroom in Elberta's house, but Elberta had offered to give up the room and sleep in the main room with Sabrina. Sabrina had spent the better part of a day helping Cecily and Randell move a washstand and a chifforobe to her aunt's cottage. Defying the mandate that all the furnishings belonged to the creditors, she had taken these two furnishings.

The question of how to care for her father was always

present. She could not afford to pay the wages of any of the servants, so she and her aunt would have to do everything for the sick man.

Sabrina was physically tired and emotionally drained. More than once at night she had given way to tears but had managed to keep such scenes from her aunt and from everyone else.

Wearily she left her aunt's house and went back home to try to cheer her father up. Elberta had been taking care of her brother while Sabrina worked at the cottage, and now Elberta met Sabrina at the door. She knew at once that something terrible had happened.

"Sabrina—" Elberta was rarely at a loss for words, but now she struggled to get them out as tears formed in her eyes and ran down her cheeks. "He's gone, Sabrina! It happened no more than thirty minutes ago."

Sabrina Fairfax knew then the depths of despair. She was now not only poor but alone, as well! Except for this gloomy woman who stood before her, she had not a relative in the world. She silently followed her aunt to her father's bedroom and looked down at his peaceful face. *He looks so rested now,* she thought. *He's better off out of all this. He could never have borne it!*

The Necklace

Four

$\mathscr{S}$abrina straightened her back and groaned. She looked at the wood she had split and stacked and said, "Well, there, it's done. If Father saw me splitting wood, he would turn over in his grave." Moving slowly, she walked around the back of the cottage and leaned the ax against the step. She looked down the row of houses all so close together, marveling once again that there was barely room for a person to pass between them. Each yard had a line for hanging clothes, and the cold breeze filled the various sheets, dresses, shirts, and unmentionables, making them dance together. *They look like a line of ghosts,* she thought.

A group of young children were playing a game of ring around the rosie in the next yard, and she leaned against the tiny porch and watched them. A tinge of envy came to her as she realized that she had not known such happiness since her father had died. She had been thrust into adulthood, poverty, and hard labor all at the same time.

She could not stop thinking about the funeral and how few of her father's old "friends" had attended. The church had been less than a quarter full, and the funeral service had been a perfunctory affair, bringing no comfort at all to Sabrina. She thought of the grave, where there had barely been enough money for a small stone, nothing like the magnificent statuary that adorned the graves of Sir Roger Fairfax's ancestors. Her aunt, Elberta, had wanted to put no stone at all there, for there was so little money, and the two had argued over this. Sabrina had won that argument, but it had been practically the last one.

A sound overhead caught her attention, and she looked up into the cold sky. A flock of geese were winging their way toward the west, and she watched their flight until they disappeared. "I wish I could fly away like you," she muttered. Then she shook her head in disgust. *I've got to stop talking to myself. It's getting to be a bad habit.* It was, as a matter of fact, a long-standing habit, but it had never bothered Sabrina until recently.

Sabrina was finding life with her aunt nearly intolerable, for Elberta was not an easy woman to live with—and that was putting it mildly. She was a miserly woman, and although Sabrina realized this was a necessity, she could not help resenting it. She had managed to come out of the wreckage of the financial morass her father had left with less than a hundred pounds, and she had given a quarter of this to her aunt. Sabrina hoarded the rest, not telling Elberta of it, and every night before she went to bed she took out the diamond necklace and the ruby ring and held them in her hands for a long time. At least here was something more than abject poverty.

Now Sabrina turned back wearily into the house and began to gather the ingredients for a simple stew. Her aunt had gone down the street to visit a sick neighbor and had charged Sabrina with going to the greengrocer and the butcher to get a few groceries. She had given her a few coins, and Sabrina had spent them all. But now as she stood looking at the tiny morsel of meat she had been able to buy, the memory of the hams and legs of mutton and sides of bacon that used to adorn the kitchen in her old home came to her. The small bit she had brought home today would have gotten lost or thrown away as excess in that kitchen!

The afternoon sun was sinking toward the horizon, and Sabrina knew that if she did not start the meal that her Aunt Elberta would not let her forget it. She had already received many lectures on how she was not a lady of property now and would have to learn to work along with the rest of them!

A touch on her calf startled her, and she looked down to see Ulysses staring up at her. "Hungry, are you? Well, here's a bit because you're such a good boy!" Ulysses took the bit of meat from her hand. She stroked his fur, thinking of the argument she'd had with her aunt over the cat. Elberta had insisted she get rid of Ulysses, that it would be an extra expense, but Sabrina had won the argument. She stooped to pick up the cat. "You're my best friend, aren't you?" She felt him purr and held him tightly until he protested, then put him down and turned her attention to the meal.

Sabrina had never learned how to cook and had made several mistakes that wasted food, burning a steak beyond the state of edibility, for one, and now as she sat at the table cutting up vegetables for the stew, she suddenly felt the enormity of her downfall. For short periods of time she was able to forget it, but then the thought of where she had been and where she now was would come on her and almost crush her with an intolerable weight.

Suddenly she heard a knock and with a start realized she had been sitting there bitterly thinking of her life and making no progress on the stew for some time. She got to her feet and wiped her hands on her apron. She wore a scarf around her hair, for bathing was a luxury she had learned to live without. Elberta had no tub, and the only bathing possible was with a basin.

Sabrina strode to the door and opened it to see Sir Charles Stratton standing there.

"Hello, Sabrina."

"Hello, Charles." Sabrina was suddenly aware of the difference in Stratton's attitude. He had taken his hat off, but he was studying her with distaste. *No wonder,* she thought. *I look like a charwoman.* "Come in, Charles."

"I can't stay but a moment," Stratton said as he stepped inside.

"Won't you have a seat?"

"No, thank you, I just came by to see if there was anything I could do for you. How are you getting on?"

"Very well."

"I know it's been very hard on you."

Sabrina shrugged her shoulders. "It hasn't been easy."

"I thought I had better come by and see what I could do in the way of finances."

Sabrina's head lifted. "What do you mean 'in the way of finances'?"

"Well, let's be honest with each other, Sabrina," Stratton said. He moved his hat around in his hands nervously. "I know your father made some unwise decisions."

"It seems everyone knows that."

"Well, it's common talk."

"I'm sure it is. Now, what is the intent of your visit?"

"Well, you must need money, my dear." Stratton reached into his inner pocket and came out with an envelope. "I've thought a great deal about it, and I want you to have this." He extended the envelope and stood waiting expectantly.

For one moment Sabrina almost reached out and took the envelope. She certainly needed money badly enough. And she was not really angry with Charles Stratton. Sabrina was not naïve where people were concerned. She might not know how to cook, but she had been born with a sense of what people were like. Ever since she was a young girl she had found this talent to be very useful.

"What you're saying is good-bye, isn't it, Charles?"

"Why, of course not!"

But Sabrina knew better. Charles Stratton would never marry a penniless woman. Sabrina Fairfax, the daughter of a wealthy man, was one thing, but Sabrina Fairfax, a penniless woman, was another. Sabrina was well aware that Charles had wrestled with trying to find a way to say good-bye to her gracefully. She understood instantly that his offer of money seemed to him the easiest way of doing it. This did not surprise her. Charles was no different from most men, she had long ago decided. A woman to him was an ornament, and if the ornament came with a fortune, why, so much the better. But as much as Sabrina needed the money, she would not accept it.

"Thank you, Charles. It was kind of you to offer, but I can't accept it."

Stratton's jaw dropped. "Don't be foolish, Sabrina!" he said sharply. "You need the money. Take it."

"Thank you, Charles. I think you'd better go now."

A flush suffused his cheeks. Angrily he stuffed the envelope back into his pocket and said stiffly, "Well, I trust you'll have a good day."

"Thank you for coming by, Charles."

Stratton whirled and jammed his hat down over his head. He jerked the door open and let it slam behind him with a resounding bang.

"Well, good-bye to you, Sir Charles," Sabrina said aloud. She went back to the table and resumed cutting vegetables. She was surprised to find herself singularly undisturbed by the conversation. She had already said good-bye in her mind to Charles Stratton, knowing that he would never pursue her now that she had lost her fortune.

She had finished chopping the vegetables and put the stew on the fire when she heard the door closing. Aunt Elberta came in and said, "I'm worried about Mrs. Peterson. That's a bad sickness she's got. We'll have to take her some of the stew." She lifted the lid on the pot. "You've got too many carrots in there."

"I'm sorry, Aunt Elberta."

Elberta stared with dismay into the pot. "And you cut them up too small. You have to leave them larger than that or they'll just dissolve."

"I'll learn how, I suppose, in time."

Elberta shook her head with disapproval. "Did you finish splitting and stacking the wood as I asked you to do?"

"Yes, it's all done." Sabrina was careful to always answer Elberta in an even tone. The woman was extremely hard to live with, but no one else had volunteered to take her in.

"Did anyone call?"

"Charles Stratton."

"Sir Charles! He came here?"

"Yes, he did."

"What did he want? Did he ask you out?"

"He came to say good-bye."

"What do you mean good-bye?"

Sabrina was tired. She had worked hard all morning at menial tasks. She was a strong young woman, but housework was not something she could do with much cheer. It always discouraged her and reminded her that she no longer had servants. She said coolly, "That was what he really came for. He offered to buy me off."

"Buy you off! What are you talking about?"

"He offered to give me money so that he would have a clear conscience for not having anything else to do with me, Aunt Elberta."

"He didn't say anything like that. He couldn't! He's too much of a gentleman."

"He didn't say it out loud, but that's what it was for."

"How much did he give you?"

The avarice in her aunt's voice was obvious. "I don't know. I wouldn't take it."

Anger danced in Elberta's eyes. "Didn't take it! Why not? Have you lost your mind? You need all the money you can get."

"I don't need his money."

"You're not too proud to come and live off *my* charity! I can't see why you're too proud to take money from him."

The barbed remark stirred Sabrina's anger. She started to answer but then realized that if she answered as she was tempted to there would be an unpleasant period lasting for several days. Elberta could not take being crossed, and she knew how to make life totally unbearable. "I just couldn't take it," Sabrina said quietly, then got up and went outside. She buried her head in her hands and struggled against the tears that threatened to come. "I've got to stay here," she said. "There's no place else for me to go."

———

For the next few weeks Sabrina managed to endure her aunt Elberta's endless criticism. Sabrina was a determined young woman and always thought she could do anything she set her mind to. She got up each morning mentally prepared for her aunt's cutting remarks and constant criticism. She had long ago given up hope of doing anything that pleased the woman. The only thing she could do now was try to keep as much peace as possible between them.

She had, during this time, met with two of her old friends, but it had been a painful meeting in each case. Both of them had tried to appear as though nothing had happened, but it was obvious to Sabrina that she was now not one whose friendship was highly regarded. As a matter of fact, she saw that she embarrassed both of them as they tried to show a sprightly interest. Why should they be interested in her life? Were they interested in making a few pence to buy food for two women? Could they take any possible interest in making old clothes over to last longer?

Sabrina gained some wisdom from these two encounters. She saw in her friends the woman she once had been. "I would have done exactly the same if one of them had been in my position and I still had money," she muttered. This came as a bitter truth to Sabrina. She had led a shallow, selfish life without realizing it, and now she was reaping some of the results.

One late February day the pastor came to visit. She seated him by the fire, and he twisted his hat nervously between sips of his tea. His name was Simms, and Sabrina had seen him only in the pulpit, except on two occasions when he had called at the house. That had been months ago, and now as Rev. Simms sat in her aunt's humble cottage, Sabrina realized that he was at a loss. His parish was composed primarily of wealthy people, and he knew well how to deal with their problems. But as she watched him squirm and try to make conversation, she realized he had no idea at all what to say to her.

Finally, after a five-minute struggle to keep the conversation going, Rev. Simms put his cup down and said, "I'm so very sorry for your loss, Miss Fairfax. Your father was a good man."

"Yes, he was," Sabrina said and offered no more.

Simms looked around the room, which offered no evidence of wealth, and said, "I trust that you're—" He broke off and then stood to his feet. "If there's anything, my dear Miss Fairfax, that I can do, I pray that you will let me know."

"Of course, Rev. Simms."

Simms was turning his hat even more rapidly, and Sabrina knew that he was not yet finished with his mission. He had come, she realized, with something definite to say and wondered what in the world it could be.

"I think I should mention that we have a certain fund, which is under my hand."

"A fund? What kind of fund, Rev. Simms?"

"Well, it's—it's for those who are in need."

"The paupers' fund," Sabrina said, and polar ice was never colder than her eyes. "Thank you, Reverend. I'm not quite a pauper yet."

"Oh, I didn't mean to offend you, but obviously—"

"Thank you for coming by, sir." She ushered the clergyman out and refrained from slamming the door. Instead, she forced herself to close it gently, then stiffened and leaned back against it. She felt like screaming and cursing and pulling her hair, but again she refrained from following her first instinct. "He meant well," she whispered. "But deliver me from people who mean well!"

When Sabrina had moved out of the house, she had dumped all of the papers from her father's desk drawers into a bag with the intention of sorting through them later. With her aunt gone for the morning, now was as good a time as any. There were letters from people of all sorts—some from twenty and thirty years earlier—bills, notes, and old legal documents, most of them musty with age.

Sabrina had no thought of finding anything worthwhile, but she checked every document just in case it was something she had need of. She read some of the love letters that her parents had sent to each other, trying to go back to the time when her mother had been alive. She missed her mother, who had been a soft-spoken, gentle woman who had left this earth at the age of thirty-three. She went over the lines of one tender love letter, thinking of the young woman who had written it and of the man who had received it, and wished that they were both still alive.

She placed the letter with the stack of some fifteen or so items that were worth keeping. The larger pile was full of worthless things destined for the fire.

She picked up the next item, which was a rather large envelope, and pulled two pieces from it. One proved to be a map.

When she unfolded it, she did not recognize any of the places on the map, but a section of it was traced out with a heavy black line. She saw the names *Holston* and *Cumberland*. She knew that Cumberland was in England, but she had never heard of Holston.

She wondered at the significance of the map for some time before turning to the other smaller sheet of paper that had been in the same envelope. She started reading it and realized that it was a deed. She was not, of course, an expert in law, but the deed plainly said that the property in question had been sold to Roger Fairfax, and it included the legal description. It seemed to be a rather large tract of land—some two thousand acres!

A sudden hope came to Sabrina. "Two thousand acres! That must be worth *something*. And since the deed's here, the lawyers and the creditors didn't get it."

She read the deed more excitedly, and she saw that it had been signed in North Carolina. The name sounded familiar, but she could not place it. For a long time Sabrina sat there studying the map. There didn't seem to be any large cities on it, but there were many rivers with strange names. Finally she realized with a shock that this land was not in England at all but in another country.

But what other country? She could not tell, but she would go tomorrow to Mr. Franks. "He'll know where it is," she whispered. "Maybe it'll sell for enough money so I can get out of here and start a new life."

The wind was chilled as Sabrina walked along the shore of the River Thames. Fishing boats were bobbing up and down, for the river was rough. The clouds rolled dirty and dark over the horizon, and the wind came ashore, making a keening noise.

Sabrina drew her coat tighter around her throat as she went over her conversation with Mr. Franks once more in her mind. When she had shown the map and the deed to Mr. Franks, he had taken one look and said, "Why, this is in the Colonies, Miss Sabrina."

"The Colonies!" Sabrina had thought little about the Colonies.

"The deed is clear, Miss Fairfax, as much as I can tell from this far away. But, of course, things have been in a flux in that part of the world for some time. Especially the land west of the original Colonies. One would simply have to go there to find out. The land may be very valuable, or it may be worth nothing—or the deed may even be questionable. Impossible to say from this distance."

Sabrina stopped and stood there looking out at the river. She tried to imagine that it was the Atlantic Ocean and she was looking across at the new nation that had been borne out of the Revolution. She knew so little about that land. There were wild Indians there, she knew that much. She had heard there were large cities along the seaboard, but Franks had told her that this land lay far away, a rough land. She had never thought of leaving England, but now there was nothing here for her.

I could sell the diamonds to get enough money for my fare to go to America. The land may be worth a great deal. The thought took her by surprise and disturbed her greatly. She couldn't leave London! This was the only home she had ever known. She turned and walked quickly away from the river and tried to put the alien thought out of her mind. She was afraid, and she knew it. The idea of going to a strange land, knowing no one, with no profession, no friends, no relatives. Who wouldn't be frightened?

Suddenly she realized she was passing by the barge where she had seen the fight and thought of the man who had been beaten down. He had fought until he could not fight any longer. She stopped and stared at the barge. All signs of the fight were gone, but she remembered his courage and his strange name—Zion, was it?

He's from the lower class, she thought, *but he has more courage than I have.*

Sabrina argued with herself for several minutes. Finally she decided, "What have I got to lose? I have nothing here—no belongings, no family, no land. I might as well go. Even if I discover that the land isn't really mine, I haven't lost anything! At that instant she made up her mind. "I'm going to sell the necklace and go to America!"

PART II

Sion

June 1791 – March 1792

Back to the Mines

Five

As soon as Sion Kenyon entered the house of his employer, Cradoc Evans, he knew that what he had feared had come to pass.

"Come in, Sion—may we have a small drink, is it?"

"To be sure, Mr. Evans."

At Evans's gesture Sion took a seat and glanced around the kitchen. Mrs. Evans was not there, which was unusual. He suspected that Cradoc had sent her away so she would not have to be witness to the scene that might be painful.

"There we are, my boy. Drink it off!"

Sion drank the small beer, wiped his mouth with the back of his sleeve, and said quietly, "Very good it is, Mr. Evans. You always make the best small beer in all of Wales."

"Kind of you to say so, it is," Evans said. He turned the large cup around nervously in his hands. Finally he looked at his friend with troubled eyes. "It's sorry I am to have to tell you this, Sion, but you'll not be able to stay in this place."

"You sold it, then?"

"Aye. I agreed with Thomas Powell yesterday. He'll be taking over in a week." With a futile wave of his hand, Evans added, "Sorry I am to have to tell you this."

"I've been expecting it."

"Indeed, I suppose you have. Molly and I have been fearful to tell you. You've become like a son to us. Indeed you have, Sion."

"You've been very good to me, sir. I remember the first day I came here. I had no more knowledge of farming than a stone."

"That you did not, but you caught on quick. Quicker than anyone I ever saw."

Sion Kenyon had lost his mother to cholera when he was just a lad and his father to a mining accident not much later. He had come to work for Cradoc Evans and his wife just outside the village of Carmarthen. The farm had become a home to him, and Cradoc and Molly Evans had become more like parents than employers. They were growing older now, though. Cradoc was troubled with rheumatism and able to do very little except make the small beer he so enjoyed.

They had first mentioned moving over a year ago, when Cradoc had moaned in pain as he tried to work in the field. "I'll not be able to do this much longer, Sion. Molly and I will have to go stay with my brother, and it pains me greatly."

Since then Sion had known that the day would come when the farm would be sold. Now as he sat with the man who was a second father to him, he took another sip of the frothy liquid and said, "I'm grieved you're in bad health, you and your dear wife."

"Well, God has been good to us. He has given us a long and good life. We had no children, but we had you, Sion. That's meant a lot to Molly and me."

The two men sat there quietly enjoying each other's companionship in the kitchen. It was a quiet hour, but Sion well knew that he had turned a corner in his life. After a time Sion leaned forward and pressed the arm of Cradoc Evans that was stretched out on the table. "You'll not be worrying about me. I'll make out fine."

"I know you will. You're a good man, Sion. I never saw anyone better with a farm. When you took over two years ago, I wasn't sure. But you've not made a mistake that I know of."

Sion laughed. He was a well-built individual with light brown hair and brown eyes. He ran his fingers along the scar on the side of his neck as he remembered the day he got that scar. He had been down in the mines leading a pony out as he pulled a cart full of coal. A timber broke and fell onto Sion's neck, leaving a jagged slash, and his father simply put some coal dust on it and laughed, saying, "There you are, me boy. You'll have a fine scar now to show you're a miner."

Sion ran his forefinger along the scar absentmindedly, a habit he had tried to break himself of. When deep thought came upon him, or a decision had to be made, he found himself stroking the scar.

"I talked to the new owner and told him what a good man you are about a farm, but he has two grown sons of his own. They'll all be coming here to do the farming. So there it is. No place for you, I'm afraid."

"No matter. I'm strong, and the good Lord will look out for me."

"That He will. I thought, perhaps, you'd be going back to the mines."

"A thing I'd never do!"

"You disliked the mines so much, then?"

"They killed my dad, and it's no job for a human being."

Evans shook his head. "Many a Welshman would fight you over that, to be sure."

"They work in the mines because they have to. There's nothing else to do in this land. It's either farming or coal mining, especially in this valley."

Cradoc Evans leaned forward and put his hand out. It was frail now, although it had been strong ten years ago when Sion Kenyon had first gripped it. Now age had had its way with Cradoc, and Sion was careful to hold it gently. "You'll be leaving the valley, then?"

"I'll try to find work here. This is the only place I know. A man hates to be torn up from his roots."

"Aye, the Scripture says, 'As a bird that wandereth from her nest, so is a man that wandereth from his place.' "

"I'll not be wandering—but no mines for me, not unless it's a matter of staying alive!"

The sun cast its pale gold light down over the valley, a great wash of antiseptic light. The trees that Sion passed on his way down the winding road shed shadows on the ground like columns. The landscape had a tawny hue. The reds and golds were long gone, brought down by wind. Far to the west the ancient hills hunched as the north wind broke upon them.

The rains had fallen earlier, and now the air was cold. Sion looked across the way, and to him the hills in their sullen haze seemed to brood some brutal thought. He pulled his coat tighter around his throat and trudged along the road, filled with nothing much except a desire for warmth and food. For the past two weeks he had walked not only the immediate area, where he knew everyone, but the neighboring villages as well. Times were hard, and he had found no permanent work—only a few jobs by the day that paid a few farthings.

A large yellow dog rushed out from the house that lay to his right, filling the air with a rapid staccato of barking. Sion was good with animals and simply stood and waited until the animal reached him. Then he stretched out his hand and said, "Here, boy." The dog stared at him for a moment, absolutely still, then cautiously the animal advanced. Sion did not move until the dog had sniffed his hand thoroughly. Carefully Sion stroked his head.

"You're a fine one," he said as he looked up at the house. "This is my last hope," he muttered, and the dog whined at his tone. "Not your fault, old boy, but it's been a rough time for me." He straightened up and started toward the house. Smoke was rising in a wreath of gray from the chimney. It was soon caught by the cold wind and dissipated. Three cows were in a pen to the left of the house, and they put their heads over the fence and lowed at him as if they were expecting their dinner.

Sion stepped onto the porch, his bedroll over his shoulder, and felt the weariness that afflicted his soul more than his body. His body was strong enough, but the constant series of rejections had worn him down. It had been hard for him to take. He had long been an amateur pugilist and had learned to suffer hard blows to his body, but the blows to his spirit hurt worse.

He knocked on the door sharply. No one came for a moment, then finally a man opened the door. "Yes, what will it be?"

"I am looking for Angor Grufydd."

Something changed in the man's face. "Me father," he said, "but you'll not have heard. He passed on two years ago."

Quickly Sion said, "Sorry, I am. I didn't know your father,

but he was a good friend of my own dad a long time ago. They worked together in the mines."

"And what might your name be?"

"Sion Kenyon. My father's name was Hugh."

"Why, me father spoke of him many times." The speaker was a man of thirty or thirty-five with dark hair and eyes. He was shorter than Sion but trim, and the scars turned black with coal dust around his face. The black ground into his hands told Sion that he was a miner.

"I'm Rees Grufydd. Come in and warm yourself at the fire. Will a cup of tea go down well?"

"I wouldn't want to be a bother."

"Bother! Well, devil fly off, if it ever becomes a bother for Rees Grufydd to give a man a cup of tea, I'd rue the day. Come in! Come in!"

Sion stepped in and took in the main room, which contained a fireplace, a table, a few cabinets nailed to the wall on one end, and several chairs and a sad relic of a couch on the other. The walls were covered with pictures clipped out of magazines, as well as one painting of a young couple.

Rees saw his glance and said, "That's me dad and mum painted a year after they were married."

"You look very much like your father."

"So they say."

A pretty woman with two children came in from outside.

"Here, this is me wife, Glenda."

"I'm glad to know you, sir." Glenda Grufydd was a tall woman with bright blue eyes and red hair. She smiled and said, "And these are our two children. This is Ysbail, and this is Merin, our son."

Ysbail was a girl of twelve or thirteen—the exact image of her mother with bright blue eyes and red hair. She nodded as she examined Sion carefully. Merin appeared to be about six. He was a sturdy young man with brown hair and warm brown eyes. They both greeted Sion politely.

"Come and take a seat by the fire. Dinner will be ready soon. Me wife's a terrible cook, but no matter." He winked at Sion, and his lip twitched with a grin.

"I never notice you turning anything down!" Glenda laughed.

"Oh, I couldn't do that. It would be an imposition."

"None of that," Rees insisted. "Have a seat, and I'll tell you something that, perhaps, you don't know about your own father."

Sion was curious, and he took the offered seat. He could smell fresh meat cooking, and his stomach contracted, for he had had no substantial meal for two days. Only bits and pieces that couldn't sustain a man. He sat down and smiled at the boy and girl who had stationed themselves so they could see his face. "Did you know my father?" Sion asked Gruyfdd.

"No, but me father talked about him a lot." Rees sat down across from Sion and filled a pipe as he talked. "The two were great friends."

"So my father told me."

"But I wonder, did he tell you that he saved me own father's life?"

"No, he never said a word about that."

"Well, he did. There was a cave-in, and me father was caught along with three others. The gas was bad. They were dying. I've heard Father tell the story so many times. He was lying there unable to move, pinned down by a heavy timber, and he tried to keep the spirits of the other two men up." Rees puffed on his pipe, sending miniature clouds of purple smoke upward. "And then Father said he heard a noise, and he knew someone was coming. Ah, bless me, that was a fine time for him. He said he'd never heard such a sweet sound in all his life."

The fire crackled in the fireplace, and the smell of fresh food and the welcome he had received warmed Sion Kenyon. "It was my father, was it?"

"Indeed it was! Me father said yours came in like a giant throwing rocks and timbers away. When he got to him, he said, 'Well, there's a pretty mess you've got yourself into!' and he laughed, Father said. My father said that was the best laugh he ever heard, and he knew that God had sent him."

"My father never told me that."

"Well, he should have. He lifted the timber off me father as if it were a matchstick, then got him out of there and went back for the other two. That was a long time ago, but me father remembered it always. And so do I in a way. And so should you. Your father was a man of great courage."

"Indeed he was. I lost him to another mine accident almost ten years ago."

"Man, it's sorry I am to hear that. But he's with the good Lord now, I trust."

"Yes, he and my mum were both fine Christians. I try to follow their example."

"I try to follow the example of my parents, as well. Now tell me something about yourself. Where have you been living all these years? Where are you headed?"

Sion spoke of his life simply and quickly and without any self-pity whatsoever. He finished by saying, "And so I've been tramping around looking for work on a farm."

"Hard times for the farmers."

"So I've discovered."

At that moment Glenda Grufydd interrupted them. "Come and eat before I throw it to the pig."

"Don't do that, me darling," Rees laughed. He got up and said, "Come along, Sion. Traveling makes a man hungry."

Indeed traveling had made Sion hungry, and after Rees asked a quick blessing, he applied himself to the food—boiled mutton, cabbage, cheese, and home-baked bread. He ate only a little until Rees urged him on.

"A big fellow like you can eat more than that. How much do you weigh?"

"About thirteen stone when I'm not thinned down. A little less than that now."

"And would you be thinning down for a reason, then?"

"Merin, don't be impertinent!"

"It's all right, Mrs. Grufydd." Sion turned to the boy and said, "Yes, son, I do a bit of friendly boxing."

"Ah, you are a pugilist, then," Rees said, his eyes lighting up. "I do a little of that line myself."

"And you have no business doing it!" Glenda snapped. "A grown man scuffling and coming home with his nose bloody!"

"You see how it is, Sion? Women don't understand these things."

Suddenly Sion laughed. It made him look even younger than his twenty-three years. "I'm much in the way of your missus," he said. "I've come home so bruised I could hardly turn over. I wonder what makes a man make a fool of himself like that."

"Why, it's sport, man—it's sport!"

"Sport indeed!" Glenda shook her head. "If I had my way, it would be against the law."

"It *is* against the law in some places, I hear," Sion said.

"Some of our counties have the same law, but that's for professionals."

Sion enjoyed the meal and afterward rose, saying, "A better meal I've never had, Mrs. Grufydd."

"Where will you be going?" Rees asked. "Are you looking for work?"

"Aye. I came to see your father. I knew he was a manager at one time."

"That he was, and if it's to the mines you need to go, I can help you."

"I always said I'd never go back to the mines again. I was a boy when I was last there, but it was an unpleasant time for me."

"The mines are hard, but a man does what he must. Tomorrow morning you'll go with me. I think it will be fine. There have been no layoffs lately and no strikes."

"I'll meet you here at dawn, then, is it?"

"Where will you be staying?" Rees demanded.

"I'll find a place."

"We have a small room in the attic. It's not much, but it's warm. We can fix you up there."

"Would it put you out?"

"You'll put Ysbail and Merin out. It's their playhouse."

"I'd be sorry to do that."

"It's all right," Ysbail said. "I'll help make you a place."

"There you are. You've got a volunteer, and Merin will help, too, won't you, boy?"

"Yes, sir, I will. Can I go to the fight next time you go, Daw?"

"No, you cannot. But it's fishing we may go when the weather breaks. Now, come along. We'll get this man settled in like a king on his throne!"

————————

Sion entered the cage and felt the same fear he'd experienced as a boy of nine. Going down into the earth was not a thing for human beings to do, as far as he was concerned. He crowded in with the other men, shoulder to shoulder with Rees Grufydd as he waited for the stomach-wrenching descent into the mine. It began before he was ready, the cage simply dropping out beneath his feet. He took an involuntary breath and heard Rees's whisper, "Some things never change, and going down to the darkness is one of them. A man would be a fool not to feel something."

The cage picked up speed until Sion felt like he was floating. He remembered this sensation and how hard it had been to keep from crying out each time the cage went down when he had been a boy. His own father had stood beside him then and had always kept a hand on his shoulder during those days.

The cage stopped with a violence that made Sion's knees bend, and then he followed the miners as they stepped out. Sion broke out into a sweat as he surveyed the scene illuminated with the pale glow of lamps. He had been assigned to work with Rees, and he knew he was on trial. They made their way through a long series of tunnels supported by huge black pillars of coal left to support the ceiling.

Finally Rees said, "Here's where we begin. You never dug coal before, Sion?"

"No."

"It's hard work, but it'll put bread on the table. Watch me for a moment."

There was little skill to the work but a great deal of physical labor. Some of the seams were so small that Sion had to practically crawl in and swing the pick with only the strength of his arm. Long before noon the muscles of his arms, shoulders, back, and stomach cried out, for he wasn't accustomed to such intense upper-body work.

After what seemed an eternity, they stopped to drink some of the cold tea they had brought in their lunch pails. "Your stomach aching?" Rees said.

"A bit."

"Think of it this way, it'll be good training. Mining puts the stomach muscles on a man who can take a good blow to the belly."

"A hard way to get in training." Sion looked around and could see only a few of his fellow miners. The pale headlights glimmered, casting almost no light. He turned to Rees and said, "I was always afraid when I was a pit boy."

"A man can be afraid. That's not the question. What he does with the fear? That's what's important."

Sion looked up. "The whole thing could come crashing down."

"That it could, and if you were topside, you could be struck by lightning. We're in God's hands."

"You're right. Even way down below the earth where everything is black and dirty, God is still in charge."

"Aye. Christ is here as much as He is topside."

All day the two worked close together, and when they totaled up the weight of the coal they had sent to the top, Rees was shocked. "Why, you've almost got as much as I have!"

"That may be true, but I don't think I'll be able to get out of bed tomorrow," Sion said ruefully. "I'll be sore as a boil."

"You're a strong man. Come along. Glenda will have a good supper for us tonight."

———

Sion darted to his right just as Ysbail pivoted and dashed off the other way, eluding his outstretched arm.

"You're slow, Sion. You couldn't catch a fly!" she taunted.

"You just wait. I'll get you, and when I do, I'm going to pull that red hair of yours out one hair at a time."

Playing tag was just one of the many games that Sion played with the Grufydd children. There was little to do at night in the valley, and usually the men were tired enough that they wanted no more activity. But Sion had always liked games, and he delighted both Ysbail and Merin with his willingness to play with them. Rees loved to read, and Glenda was always sewing. But the children always found a willing play partner in Sion.

Today Sion was keeping the children occupied while Glenda packed a picnic lunch to take with them to the fair. Rees was reading his Bible while occasionally glancing up at the game of tag.

Sion whirled and pinioned Merin. "I've got you, boy! You're it!" Ysbail moved in close to taunt her brother, and Sion caught her with his free hand. "And I've got you! You both will have to be it now."

"Let me go!" Ysbail cried, but Sion laughed as he held tight to both of them.

"I'm going to teach you a lesson for being so easy to catch." He began to spin in a circle, and Merin laughed with delight while Ysbail screamed at him to let her down. Finally he got dizzy and stopped. He put the two down and noticed Rees and Glenda watching with smiles. "These youngsters of yours are going to wear me out."

"You shouldn't pick me up like that!" Ysbail cried. "It's not genteel."

"Not genteel! Why, is running and screeching genteel?"

"That's different."

"Come, now. It was just a game." Sion smiled. He put his arm around the girl. "Don't be mad. Let's have a smile, can't we?"

Ysbail tried to frown, but Sion poked her in the ribs and she squealed, for she was very ticklish. "There's my girl. Beautiful smile!"

Glenda came into the room to announce that the picnic lunch was packed and she was ready.

Rees winked at Ysbail and said, "Go put your prettiest dress on. There may be some young fellow there you could trap."

"I'd have no boy I had to trap!" Ysbail said defiantly.

"Well, I'll pick one out for you and encourage him to say

hello to you," teased Sion. "A homely child like you needs all the help she can get."

Rees laughed. "There, Ysbail. Now you know you're a homely child. Go get ready."

Ysbail gave Sion a furious look, but he winked at her and whispered, "I may buy you some lemonade if you'll sweeten up."

For the four months that Sion had lived with the Grufydds he had found a warmth and a pleasure he had never known before. Mr. and Mrs. Evans had been like parents to him, but he was enjoying being a part of a younger, fun-loving family. There was a gentle teasing going on constantly between the adults, and the children adored their parents. They had come to adore Sion, too.

Ysbail stomped off but returned in less than three minutes dressed in her fancy dress.

"Is everybody ready now?" asked Rees.

"I'm ready," said Merin. "Can I have some money for lemonade and a candy apple?"

"We'll see when we get there," Glenda said.

Sion said, "You should have asked me. I've got a pocketful of money."

Merin asked Sion, "Will you let me play at some of the games? I may win a prize."

"I don't see why not. It's fair day, isn't it?"

"You spoil these children," Glenda said and tried unsuccessfully to frown. "Indeed you do."

The fair had brought everyone out. It was a glorious October day, and everyone was glad to see the sun. The whole land smelled fresh, and the green was so brilliant it almost hurt the eyes.

The Grufydds arrived at the fair, where it seemed they knew everyone. Sion had met many people and spoke pleasantly to those he knew. He had spent little of his wages and had determined that this day would be memorable for Ysbail and Merin. And, indeed, he made it so. After two hours they had eaten themselves almost to the point of insensibility, and

Glenda said firmly, "No more to eat, now, you hear me! And shame on you, Sion Kenyon, for abusing these poor children!"

"Well, I feel sorry for them. Having such cruel parents must be hard on them. They need a kind uncle to break the monotony of all the meanness you and Rees pour on them."

"Why, you go scratch!" Glenda frowned, and then she had to laugh. "Go find yourself a nice, pretty young girl to bother."

"Not before the contest," Rees said.

"Contest? What contest is that?"

"Well, haven't you heard? There's a pugilistic exhibition. The ex-champion of Wales is here. He's a little bit long in the tooth now, but in his heyday he was a master. He's here to give an exhibition, and I've arranged for Sion here to have a go at him."

Sion turned suddenly. "You've done what?"

"You're going to box the ex-champion of all Wales. It'll be an honor for you."

"You didn't do that really, did you, Rees?" Glenda asked.

"Why, certainly I did! That's one reason I came to the fair." He doubled his fists up and struck Sion on the shoulders. "I've seen enough of you to think you can hold your own."

"Those were just amateur bouts. Nothing serious." Sion had boxed with a few of Rees's neighbors—all miners and husky men. It had been no contest. He had been too fast for any of them, and he had been careful not to get hurt.

"Don't do it, Sion!" Ysbail cried. "He'll hurt you."

"Hurt me! An old man hurt me? What must you be thinking of, Ysbail? Well, I'll have to just show you what it's like to be a real boxer." He winked at Rees and said, "All right. Where's this former champion?"

The ex-champion of Wales, Robert Morgan, was puffing from exertion. The red spot on his right cheek glowed where he had been punched as he doggedly pursued the younger man who retreated before him. "I didn't come to do a dance, young chap. Stand still."

Sion laughed. "If I stand still, you will break my nose and bloody my face."

Robert Morgan threw a punch forward that would have demolished most men, but Sion was too quick. He simply moved his head and let the punch sail over him. He tapped the older man sharply in the chest and then sent a right that had some power. It stopped the man for a moment, and finally Robert looked out at the crowd and said, "Well, dear friends, this was to be an exhibition, but I can't keep up with this young lad, so I suppose the exhibition's over."

The crowd clapped and cheered, for the champion had done well. He had boxed with two men before Sion and had beaten them soundly, but he had barely managed to lay a fist on Sion.

A short, thickset man came forward and said, "He's a will-o'-the-wisp, isn't he, Robert?"

"Aye, that he is. If he could hit as well as he can dodge, he'd be the new champion of Wales."

Turning to Sion as he stepped out of the ring, the man said, "My name's Eric Craven. I manage fighters. I'd like for you to think about coming with me."

Sion stared at the man as he put his shirt back on. "Be a pugilist?"

"Yes. There's real money in it for a good man. I could teach you how to hit. I can tell you're a strong enough bloke."

"He can hit like a mule," Rees said, coming up to stand beside them. "But I doubt if you'll make a pugilist out of him."

"That's right," Sion said. He looked over and saw Ysbail staring at him with wide eyes. He winked at her and then turned to say to the manager, "The only thing worse than going down in the mines would be to become a professional bruiser. Thanks—but no thanks."

A Man of Honor

Six

*T*he explosion came so quickly and so unexpectedly that Sion could not figure out what was happening. He had left the innermost part of the mine where he had been working next to Rees to get a new lamp, for his own wasn't burning properly. He was halfway back to the elevator shaft when suddenly it was as if a giant had sneezed behind him. A sibilant *whoosh* pushed at his back with a force that drove him forward.

Explosion!

Sion caught his balance and heard men's voices crying out. He knew that when an explosion occurred in a mine, it was usually the result of the gas from the coal itself that would creep into hidden crevices, and even such a thing as the light from a miner's headlamp could touch it off.

A rumbling sound came low, as if the earth were groaning, and the foreman was screaming orders, trying to organize a rescue party.

Sion had heard enough stories about mine disasters to know that timing was critical. Without thought Sion dashed forward. His light was gone, and he had to feel his way. He ran head on into a timber, opening a wound over his eyebrow, and felt the blood running down his face, but he ignored it. Shoving the timber aside, he remembered what it was like to play blind man's bluff. This was like that, only he was searching for a man who had befriended him and shown him kindness. There were others, he knew, whom he was not as close to, but his main thought was on Rees Grufydd. As he scrambled over the fallen coal and timbers, bruising himself and scratching his face and hands, he threw himself forward wildly. Finally, when he thought he was almost to the place where he had last seen his friend, he called out the man's name.

He listened hard, but heard no answer. Groaning timbers were threatening to give way, and as he moved forward, one of them did with a crash.

If I had been under that one, it would have been over for old Sion Kenyon! The thought flitted through his mind, but he ignored it. He kept crawling and calling out, and finally he heard a faint whisper.

"Keep talking so I can find you, Rees."

The sound continued, and Sion scrambled toward it. He rammed his head against a timber and blinked away the pain, but then he heard his own name called, and a joy rose up in him.

"Where are you, friend?"

"Right here."

Feeling his way in the stygian darkness, Sion's hands fell on something warm, and he knew he had found his man. He whispered fiercely, "Are you all right, old chap?"

"I'm glad—you came."

"Let me see what this is." Feeling his way carefully lest he bring more timbers down, Sion discovered that a timber had fallen across Rees's legs. Part of the coal had half buried him, as well, so that only his face was exposed. Quickly Sion began to clear away the coal.

"That's—better. It felt like the whole earth were crushing me."

"Hold still now. Let's see about this timber." When he had the coal cleared away, Sion ran his hands along the rough lumber and found it was one of the eight-by-eight timbers used to shore up the ceiling. He felt along the length of it and found it splintered at one end. Putting his arms around it, he tried to hoist it and felt it heave and creak, but he could not move it.

"I'll have to clear the coal from off the timber before I can get you out of here, Rees."

He worked quickly, afraid for the gas, which could still be present. A man could die from the gas as well as from the roof crashing in on him.

Finally he had the timber. He crawled under it, got his legs beneath him, and placing his hands on his thighs, he began to straighten up. At first it did not move, but then it creaked and then he felt it give a fraction. Concentrating all of his strength, he rose slowly only a fraction of an inch and then another—and then another. The timber was clear, but to keep it from falling on Rees again required every bit of strength Sion had. He moved his feet carefully until he had worked the end of the timber clear, then slowly lowered his body until he was on his knees. Finally he lowered it to the floor of the tunnel with a shrug.

Turning at once, he went back and said, "Now, we'll have you out of here." He started to put his arms around Rees, and the man groaned. "What is it, Rees?"

"Me leg. It's broken."

"I'll be as gentle as I can, but we've got to get out of this tunnel."

As if in echo to his words, there was a crash as another part of the tunnel farther down gave in. "I'll have to hurt you, I'm afraid."

"That's all right," Rees whispered. But when Sion picked him up, he muffled a cry and then went limp.

"Better that you're out of it, my friend," Sion said. He struggled back out of the tunnel, and as he moved, he passed the foreman.

"Who's that?" he demanded.

"It's Rees."

"Is he hurt bad?"

"Leg is broken, I think."

"Get him out of here," the foreman said grimly. "Then come back and give us a hand if you can."

By the time Sion got Rees back to the elevator, men were coming down to join the rescue effort. He considered helping them but wanted to get Rees to a doctor quickly. He carried him onto the elevator and waited, sitting beside him.

Rees began to stir and muttered, "Where is this?"

"On the elevator. You'll be all right, Rees."

Rees did not speak again, and soon the elevator lifted them back to daylight. By the time they came out Rees was gritting his teeth against the pain. "You can go back and help the others."

"I will, but first we'll see that this leg is taken care of."

Rees put his hand out, and Sion took it. Rees said quietly, "Your dad saved mine, and now you saved me. Looks like you Kenyons have a habit of taking care of the Grufydds."

"Little enough to do."

"No, not little. You can be sure I'll tell me grandchildren about how you came out of the darkness to save me."

Rees sat in a chair with his right leg on another chair, a cushion under it. His leg had been broken in three places, two above the knee and one below. His face was cloudy as he said, "Blast the leg! A man can't sit around forever."

"It hasn't been forever, Rees," Sion said. He was eating the porridge that Glenda had put before him, along with several pieces of bacon and fresh bread. It was still dark outside, but he ate heartily, knowing he would need his breakfast. During the three weeks that Rees had been recuperating, Sion had worked even harder, for he was now the breadwinner of the Grufydd family. He knew it did not sit well with Rees, for he came from a long line of independent men, but he had little choice.

Glenda had whispered once to Sion, "God sent you here, Sion, to take care of us and to save my man." Sion was not as sure of the workings of God as Glenda or Rees, who often thanked God for Sion's presence when the mine had collapsed. Only two miners had died, for the rescue had been quick and the explosion had not been as fierce as some. Still, Rees was not going to mine any coal for some time, and he was restive under the notion. He toyed now with his porridge, a scowl on his face.

"What's the matter? Merin asked. "Aren't you hungry, Pa?"

Rees snapped at his child, and Merin's face showed a hurt expression.

"Don't bother your father, Merin," Sion said.

"I wasn't bothering him. I just asked why he wasn't eating."

Rees looked ashamed and apologized to his son. "Don't

pay any attention to me, Merin. I'm just in a bad humor."

"Does your leg hurt today?" Ysbail asked, a worried expression on her youthful face.

"Not a bit."

Glenda gave her husband a look. "There's no point in lying about it. Of course it hurts."

"Well, just a bit, maybe, but I don't mind that. It's not being able to work that eats away at me."

"Doesn't the Bible say something about having patience?" Sion jibed, smiling across the table at his friend.

"I don't want to be reminded of that. A man's not a man if he doesn't go out and work."

"You'll be back at work soon enough. We just have to give it some time."

Rees ate slowly and then finally looked up. "I heard you had another round with the manager over the safety requirement."

"I did have a word with him. The company's not doing enough to take care of its men."

"They never do!" Glenda said shortly. She was making a lunch for Sion, and she poured some cold tea into a jar and put a lid on it carefully. "Little do they care what happens to our men down in the bowels of the earth. They can always find more men."

"Now, don't be bitter," Rees said. "Things will get better."

"What did you say to the manager?" Glenda demanded.

"Well, I just wanted to remind him that the miners' union has made some requests and that management had agreed to them. But they haven't been done."

"I bet he didn't like that. He's all for the company and never for the men," Rees grumbled.

"Well, it did get a bit heated. Some of the men started talking about a strike, and I tried to squash that."

The fear of a strike was very real, for when the miners went on strike, there was no money coming in, and few of the miners had enough cash on hand to see them through a long strike. The mine owners were well aware of this. They lived in the big cities, living off the sweat of those who groveled beneath the earth, bringing out the black coal. A strike had never been a good option for miners, Sion realized, and probably never would be.

He got up, saying, "I'm off. Thank you, Glenda." He took his lunch and reached over to tug gently at Ysbail's hair. "You be sweet today—like me."

Ysbail pushed his hand away and caught his eye. "Be careful, Sion."

"Careful I am," Sion nodded, stroking her hair. Then he reached over and tugged a twig of Merin's hair. "And, old man, you take care of your dad, you hear me?"

"I will. When you come home tonight, will you play drafts with me?"

"That I will. You're getting too good for me, though. Beat me three games last night, you did." Sion winked at Glenda and said, "Make him behave himself."

"That's more than I can answer for!"

Rees said, "I wish I were going with you."

"The day will come. You catch up on your Bible reading. Have something good from the Word for me tonight."

"I'll do my best."

————————

Exactly one week after that day, as Sion reached the mine he was met by the manager, who blocked his way. "You won't be needed here."

"What's that supposed to mean? I've cut out more coal than any man on the shift."

"You're a troublemaker, Kenyon. Here's your pay. Now get out!"

"Wait a minute, now. I haven't made any trouble, and Rees is depending on me to keep his family going until he's able to get back to work."

"You should have thought of that before you started talking strike!"

Heat rose in Sion. "I haven't said a word about a strike! As a matter of fact, I've spoken against it."

"I'm not arguing with you. Now get out!"

Sion was tempted to strike out at the manager, but he knew the man had not made this decision. The owners had heard of

Sion's activities and had callously instructed the manager to get rid of him. The same thing had happened before to other men who had campaigned for better working conditions. Sion took the envelope the manager was holding out to him without a word and left the mine.

He made his way back to the house, and as soon as he stepped inside, Rees knew everything. "They let you go, did they?"

"Aye. They said I was agitating for a strike, but that's a lie."

Rees shook his head sadly. "It's a cruel place, the mines. The executives wear their white shirts and their diamonds and eat in their fancy places and live in their fine homes, but they care little for the likes of us."

Sion caught a glimpse of Glenda's face and saw the fear that was there. He said, "I've got a plan. I'm going to London. There's work there, they say, and I'll send back money to keep you going until you're on your feet."

Rees turned his face away, his features working. "I hate to take charity."

"You took me in when I had nothing and made me part of your family. At least, that's how I feel about it. Now it's my turn."

Rees did not answer for a time. Finally he said, "I don't know what we would have done without you these days. I don't know what we'd do without you in the future. I'll say it again. God sent you to take care of us, Sion Kenyon."

Sion shrugged off the words and smiled. "Well, there's no use putting it off. I'll go gather my things and then I'll be off."

Glenda came and put her hand on his arm. "It's grateful I am to you, Sion."

Sion felt then the weight of what he had taken on. He had no skills except farming and mining, and he knew that neither one was in demand. The well-being of this family, maybe even the survival, rested on him, and the thought overwhelmed him. He said with more cheer than he felt, "Why, it'll be a vacation for me. I'll find a good job, and every week I'll send the pay back, except what I need to live on, just until you're able to go back to work, Rees."

Rees shook his head. "It's more blessed to give than it is to receive, but it's bloody hard for a man like me to take all of the receiving and do none of the giving."

"It won't be forever. Maybe I'll come back. The manager may change his mind."

"They never forget," Rees said stonily.

Sion left all the money he had except enough to live on for a week and for his passage. He hated good-byes, so he tried to make them brief. As he hugged the children, he saw how grieved they were. "Don't you worry, now," he assured them. "We're friends always."

"But you'll be gone," Merin cried.

"Aye, but friends are friends even when they're apart. It's writing you I'll be, and you must answer."

"I'll write you," Ysbail said, and tears showed in her eyes.

Sion put his arms around the two again before straightening up. He picked up his bundle of belongings, shook hands with Rees, and laid his hand on Glenda's shoulder. "No fear now. It'll all be well."

He left the cottage and started walking along the road. Almost immediately a farmer picked him up who was going to the coast, and he thought about his friends with a heavy heart as he bounced along on the seat. *I hate to leave,* he thought, *but they're depending on me. God help me to do the right thing. Open some way where I can take care of Rees and his family.*

London was big and loud and confusing. Sion, who had known the quiet of the countryside and the pleasant hum of small villages, was almost deafened by the noise of the place. He spent a day looking for work, but soon admitted that his heart wasn't in it—he had no interest in living in the big city. The next day he made his way out of the city and began traveling around the small villages looking for work on the farms. He quickly found that things were as bad in England as they were in Wales, and there were no coal mines as a last resort.

After a week of taking whatever work he could get—an afternoon here, a morning there—he soon discovered there would be no way he could support himself and send enough money back to keep Rees's family going.

Finally he made his way back to London and went from business to business, more seriously this time, but he had no skills to offer. He was growing desperate after three days of this when he overheard one of the men in a tavern where he had bought a cheap meal speak of a boxing match that was to come. The man's words made him remember the boxing match with the former champion of Wales and the manager who had offered to handle him as a pugilist.

Ordinarily Sion would not have considered such a thing, but desperation was on him now. He paid close attention to the conversation and discovered that the fight would be held the next afternoon. He also heard the men mention that the pugilist was staying at the Green Dragon Inn.

Sion Kenyon was not a man of impulse, and yet as he finished his meal slowly, he knew that this was something he had to try. He had never lost a fight in his life, and now, after enjoying a steady diet of Glenda Grufydd's good cooking and the hard work in the mines, he knew he was hard as nails and as fit as he would ever be. He had always liked amateur boxing but never once had the thought of fighting for money occurred to him. He remembered saying to the manager of the fighter in Wales, *"If there's one thing worse than the mines, it's fighting for money."* Now, however, there was no choice.

He paid his bill and asked, "Where would the Green Dragon be? Could you tell me, sir?" He listened to the instructions and left the tavern.

Twenty minutes later he was standing outside the Green Dragon, looking up at the sign. The dragon was rather anemic looking. It had once been green, but now it was very pale and seemed tired and quite unimpressive. Walking inside, he found the owner and said, "I'm looking for Earl Duggans."

"The Bristol Mangler? That's him over at the table. You didn't come to start a fight with him, I hope?"

"No, nothing like that. Just a word with him."

Approaching the table where two men sat eating, Sion noted that the Mangler was a big man with the brutalized features of his trade. His ears were shapeless balloons of flesh. His deep chest bulged, and the muscles of his arms strained against his sleeves.

"Pardon me. Could I have a word with you two gentlemen?"

"What is it?" the Mangler said, turning to look at him. He had amazingly bright blue eyes, and despite his fearsome appearance had a mild, rather gentle voice.

"My name is Sion Kenyon. I've just come from Wales."

"From Wales. I can hear it in your voice." The other man was small and thin with a mustache that covered his upper lip. He was wearing fine clothes, and diamonds glittered from his left hand and from a pin in his coat. "I come from Wales myself. Which part are you from?"

"I come from Carmarthen."

"I know it well. What can we do for you, sir?"

"I want to become a fighter."

Both men seemed surprised, and the smaller of the two men said, "My name is Ned Chaps. I'm Earl's manager." He took out a cigar, lit it, and studied Sion carefully. "What makes you think you can fight?"

Sion stood there feeling foolish. He shook his head, saying, "I guess I'm not sure myself. All I've ever done is amateur—but I've never been beaten."

Earl Duggans smiled with broad lips that had been flattened by many blows. "You've got nerve, I'll say that for you." He looked across the table and said, "You've been wantin' another boy. Why don't we give 'im a try?"

Ned Chaps lifted his goblet and drank slowly. Then he smiled. "Do you want to have a go at Earl here?"

"Yes, sir. That's all I ask. I know I'm not a champion, but I can win against some, I'm sure."

"Well, he's modest and well spoken, like a good man from Wales. I like that. We'll be doing some training about three o'clock this afternoon." He named the spot and said, "Come around, and we'll give you a try."

"Thank you, Mr. Chaps. I'll be there."

"Well, you shape up well," Chaps said as he walked around Sion. He poked at the muscles of his chest and pinched his biceps. "Hard as the coal you've been digging. Look at that, Earl. You get them stomach muscles by digging coal, believe it or not."

Earl Duggans, the Bristol Mangler, was stripped to the waist. He wore a pair of silk tights and black shoes. "He looks good. We'll see if he's got anything."

Sion had no tights. He had simply taken off his shirt. A crowd of men had collected to see the Mangler work out, and now Ned Chaps raised his voice. "Glad you could come, gentlemen. We have a young man here who thinks he wants to be a fighter. The Mangler will probably change his mind in the next few minutes." He waited until the laughter died down and then said, "All right. Let's see what you've got, Sion Kenyon."

Sion lifted his hands, his fists clenched, and saw something change in the face of Earl Duggans. He had seemed pleasant and gentle when he was having his meal, but now that Sion was in the ring opposite him, he looked angry. It was this anger plus a tremendous strength and endurance that had made him one of the contenders for the championship of England. He moved forward very fast for such a big man. He weighed over two hundred pounds, and his blow, which merely grazed Sion's chest, had such power in it that Sion knew he was in for a struggle. He also knew he'd better get moving, so as the blow struck his chest, he jumped forward, and his left fist flickered out, catching Duggans on the forehead with enough power to stop him cold. A murmur went around the small crowd, and the Mangler grinned.

"You're fast. I can see that."

Sion did not answer, for he knew that to impress Ned Chaps he had to at least show potential. He took several blows to his torso but managed to stay on his feet.

Sion was a faster man than Duggans, and he needed all of his speed and all of his skill. Despite his quickness, he took a great many hard blows. He could have avoided these simply by dodging and weaving, but he knew that was not what Chaps was looking for. Time and again he sent hard blows toward the champion. It was like striking a tree trunk. However, from time to time, when he got a blow in at the midsection, right where the ribs meet over the stomach, he was rewarded by hearing grunts from Duggans.

Finally he was caught by surprise by a blow directly to his jaw. It drove him backward, and he heard a cry go up from the observers. His head was swimming, but he shook it and came up in a position to fight.

Duggans said, "He can take a punch, Ned. Do you want to go on with this?"

"What do you think, Earl?"

"I think you ought to give him a try." He dropped his hands and came forward. "There's many a man taking money for fighting that haven't got what you've got, lad. What'd you say your name was?"

"Sion."

"Zion?" He pronounced it with a *Z*.

"No. Sion with an *S*."

"That's a good Welsh name," Ned Chaps said as he came over with a pleased expression. "I'll arrange a bout the same time Earl has his. We'll see how it goes. You need any money?"

"Aye, a little. I'm helping a friend back in Wales."

"Helping a friend? Well, here's a bit you can help him with. We'll fix you a place to stay. You can be Earl's sparring partner. He needs to see some of that quickness for this bout coming up."

"Thank you, Mr. Chaps."

"You hear that? He's got manners, Earl."

"He can have manners enough for both of us." Earl grinned.

"That's right. Never mind your manners in a fight," Chaps said. "That's lesson number one."

————

Four months of fighting all over England had made a difference in the way that Sion Kenyon thought. He had won most of his bouts, but he had also lost a few, two of them by knockouts.

"The more experienced you get, the better you get," Chaps said. "Tell me. Do you like to fight?"

"No, I don't."

"I thought so. Well, it's a hard life. Not much worse than coal mining, is it?"

"About the same, I'd say. I'd hate to do either of them for the rest of my life."

"Become a champion, and then you'll be rich and make me rich, too."

The worst time that Sion had during this period came at the end of it when he fought a forty-two round fight against Benjamin Brain on a barge anchored to a wharf on the River Thames. He was badly beaten and unable to fight for the next month. Chaps had cleaned him up after they got back to the inn and said, "It was my fault, Sion. I overmatched you. Another year or two, and you'll take this mate. You did fine. Just fine."

Sion was dizzy and ached all over from the battering he had taken from Big Ben. He took the money that Chaps offered him and spoke his thanks. "There was a chap on the wharf who gave me ten pounds. If he'd give ten pounds to a loser, think what he'd give to a winner."

Sion paid little attention to the words. He was thinking of the last letter he had received from Glenda. She did all of the writing at the dictation of her husband, and she had added a footnote that read, *Another month, and Rees will be able to go back to work. I can't tell you how much in your debt we are, Sion. You have fed us and clothed us and kept us going, and God will bless you for it.*

Sion looked up at Ned and said, "You know, Ned, when I don't have to send money to my friend and his family, I won't be doing this anymore."

Ned Chaps studied the battered features of the young man. "It's bad business for me to say so, but I think that would be a good decision. Many a man I know is walking around with only half a brain. I wouldn't want that to happen to you, Sion. Not to a fellow Welshman."

"We understand each other, then. When I don't need to do this anymore, I'll walk away from it."

"That's fine. You do it, then."

Strange Encounter

Seven

Sir Bartley Gordon looked strangely out of place among the milling crowd in the empty factory building that had gathered to watch two chickens try to kill each other. Most of the spectators were roughly and crudely dressed, but Gordon, a member of the aristocracy, looked almost like a peacock in his fine feathers. He wore a pair of snow-white silk stockings, a waistcoat that would have put Joseph's coat of many colors to shame, and a frock coat with turned-back sleeves and studded with mother-of-pearl buttons down the front. Around his neck a crimson scarf blazed colorfully enough almost to blind the onlookers, and to crown his outfit a large ostrich plume rose high out of his three-cornered hat.

As Gordon watched the two birds encounter each other in a vicious melee, his face was tight with anticipation. Gordon was flanked by two members of an obviously lower-class station. Rook Gere was a big, hulking brute with a thick neck and large hamlike hands. Charlie Yule was a thin man with a catfish mouth and a sly expression. All three of the men were half drunk.

As a cry of victory went up from the winners and a moan of defeat from the losers, Gere said, "Too bad, Gordon. You bet on the wrong one."

"The bird was a coward!" Gordon snorted. He pulled a flask from his inside pocket and worked his throat convulsively as he swallowed. He did not offer the others a drink from the silver flask, but they had brought their own and helped themselves as the handlers of the birds, both winner and loser, went in to collect their charges. The loser lay slashed to pieces by the razor-sharp steel spurs attached to the heels of the other.

The crowd milled around waiting for the next event, but Gordon was disgusted. He had lost money—a great deal of it—on this visit, and now he muttered, "I'm sick of this place. The birds are no good."

"Too right," Charlie Yule agreed. "Let's go find some more action."

The three men left the building and found themselves in a pea-soup fog. London was a murky place indeed when the fog came rolling in to mingle with the cinders and smoke from the thousands of chimneys that burned the black coal dug from the bowels of the earth. The air was particularly foul today, the smoke seeming to fall out of the chimneys instead of rising up into the air and dissipating. The men shouldered their way along, Gordon flanked by his two lieutenants, shoving anyone they happened to encounter out of the way. More than once they were accosted by one of the many harlots who worked in this section of London. Gere said once, "What do you say we have a go at these women?"

"I'm not anxious to get the pox!" Gordon snapped.

The city of London was an excellent place to encounter the pox, for prostitutes swarmed the city streets. But Gordon had been infected twice already and had no desire to go through the terribly painful cure once again. The three men stopped at a tavern and drank for a while, and by the time they staggered out, the streets were less crowded, but the sounds coming from the inns and taverns that lined both sides of the avenue were loud. Sir Bartley Gordon was still in a foul mood, angry at having suffered such losses at the cockfight. When this happened he usually struck out at someone vulnerable. His power, money, and high connections had saved him from paying for this sort of behavior, but now he blinked and stared through the murky fog, ready to exercise his will on anyone weaker.

Sabrina took the bank notes from the small gray-haired man and handed over the necklace. "Thank you," she murmured and tucked the bills into a small reticule.

The jeweler shook his head. "Not wise to walk the streets with that much cash, miss."

"I'm only going a short way. I'll be all right."

"If you were wise, you'd leave that cash here and pick it up in the morning."

Sabrina shook her head. She had left her aunt's house earlier after having a furious argument with her. Elberta had informed her that she was insane to leave England, that she would be scalped by the red Indians, but Sabrina had paid her no heed. Her mind was made up, and she was anxious for the adventure to begin. Now that she had the cash in hand, she did not want to turn loose of it. She was not an expert in bargaining, but she had held out for a good price for the diamond necklace. She felt the weight of the money and the pleasant plumpness of the reticule and felt that she was not ready to surrender it even for one night.

"I'll be fine. Thank you, sir," said Sabrina as she left the store.

Nervously she peered through the fog for a hackney carriage, but there seemed to be none on this narrow, twisted street. She straightened her back and walked on, passing many inns and taverns. The sounds of the city seemed to be muffled by the heavy blanket of fog. Suddenly three dark forms loomed up in front of her. She shrank back against the shop that banked the street and allowed them to pass, but instead the smaller of the men suddenly turned to confront her. The two other men, one of them very large and the other tall and thin, formed a half circle around her. "Well, now, what have we here? A lady of the evening, no doubt."

"Let me pass," Sabrina said as firmly as she could. She was aware of the reticule filled with money, and fear came on her as she thought of what could happen in a situation like this. She berated herself for not giving heed to the jeweler's advice, but now tried to appear more confident than she felt. "Get out of my way!" she demanded.

The smaller of the men, she saw, was dressed in an expensive, ornate outfit. Taking a good look at his face, she suddenly recognized the man, for she had met him briefly at social functions. "Pardon me, Sir Bartley. I must hurry."

Bartley Gordon was very drunk. He peered at the woman closely. "You know me?"

"Yes. I'm Miss Fairfax. We've met several times."

"Well, it is indeed Miss Fairfax!" He stepped closer, and Sabrina could smell the raw alcohol on his breath. He was smiling at her crookedly, and there was something sinister about the man that frightened her. "You wouldn't give me a dance the last time we met in Bath. Perhaps we'll have one now."

"Please let me go. I'm late."

"There's no hurry." Gordon took her arm and turned to give Gere a wink. "This lady refused the pleasure of my company. Can you believe that, Gere?"

"Hard to believe, Sir Bartley. But she can't refuse you now." Gere laughed coarsely and said, "Go on and have your dance."

Gordon was obviously enjoying his moment. When Sabrina tried to pull away, he closed his hand and held her tightly. "Now, there's no hurry." He laughed drunkenly and turned to nod at Yule. "She won't be so proud now. Her father lost all his money. From what I heard you were thrown out on the streets. Well, you and I may be able to fix that." He pulled her closer and tried to kiss her, but Sabrina turned her head and shoved him away.

"You're not a gentleman! You never were!"

The words inflamed Gordon. "Not a gentleman! Well, you're not a lady, so that makes us even. Come along. You can show me a good time. Maybe I can make up some of the money your fool of a father threw away."

Rook Gere suddenly laughed. "She's got a purse there. Me and Yule will take that, and you can have her, Sir Bartley."

"That sounds fair enough. Come along, sweetheart."

Sabrina suddenly screamed at the top of her lungs. "Please, somebody help me! Somebody come—please!"

Gordon slapped her across the side of the face, and the cry was broken off. "Shut your mouth, wench!" he snarled. "You had your fun with me, and now it's my turn to get some of my own back!" He started dragging her toward the mouth of an alley that opened darkly ten feet away. Sabrina continued to cry out for help, but again he cuffed her, and she fought him with all of her strength.

Gere and Yule laughed, and it was Yule who said, "Let's

have that reticule, woman. It'll get in your way while you're having your dance with your gentleman friend here."

Yule reached out and made a grab for the reticule, but Sabrina jerked it back and with a catlike swipe ran her fingernails down the side of his face. They broke the skin, and Yule let out a screeching cry. He cursed and said, "Come on, Rook, help me get that bag."

Black terror filled Sabrina. She had never in her life been threatened in any way, and now she knew that the very worst awaited her. She cried out again and this time tried to dodge as Sir Bartley Gordon struck at her with his fist. One of his blows caught her high on the forehead, and stars suddenly wheeled in front of her eyes. She fell back against the brick wall of the building and felt the hands of one of the men pulling at her reticule—but at the same time she heard a new voice.

"All right, you three—scratch for it!"

Sabrina turned and saw that a man had appeared out of the fog and now stood confronting the three who were gathered around her. "Please help me!" she cried.

"On your way, fellow!" Bartley Gordon snapped. "This is none of your affair!"

"I'll go, and I'll just take the lady with me."

Sabrina could not see the face of the speaker clearly, but she noticed a slight foreign quality to his speech. He didn't appear to be carrying a weapon. She started to get up off the ground, saying, "Help me get away!"

Rook Gere clamped his huge hand on her arm. "Stay right where you are!" he growled and then turned to face the newcomer. "Get out of here or I'll break your face!"

Sabrina was aware of the crushing power of this man. His hand on her arm was so powerful that it was paralyzing her. She tried to pull away, but she might as well have been encased in cement.

"I'll give you one more chance and that's all. Now let the lady go."

"Beat him down, Gere!" Bartley Gordon screamed. "He's only one."

Sabrina felt her arm released and staggered, but she was instantly grabbed by Gordon. She struggled against him but kept her eyes fixed on the scene before her. The monstrous man advanced toward the newcomer. She did not see what happened next, so quick was the movement, but she heard a sudden woosh accompanied by several other solid, meaty-sounding blows. She saw Rook driven backward against the wall, and then the stranger struck him in the face, sending him down. The stranger whirled and landed a hard right on the chin of the other man, who had moved in behind him.

Now he turned to Sir Bartley. "Let go of her," he said as he took a step closer. Gordon did not move, and the stranger suddenly struck out. His fist caught Gordon right under the heart, and he uttered a short, piercing gasp and staggered backward.

Sabrina, now that she was free, moved away, and the man who had come out of the fog directed, "Down this way, miss."

"Stop right where you are!"

Sabrina turned her head and saw that Sir Bartley Gordon had pulled a small pistol from under his coat. She heard the click as he pulled the hammer back and said, "I'll kill you if you don't leave right now. The lady stays here!"

Sabrina froze with fear. She had never been in such a deadly situation, and she felt herself growing faint.

"Put the gun away."

"I'll put *you* away!" Bartley screamed. He lifted the pistol, and perhaps by accident or perhaps intentionally, his finger tightened on the trigger. The explosion seemed very loud to Sabrina, who saw the stranger lunge forward and grab the pistol from Gordon, then strike him full in the face. The force of the blow drove Gordon back, and he fell full length.

The stranger turned his eyes to the two men who were struggling to their feet, then said quietly, "We'd best go at once, miss."

But they had no chance to leave, for suddenly four men appeared. "What's all this?" the largest of them said.

"These men were trying—" Sabrina had no opportunity to finish, for Sir Gordon had scrambled to his feet and was screaming.

"This man was trying to rob me! I shot at him, but I missed."

"What's your name?" one of the watchmen said. The other

three had surrounded the group and stood watchfully. They all carried large billy clubs, and one of them had a pistol in his hand.

"I'm Sir Bartley Gordon, and I demand you arrest this fellow! He's a cutpurse."

"That's not so!" Sabrina said hotly.

"She was in it with him. She came out and accosted us. She's a harlot! Take them in at once!"

The man said, "We'll go down and get this straightened out." He picked up the pistol that was lying on the street and looked at it. "What do you know about this?" he asked the stranger.

"These three men were trying to abuse this lady, and I tried to help. This one pulled the pistol and shot at me, so I knocked him down."

"What about the other two? You knocked them down, too?"

"That's the way it was," Sabrina said quickly.

"Well, we can't do anything in the middle of the street." The sergeant looked around at the small crowd that had gathered to see the action. "Come along. We'll let the magistrate decide about all this."

The magistrate was a feeble man who should not have been in charge of anything. The only thing he really heard when the watchman explained the situation was Bartley Gordon's title: *Sir.* Judge Isaac Jones was a worshiper of the upper classes and could not conceive of anything being done wrong by such a one as this. He listened as Sir Bartley explained how he and his companions had been accosted by the two, and then he turned his attention in a halfhearted fashion to hear the story of the accused. "What's your name?" he said in a surly tone.

"Sion Kenyon."

At that moment Sabrina suddenly realized why the man had seemed so familiar. She had not had time to exchange a word with him, but when they had come into the light of the station he had looked familiar. She remembered suddenly that this was the man she had seen in the prizefight on the River

Thames, the one she had given ten pounds to. She stared at him in disbelief, but she had no time to do more than that, for the judge said roughly, "Robbing is a serious business in London. You'll pay for it. I'll bind you over for trial next Thursday. Case dismissed."

"But, Judge, he didn't do it!" Sabrina exclaimed.

"She's in it with him," Sir Bartley retorted.

"You have no proof of any of this. Just their word," Sabrina said.

"I'm holding this man! Get out of here, and if I see you again, I'll show you how rough I can be on harlots walking the streets of our fair city!"

Anger laced through Sabrina at the injustice of the situation. She turned to face the man who had come to her rescue and said, "I'll find some legal help for you."

"Thank you, miss," was all he said.

As Sabrina turned and left the station, she found herself weak. The reticule still dangled from her wrist, but if Sion Kenyon had not appeared out of the darkness of the night, she well knew what her condition would be at this moment. *I've got to help him,* she thought desperately. *I've got to do something!*

Before this whole mess started, Sabrina had purchased passage on a ship that would leave tomorrow for Portsmouth, Virginia. After studying her deed and a map of the New World, she had determined that it would be fairly simple to find her way to the land that now belonged to her. Now she thought again how strange it was that she had encountered the boxer that she had witnessed not too long ago on the barge. She was not a great believer in providence, but she well knew he had saved her from a terrible fate.

She headed for the court where the trial would take place. She had never been to a trial of any kind, and she was unhappy with the barrister she had hired to help Sion Kenyon in his battle. His name was Everett Slavins, and she knew nothing about him—she had simply asked for someone in the office who could help her friend. Slavins had been unimpressive, but his fee had been impressive enough. He had listened to her story and said finally, "Miss Fairfax, I will go to appear for your friend, but I'll tell you now there's little hope."

"But he didn't do it."

"But Sir Bartley Gordon says he did."

"Well, I say he didn't, and I'm an impartial witness!"

"The judge that Kenyon will appear before will believe Gordon, and you can believe me on that."

Sabrina had paid the minimum fee for which Slavins had agreed to appear in court. He had warned her it would be a very brief appearance, for his fee was nominal.

Now as she entered the courtroom, Sabrina took her seat. She found a noisy, loud crowd and sat through several cases. The judge sat on a high platform, wearing his white wig and black robe. He said little, but there was a harshness about him that spoke of long practice at putting people in jail or sentencing them to the gallows. Finally Kenyon was led in, and Sabrina saw his eyes go over the courtroom. He found her, and when their eyes met, she tried to smile. He returned the smile rather tightly before sitting down beside Slavins.

The trial was not what Sabrina had expected. The judge listened as the prosecutor stated the case and made an impassioned plea for ridding the streets of riffraff so that innocent people would be free to walk in London without fear of being robbed or murdered.

A handsomely dressed Sir Bartley Gordon took the stand first. Speaking calmly and simply, he explained, "My two friends and I were walking along the street when this woman came out and accosted us. We thought she was a harlot, of course, and we told her to be on her way. Then this other fellow came out and put a gun on us. He demanded our money. One of my friends knocked the gun from his hand, and it went off, and there was a scuffle. That's when the watchmen arrived and took the man into custody."

Slavins rose and tried to shake Gordon's story, but Gordon simply stared at him as if he were an insect. Finally the judge said, "That will be enough badgering. Sit down, Mr. Slavins."

After Slavins sat down, the judge asked, "Do you have any defense?"

"I would like to call Sion Kenyon as my witness."

Kenyon made his way into the dock. When Slavins said, "Would you please relate what happened?" he began to speak.

Sabrina was impressed at the simplicity of his reply, for she knew it was the truth, but she could see that the judge did not agree. When the prosecuting attorney, a big bulky man named Simmons, got up, he began to demand answers.

"What do you do for a living, Mr. Kenyon?"

"I'm a pugilist."

"Oh, one of the roughs!"

This gave the key to Simmons's prosecution. Everyone knew that prizefighters were violent men and thieves as well, the very lowest class of English life. He tried to shake Kenyon's story, but when Kenyon simply stuck to it, he laughed and said, "Well, that's what you would tell, but I'm sure the judge knows whom to believe."

It was a lost cause, Sabrina recognized, and in the end the judge simply said, "I find you guilty and sentence you to ten years of hard labor.

"Oh no!" Sabrina said under her breath. She could not see Kenyon's face, for he was facing the judge, but when he was taken away, he gave her one look and a nod.

Sabrina went straight to Slavins, who was busy gathering up his papers. "I told you it would be that way," he said gloomily. "There's no hope."

"But isn't there something that can be done?"

"He was found guilty. He'll go to prison. He might get a few years off for good behavior, maybe not."

"There must be something we can do, Mr. Slavins!"

Slavins straightened up and looked at her. He felt bad about losing the case, even though it was lost before it began. He studied the woman before him and said, "There are only two things I can think of."

"What are they? I'll do anything I can to help him."

Slavins lowered his voice and leaned forward, speaking almost in a whisper. "Sometimes men who are found guilty and sentenced are pressed into service for the navy. It's a terrible life serving on one of His Majesty's war ships, but it's better than prison."

"Why, I can't do anything about that."

"Of course not, but there's another way. The prisons are full right now, and they're anxious to get rid of as many men as possible. Sometimes people take on convicted felons to serve as indentured servants."

"How does that work?"

"They agree to be responsible for the prisoner, who is obligated to serve them for a set number of years. Two or five or even ten years. At the end of that time they're set free. It's a form of slavery, in effect, and many people who are starting plantations—say in the Caribbean—need cheap help, so they take a bunch of felons with them. Pretty hard on them, they are. Work them to death most of the time."

"Would it be possible for me to do that?"

"Are you sure you want to? You'd be taking on a man you don't know."

Sabrina had already made up her mind. At the same time she was thinking of the debt she owed to the man, she was thinking also of how she needed someone as a protector. Sion Kenyon had showed that he had at least some instincts of decency, and he would have to do.

"I want to do it. Will you help me?"

"Yes, I'll draw up the papers. It's fairly simple. We can do that right now if you'd like."

"Yes. It's what I want to do."

Sion was sitting on the floor waiting to be transferred to prison, for there was no furniture in the common cell. Several of the prisoners had been quick to inform him about the hellish place it was. The cell was cold, and he had only a thin coat on. He leaned back against the hard, cold stone and thought with desperation of his condition. He had gone to the aid of a woman without thinking about the consequences, and now because of his hasty action, Rees and his family would have no help.

His thoughts were interrupted when a guard came in through the barred door and called out loudly, "Kenyon!"

"Here I am." Kenyon got to his feet.

"Come this way. You've got a visitor."

Kenyon hurried after the guard somewhat confused. He thought it might be Ned Chaps, his manager, but he knew that Chaps was gone to the north of England with the Bristol Mangler for a series of matches.

The guard led him down a corridor, turning several times, and finally opened the door and said, "In there, and let's have no trouble."

Sion was surprised to see the young woman when he entered the room. He had learned her name during his short hearing. "Hello, Miss Fairfax."

"Hello," she greeted hesitantly. "I'm sorry I got you into all this," she said. "I had hoped they would turn you loose."

"It's not your fault," Sion shrugged. He studied the woman carefully, wondering what her purpose was. Perhaps it was just to tell him she was sorry. "Don't worry about it," he added.

"Well, of course I'll worry about it, but I've come up with something that might help. Do you know anything about farming?"

"Farming! Why, I do know a bit. I worked on a farm in Wales for several years. It's what I've done most of my life."

"Have you ever heard of such a thing as an indentured servant?"

"No, miss, I haven't."

Miss Fairfax pulled the papers out of her reticule and explained the process to him. Finally she said, "I'm going to America. I have a piece of property there, but I need some help."

"And you want me to go with you as your servant? What did you call it?"

"Indentured servant. Yes, that's what I'm offering you. But let me tell you it's a dangerous place. There are Indians, and it's a long voyage, and to be truthful with you, I don't know what I'll find when I get there."

Sion had thought much of the foul hole of a prison that he'd been sentenced to, and now he said, "I'd have to have a little money, miss, from time to time—not for myself. It's for a family that I'm responsible for."

"Your wife?"

"No, I'm not married, Miss Fairfax." He went on to explain how he owed Rees a debt. "That's why I took up prizefighting. I couldn't find anything else to do. Another two or three months, and I think Rees should be fine. But I would need to send them a little bit."

"I think we can manage that. You realize that if you sign these papers, you'll be a servant. Not a slave, exactly, but you can't leave me for five years. At the end of that time, I'm to give you a sum of money and a suit of new clothes."

"I'll do it gladly, Miss Fairfax. I've always wanted to see the New World."

She put the papers down and watched as he signed them. "I'll be leaving now, but I'll be back for you first thing in the morning. The ship leaves tomorrow."

"Aye, miss."

As Sabrina left the prison, she felt a severe attack of nerves. *I'm putting myself in the hands of this man I don't even know. He did help me when I needed it, but that was only for a moment. I'll have to keep him in his place.* The thought did not comfort her, but as she went to make the final arrangements, she thought of the long voyage and of the uncertainties before her. *He'll be a help to me,* she thought. *I'll have to get him a pistol and a rifle so he'll be ready for anything.* She held her head high and thought for a moment of the New World that lay so far away. It was dark and mysterious, and she had heard so many conflicting tales. But it was her destiny now, and with a grim determination she moved forward to meet it.

PART III

The Journey

March – April 1792

A Rocky Voyage

Eight

As Sion followed Sabrina up the gangplank to board the *Caledonia,* he felt a sudden twinge of nervousness. He had never been on anything larger than a rowboat, and now as he glanced out over the gray sea that spread itself out to infinity, he suddenly realized how fragile life could be. Up until this moment he had given little thought to the voyage to far-off America, and he was not a man given to fears, yet the thought of endless miles of water and the depths beneath the ship flooded him with uneasiness.

Ahead of him Sabrina moved quickly, carrying a small wicker cage with one hand and holding on to the rail with the other. From time to time a plaintive cry came from Ulysses, who he had learned was her cat. It didn't sound like the cat was looking forward to a journey across the sea, either.

Sabrina's back was straight, Sion noticed, and he wondered, not for the first time, about this woman who now held his future in her hand. He had been around her long enough to know that she was a willful young woman accustomed to having her own way, and that she could be rather sharp at times. He was not unaware of her beauty, and as they stepped out on deck, he saw an officer turn and follow her with admiring eyes.

"Hurry up, Zion, don't be so slow!" Sabrina snapped. She looked tired, for lines of tension were around her mouth, and Sion realized that she was under a great deal of strain.

"Aye, ma'am—and my name isn't Zion."

Sabrina met his eyes. "I thought it was."

"I know that. It's Sion, with an *S*."

"But I never heard of anyone with the name of Sion."

"It's a common enough name in Wales, miss. It's the Welsh form of John."

"Well, I can't keep up with your foolish language! Come along. We'll have to find our cabin."

The officer Sion had noticed had overheard the conversation. He stepped forward, touched his hat, and bowed slightly. "I am the first mate, miss. My name is Stern. May I help you?"

Sabrina turned to face the officer and noted that he was a tall, nice-looking man of thirty or so with brown hair. "Thank you, Mr. Stern. I have a cabin."

"And your name is?"

"I am Miss Sabrina Fairfax. Here's my bill of passage."

"Come this way. I'll help you find your cabin, Miss Fairfax."

"Come along, Sion."

Sion followed the two and noticed the ship moving under his feet. Since he was accustomed to the solid earth, the idea of living on something that gave way to other elements captured his attention. He considered the ocean some sort of strange and dangerous beast to be watched carefully.

Stern led the way down a corridor. Arriving at a door with a seven carved into its face, he opened it and said, "This will be your cabin, Miss Fairfax."

"Thank you so much, Mr. Stern."

"Anything I can do to make you comfortable, I'll be glad to help you. The steward's name is Jones. He'll be by soon to welcome you aboard. Have you made many voyages?"

"No, this is my first."

"We may have a bit of weather, so you might be prepared." He turned and left, and Sabrina said, "Bring the trunk in, Sion."

Sion had trouble getting through the narrow doorway, for the trunk was bulky. He looked around and saw that the cabin was very small, containing two bunks, one over the other, a small cabinet fastened to the wall, one window, and little else. There was but one place to set the trunk, and he put it down.

"Find a place for the rest of the luggage. And I didn't get a cabin for you."

"I'll find a place. No problem. I'll see to the rest of the luggage."

Sion left and occupied himself with getting the luggage on board. He found a man with the title of bosun, a short barrel of an individual with steady gray eyes. His name was Olson, and he brusquely helped Sion find a place for the luggage.

"I'll need to find a place to sleep so I'll be out of the way, Mr. Olson."

"You can sleep down with the crew. Just find a corner wherever you can."

Sion left and for the next hour occupied himself with going over the ship. He had a curious streak in his nature and was fascinated by the tall masts with the furled sails. The maze of ropes going up to the tops of the masts and lying in coils everywhere seemed to him beyond comprehension. "Every man to his trade," he said. "These fellows would be as lost in a coal mine as I am on board this boat."

Both Sion and Sabrina were on deck when the sailors cast off the lines and the men overhead began to drop the sails. Afternoon had come, and she had expected the ship to wait until morning, but apparently morning, afternoon, and night were all the same to the sailors. Sion was back on the stern, and Sabrina was standing midship watching the sailors scurry about. As the ship began to move, she felt a strange sensation. Most of her life had been easy, until her father died, that is, and as the *Caledonia* eased out from the wharf, she glanced out over the horizon and for one moment was tempted to demand that she be put ashore. It was a natural enough reaction, for she was setting forth on a journey to a land she had never seen and knew nothing of. As the wind filled the sails and the ship picked up speed, the harbor seemed to recede. It seemed that the ship was standing still and the land was moving away.

"I trust you're settled in to your cabin, Miss Fairfax?"

Sabrina turned to find the first officer standing beside her. He had removed his cap, and the breeze ruffled his hair. His skin was tanned to the color of mahogany, which contrasted with his white uniform.

"Yes, thank you, Mr. Stern."

Stern's brown eyes surveyed the activities of the crew, and twice he barked out a command having something to do with the sails. Finally he turned and said, "You have family in America?"

"No, I don't."

"Well, there's one thing I'd better warn you about."

"And what is that, sir?"

"The Americans will likely not be too friendly. The Revolution took a lot of their people out. Anyone you meet is liable to have lost a husband or a father or son. They're not amiable toward the English. I've spent a little time in the Colonies myself." He smiled and shook his head. "But, of course, they're not colonies any longer. We managed to lose them all during the Revolution."

"I've never understood that," Sabrina said. "We have the largest standing army in the world, and of course, the largest navy, and yet a handful of farmers defeated us."

"It was quite a bitter pill for the king to swallow, but swallow it he did." Stern shook his head and twisted his mouth in a sour expression. "The Americans are a tougher breed than anyone in England figured. I had a brother who was an officer in Cornwallis's army. He told me the Americans knew how to fight."

"And our soldiers didn't?"

"Our soldiers were trained to fight in ranks in open fields, but most of the battles in America took place in forests and woods. Those American woodsmen are dead shots. He told me they could take a head off a squirrel at a hundred yards. You can imagine what they would do to a mass body of soldiers."

Sabrina was anxious to know all she could about America, and she stood there asking questions until the land was only a low-lying streak against the horizon. The ship was rising and falling now with a jerking motion, and the wind was whipping the sails around so that they popped. The ship itself made creaking noises that made her uneasy.

"It feels like the ship is falling apart."

Stern smiled. "It always seems like that to people not accustomed to ships. She's just working herself a little bit." He looked off to the west and shook his head. "We'll be in for a bit of a blow." He answered a question as a young sailor hurried by. Turning again to Sabrina, he said, "The captain would be glad to have you at his table for dinner this evening."

"What's his name?"

"Captain Jacob Drum. He's an older man. Dislikes America. Shall I come by your cabin and take you to dinner, Miss Fairfax? I've got to see to these hands."

"That would be so kind, Mr. Stern."

Sabrina sat on the single chair in her cabin holding on to the table. She looked with apprehension at the window as the ship turned suddenly, then dipped slowly. A driving rain had started, and the drops beat against the pane. The ship tilted steeply forward, and Sabrina waited until it began to rise. The "bit of weather" that the first officer had mentioned seemed violent to her, and she wondered how rough the sea would have to get before she should be really afraid. She had not seen Sion, but he had told her that he had found a place to sleep. A sense of loneliness enveloped her, and she thought of the safe harbor she had found in her aunt Elberta's house, as much as she had hated it. She remembered Elberta's parting words: *"You'll get scalped by the red Indians, mark my word! You can always come back here, but you'll have to lose some of your pride, Niece."*

Sabrina smiled with a touch of bitterness as she realized that she didn't have much pride left. No one could be proud when she was being tossed about on a wild ocean. The thought of the depths beneath the ship made her uneasy and queasy, or perhaps it was the motion of the ship. She had been warned that seasickness could afflict anyone, and she fervently hoped she would miss that ailment. Ulysses approached her and rubbed against her calf. She picked him up and cuddled him to her breast. "You're my best friend, Ulysses," she whispered. "You're all I've got now."

A knock at the door brought her to her feet. She was only two steps from the door, and when she opened it she found the first officer there.

"Ready for dinner?"

"Yes, I suppose I am, but I don't see how you can eat with the ship pitching around like this."

"Well, we sailors have to eat, ma'am, even if we have to nail our plates to the table. Come along. I'll show you the way."

Sabrina had put on a coat, for the March air seemed colder at sea than it had in London. She staggered slightly as the ship seemed to wallow, caught itself, and then righted again.

"Take my arm, Miss Fairfax."

Sabrina was glad to accept the tall officer's offer. "Is this very bad?"

"This? Oh no, not at all! It'll blow itself out by sometime tomorrow or the day after. Actually, we should have fine weather."

Sabrina accompanied Stern down the corridor, then exited out onto the deck. The wind whipped at her, and she clung tightly to Stern's arm until they had traversed a third of the ship and then went down a set of rather steep stairs. They entered a room some twelve feet wide and perhaps fifteen feet long. There were two tables there and several officers. They stood as Sabrina entered, and as she ran her eyes around the room, she noted that there were a few passengers.

"Captain Drum, may I present Miss Sabrina Fairfax. Miss Fairfax, may I present Captain Drum." Drum was a dour-looking man of fifty or so, and he bowed stiffly.

"Welcome aboard, Miss Fairfax. Will you sit here, please?"

Sabrina nodded and acknowledged Drum's greeting. She took her seat at the captain's right hand, and Lawrence Stern seated himself beside her. Drum gave her an analytical look out of a pair of cold, greenish eyes. "You're bound for America, then. Have you been there before?"

"No, sir. I've never been out of England."

"You won't like it."

Sabrina could not help but smile, and she felt Stern's elbow touch hers. He had warned her that the captain disliked America and now was warning her not to engage in an argument.

"Do you think not, Captain?"

"I think Dr. Johnson was right."

"Dr. Samuel Johnson? The man who wrote the dictionary?"

"Yes, a very wise man indeed, God rest his soul," Drum grunted. "He said the Americans should be grateful for anything we give them short of hanging—and I'm not even sure about the hanging now."

One of the passengers, a slight man sitting beside a woman who was even smaller, said, "You don't care at all for Americans, then."

"They're nothing but a race of convicts!" Drum grunted.

Drum began to speak of how worthless Americans were, but at that time the stewards began to bring the food in. Sabrina found it required all of her attention to simply control the food. The ship was tilting regularly now, and the plates and heavy goblets had a tendency to move away from her. The food was adequate—boiled mutton, beans of some indeterminate variety, and freshly baked bread. The mutton and the bread were good, but she gave up on the beans. In all truthfulness the rolling of the ship and the queasiness in her stomach had taken away her appetite.

As she tried to eat all she could, Stern whispered, "The captain lost a son and a brother in the American war. As for me, I found the Americans to be good people. But they're different from the English. You'll find them rather crude, I'm afraid. At the risk of being nosy, may I assume that your trip is not for pleasure?" He chuckled, saying, "Very few do that."

"No. I've inherited a tract of land in the wilderness."

"Oh, in the wilderness!" Stern raised his eyebrows. "Well, that will be a change for you. I've never been there, of course, but we had a carpenter on board who spent some time there. He was a fascinating fellow. He talked a great deal about the hardships of pioneer life."

"Is it very hard?"

"Well, it was when he was there, which was some time ago. According to his stories it was a struggle to keep from being eaten by bears or scalped by Indians."

Sabrina listened more than she spoke, and finally she found she could eat no more. She turned to the captain and said, "Captain Drum, would you excuse me? I'm rather tired."

"Of course. Would you see the lady to her cabin, Mr. Stern?"

"Yes, sir."

Sabrina rose, and as the two left the room, she took Stern's arm again. They made the journey across the deck, and when they stepped inside to go down the corridor, nausea struck her like a blow. She gasped, and Stern suddenly turned to her. He took one look at her face and said, "Feeling queer, Miss Fairfax?"

"Yes. I'm going to be sick, I think."

"Come along. We'll get you to your room."

Sabrina clung to his arm, and when he opened the door to her cabin, he said, "If I were you, I would lie down. We don't have a doctor on board, but there's nothing a doctor can do for seasickness anyway. I'll come by and check on you later."

Sabrina could not even answer. She barely waited until the door was closed before she leaned over and deposited her supper on the floor.

Sabrina had lost all track of time. She knew only that she had thrown up until there was nothing left to throw up. The ship tossed and rolled, and she lay flat on her bunk, too weak to do more than pull up the blanket. She was disgusted, for she knew she had made a mess. There was no maid to clean up after her, and she found herself wishing fervently she had never heard of the *Caledonia,* or of America, for that matter. A knock at the door sounded, but at the same instant the nausea came so that she could only croak an invitation.

She heard the door open and then close. Someone struck a match, and the light from a lamp mounted on the wall cast yellow shadows over the cabin. She turned her head and opened her eyes to see Sion bending over her.

"The first mate told me you were sick, miss."

Sabrina nodded and whispered, "Water, please."

"Of course." Sion disappeared, and Sabrina lay there in utter misery. She had never known such a sickness as this. It seemed as though her insides were being ripped out, and with every movement of the ship she wanted to throw up more.

The door opened again, but she did not even open her eyes. She heard movements and then the sound of water being poured from a larger vessel to a smaller one. An arm came around her, lifting her into a half-sitting position. She felt the glass at her lips and took a few sips. "No more."

"Better take a few more sips, miss."

Sabrina could not even speak. She simply lay with his arm holding her and from time to time took a sip of water.

"Lie down awhile, and I'll make the cabin presentable. If you have need again, you can use this bowl the cook gave me."

Sabrina lay there but opened her eyes long enough to see Sion cleaning up after her. Such a duty, which would have disgusted her, seemed not to trouble him.

After some time she felt herself growing sick again, and she lost the water he had given her. At once he came over and said, "Don't mind it, miss. You'll be all right soon."

"I think I'm going to die."

"No danger of that. Here, let me clean you up a little." Again Sabrina heard the sound of water being poured, then she felt a cool cloth cleaning her face. It felt good and refreshing, and she discovered that she was growing sleepy despite her illness. Several times Sion forced her to drink just sips of water, but then she dropped off into a troubled sleep.

Sometime after this she awakened and heard Sion say, "You need to eat just a little of this, miss."

"No, I can't eat."

"They tell me it's the best thing for you."

"I'll just bring it up again."

"I suppose you will, but sooner or later you'll be able to keep some down. The danger, they say, is in getting dried out and weak."

Sabrina was too weak to argue. She allowed Sion to lift her up and felt like a baby in his hands. He had a bowl of something, which turned out to be a thin broth. She managed to keep down a few swallows of it and then said, "No more."

"That's right, miss. You rest, and then we'll try a few more spoons."

Sabrina lay down, and once again he began to bathe her face with cool water. Sabrina had a feeling of utter helplessness. She was all alone except for a servant she hardly knew, bound for a land she knew nothing of, with only a vague hope of success. In despair she fretted about her future until she finally drifted off again.

————

Sabrina woke up with a feeling that life was possible. She knew it was the fourth day now since the *Caledonia* had left England, and the seasickness had occupied all of her thoughts. She had been so weak that she had feared she would die, and it had only been Sion's constant care that had pulled her through it. Now, however, she awoke and felt a strength that before had been drained out of her. She sat up in bed and noticed that the cabin was spotlessly clean. She knew that the clothing she had soiled had been washed and refolded. She had been able to change clothes several times, and now she swung her feet out of bed. As she sat up, she noted that sunlight was streaming in through the window and the ship was moving smoothly over the surface of the ocean. Standing up carefully, she found herself weak but not at all nauseated. The illness had left as quickly as it had come, but the four days in bed had innervated her.

She dressed, putting on fresh clothes, and wondered at how neatly they had been folded. She left the cabin feeling suddenly very hungry, and the first man she encountered was the first officer, Lawrence Stern. He smiled as he approached her.

"Well, you're better, I see."

"Much better."

"I'm glad to see it. You're probably hungry."

"Yes, I am. Amazingly so. I've been having to force myself to eat."

"That's the way it is. That man of yours, Kenyon, he's quite a fellow."

"How's that, sir?"

"Well, he's taken care of you fairly well, I'd say. He bullied the cooks into fixing that special broth you've been getting and the other food. And he's been washing your clothes."

Sabrina's cheeks flushed. She could think of no answer and finally said merely, "Yes, he's done very well." Looking out over the sea, she asked, "How much longer before we land?"

"Perhaps six weeks, if the wind holds. We've made good

time despite the blow. Come along. We'll have the cook make you something light. Perhaps some scrambled eggs and toast."

———————

Stern was talking with Sion, the two of them standing in the bow. The wind was cold and crisp, and Stern was commenting on Sabrina. "A very fine lady. She had a very hard time of it with the seasickness."

"Yes. I'm glad it didn't get to me."

"Have you been her servant long?"

Sion liked the first officer. He had been very helpful, and he was well aware that without Stern's help he would not have had the freedom to care for Sabrina as he had for the past four days. "Not at all. I came to her very recently."

"I can't help but be curious, and it's none of my business, but she never says anything about herself."

"I don't know her that well, Mr. Stern. I do know she's had a rough time of it lately. Her father died recently and left her very little. I also know that she's inherited some land over in America. She needed someone to help her with the farming there, and I was handy."

"I'm not sure it's wise to go to America. They don't care for the English much. She may find it unpleasant—and you too."

"It couldn't be any more unpleasant than being down in a coal mine." Sion smiled, his teeth white against his skin, which had taken on some color during the voyage. Life at sea had agreed with him, and he had found out that he liked sailing. "I expect she'll make out all right. I'll do the best I can to help her."

"Strange for a cultured young lady to be going to the wilderness."

"Well, God moves in mysterious ways to do His work."

Stern turned and studied the face of Sion Kenyon. "You're a Christian, I take it?"

"Indeed, I am."

"Well, you'll need all the religion you have. Be careful of those Indians."

"Are there a great many of them?"

"I don't know the country. I understand they've been pushed back, but they're always a danger."

At that moment Sabrina came up, and the two men turned. Stern touched his cap and said, "Well, was it a good meal, Miss Fairfax?"

"Very good."

"That's fine. You'll get your strength back after a few good meals. Well, I must be about my duties," he said as he strode off.

"He's a very fine man, miss. He was a great help to me when I was trying to take care of you."

Sabrina turned and hesitated. "I have to thank you, Sion, for taking care of me. I know it must have been unpleasant."

"Unpleasant! Why, not at all, miss."

"I think it was, but I'm very grateful to you."

Sion nodded but shrugged off her thanks. "You're welcome." He waved his hand at the sea ahead of them. "That's pretty, isn't it? I didn't think I'd like the sea, but I do. If I had started in it early, I might have made a sailor of myself."

"Do you really believe we'll be all right in America?"

"Why, of course we'll be all right, miss. Why wouldn't we be?"

"We might get butchered by Indians."

"No, I think not. God wouldn't take us there for such an end as that."

It's a Big Country

Nine

As the *Caledonia* nosed into the harbor, Sabrina stood at the rail grasping it hard, as though it needed her help to make its way inside toward the swarming docks. Portsmouth, Virginia, was not like she had imagined it, but then she had little idea of what America would be like. The harbor was busy with ships of every description, most of them lined up with their sails furled so that the bare masts looked like a forest stripped of all its branches. Smaller vessels scurried like water beetles over the surface, headed from the ships that were anchored farther out manned by sailors in brightly colored jerseys of every description. The smell of salt was in the air, but it was not the clean smell that she had learned to enjoy on the voyage, for it was tinged with the raw scent of civilization.

The weather was warmer than she had expected, much warmer than it had been when they left England. She remembered the first officer telling her that America was much farther south, and therefore, the winters were much milder, but the summers could be stifling, especially in the southern colonies. Overhead the sky was blue and hard enough to strike a match on; across it fleecy clouds were driven by a brisk wind. The hoarse squalling of the gulls that circled incessantly mingled with the shouts of the officers on board the *Caledonia*, and from the docks came the sound of a man lustily singing a song about a woman who did him wrong.

After the bout of seasickness, Sabrina had enjoyed the voyage, although she did fight with boredom most of the time. Mr. Stern, the first officer, had obviously been taken with her, and it raised Sabrina's spirits somewhat to see that despite her loss of money and position she still was able to charm a man. The two had taken strolls on the deck, and she had listened attentively as Stern told her what he knew of America. She had allowed him to kiss her once, but then she had laughed and stepped back, saying, "I have heard that sailors have a girl in every port."

Sabrina had also been somewhat puzzled by Sion Kenyon. She had actually seen very little of him, for after he had cared for her so wonderfully while she was sick, he had kept company with the sailors and some of the other passengers headed for America. Sabrina, at first, had been apprehensive that he would take advantage of the situation, fearing that because he had helped her he might feel free to move closer to her socially. This had not been the case, however. Indeed, he had deliberately shunned her company. This had brought some relief to Sabrina, but paradoxically she wondered at the man. She knew her own attractiveness, but he appeared to be totally uninterested in her. He had been polite and respectful on those occasions when they met, but nothing more.

"All passengers prepare to go ashore!"

Sabrina heard the loud voice of the bosun and straightened up. She kept her grip on the rail, however, and in that instant the fears of what lay before her rose again within her breast. During the voyage she had successfully pushed them away, covered them up with the activities of the ship, and had spent many hours reading. But now all that had changed. The swarming dock that lay before her was as alien to her as if it had been China or India. Now, once again, the feeling came to her that the wisest thing she could do was to stay on this ship and sail back to England as quickly as possible.

"Well, here's your new home." The voice came from directly behind her, and Sabrina turned to see Mr. Stern smiling at her. He waved his arm and said, "It's a big country, Miss Fairfax."

"Yes, it is."

"You'll find your place in it, I'm sure," Stern added. "But if you don't, you can always go back home again."

"I doubt that. This will have to be my home, Mr. Stern."

Stern had learned enough of Sabrina's history to feel sympathy. "Yes. Well, if that's the case, you'll make out." He had taken off his hat, and the warm April wind tumbled his hair over his forehead. He brushed it back and shook his head. "I hate to see you headed out for that raw wilderness, but I know it's something you have to do."

"Yes, it is."

He put his hand out, and she took it and felt the strength of it. "I will think of you often," he said quietly.

"And I of you. You've been kind."

When Stern turned away, calling out orders sharply to the deckhands, Sabrina felt she had lost something. He was only a chance acquaintance, but she had valued his kindness and consideration during the voyage, and now she wished futilely that he were going with her. She went searching for Sion and found him carrying her baggage from the hold up to the deck.

"I'll get your trunk, miss," he said. "You'd better watch this baggage. Some of these Americans may be thieves."

"I expect they are. Some of them, at least."

Sion suddenly smiled at her and winked almost merrily. "Just like Welshmen. Some good, some bad—Englishmen, too, I expect. I'll get the trunk."

Sabrina stood with Sion in the midst of the busy crowd holding the cage that contained Ulysses. The luggage made a small mound, and she looked around uncertainly. "I expect I'd better go try to find out something about the legal side of this land," she said.

"Maybe I'd better stay here with the luggage."

"No, let's get a carriage."

Sion looked around and saw a line of carriages. He went quickly and spoke to the driver in the first one—a tall, lean man with a sour expression on his face and a huge wad of tobacco bulging in his jaw.

"Good day, sir. We need to rent your carriage."

Before he turned to acknowledge Sion, he spat an amber stream that almost hit Sion's feet. "That's what I'm here fer. Where you goin'?"

"My mistress will give you instructions. Perhaps you could give me a hand with the luggage."

"Reckon I kin." The lanky driver stepped down and towered over Sion. He seemed to be all arms and legs, and the clothes he wore would have disgraced a beggar back in England.

Sion led him to the baggage and said, "This man will take us anywhere you please, Miss Sabrina."

"I need to go to the courthouse."

"Yep."

With this curt monosyllable the man began gathering up the bags. Sion shouldered the trunk, and Sabrina followed them to the carriage. After they were loaded, she waited for the driver to help her in, but he simply hauled himself aboard, picked up the lines, and spat again.

"Here, let me help you on," Sion said quickly. He took Sabrina's hand, put her in the backseat of the carriage, then leaped into the front seat. "I think we're ready now."

"Yep."

The driver, having started the horses forward, turned and said, "Reckon you be English."

"Aye, the lady is. I'm from Wales."

"Where's that?"

"It's a part of Great Britain—next to England."

"I fought in the war against you 'uns."

"Did you, now?"

"Yep. I kept count of the lobsterbacks I kilt. Up to seventeen and then I lost count. Reckon I must have got more'n twenty of you 'uns. Was you in that war?"

"No, I wasn't."

"Thet's good."

Sabrina, sitting in the back, listened as the driver spoke, alternately voicing his disapprobation of anyone from "across the water," as he put it, and spitting tobacco juice. She was disappointed in her first contact in America, but realistically she understood that this was the counterpart of a lower-class cockney from London. And Stern had prepared her to some extent for the crudeness of Americans.

"There it is," the driver said, pulling the horses up and waving a long arm toward a two-story brick building with a cupola on top. "You want me to wait?"

Sabrina hesitated, then said, "I don't know how long I'll be."

"Well, I gotta make a livin'."

The driver did not get down, so Sion leaped to the ground, assisted Sabrina, then unloaded the trunk and the baggage, placing them next to the building while Sabrina negotiated the fare. There was some discussion about English money, and when she came back, she said, "I'll have to get my money changed to American. I have no idea whether I overpaid him or not."

"Probably did," Sion nodded. "You go right ahead, Miss Sabrina. I'll see that no one bothers the luggage."

Sabrina entered the courthouse and stood uncertainly in the corridor. Two men walking down the hall looked at her curiously, and she realized that she was probably overdressed. She had on a dark green traveling dress with matching jacket. The dress fit tightly over the bodice, had a high neckline edged with black ribbon, and cinched in at the waist. The full skirt just touched the floor. The midthigh-length long-sleeved jacket fit snugly at the waist, buttoned up the front with large black buttons, and had a large collar edged with black ribbon.

One of the men came over and said, "How do? You lookin' for anybody special?"

"Yes. I need someone who can tell me about a title to some land."

"Reckon you'll need to talk to Dwight."

"Dwight?"

"Yes. Dwight Camrose. He's in the last office down the hall to the right."

"Thank you, sir."

"Right welcome, miss."

Sabrina felt the eyes of the two men follow her as she walked down the rather dirty corridor. When she stepped inside the door indicated by the man, she found herself in an outer office with several chairs and a long counter. A clerk was standing behind the counter smoking a pipe, and he greeted her.

"Yes, miss. Can I help you?"

"I need to see Mr. Camrose."

"About what?"

"It concerns a title to some land."

"Have a seat over there, miss. He'll be with you directly."

"Thank you."

Sabrina took her seat and waited, but the "directly" turned out to be much longer than she had anticipated. Finally a man came out of the office, puffing furiously on a cigar and pulling a straw hat down to his ears. As soon as he left, the clerk nodded at Sabrina.

"I reckon you can go in now, miss."

"Thank you."

Sabrina entered the office and found a short, rotund man wearing a snuff-brown suit standing by a large map, making some sort of insignia on it. He did not turn around for a time so she stood until finally he put down his pen and turned to face her. "Well, what can I do for you, miss?"

"My name is Miss Sabrina Fairfax. I've just arrived from England, and I need some information about some land that I own in—" and here she consulted her deed—"the Territory of the United States South of the River Ohio."

"Well, you're in the wrong place for that."

"I know, but I thought you might give me some help on the procedures."

Camrose pulled a plug of tobacco out of his pocket. He bit off an enormous bite, tucked it into his jaw, and said, "I guess maybe I can do that, but I can tell you right now you're going to have to go to where the land's at to make sure."

"I inherited the land, and I'm not even sure exactly where it is."

"Let me see that title."

Sabrina handed her papers over to Camrose and watched as he studied them.

"If you'll step over here, I'll be glad to show you where this here piece is at." He stepped to the wall, and Sabrina moved closer. The map she saw was so filled with lines and names it confused her, but Camrose clarified the matter at once. "Your claim is here," he said, touching the map with his forefinger. "It's close to a settlement called Holston."

"I've been somewhat concerned, Mr. Camrose, about the legality of this title."

"Well might you be, Miss Fairfax. You're not the only one. The trouble is the titles have been passed around so much it's hard to tell anymore. Of course, the Indians lived on it once, and they got a claim. North Carolina owned it at one time. They got a claim. There was a brute who tried to start a new state called Franklin. He claimed the land. And now the government of the United States has a claim. You'll just have to head for this property and get yourself a good lawyer."

"Can you tell me anything at all about what this property is like?"

"No, miss, I can't. It might be cleared. It might be nothin' but trees and mountains. The only way to tell is to go. I can tell you one thing, though. The title may be good, but Indians can't read titles very good. It's too dangerous for you, if you want my opinion."

"I have to go there," Sabrina said simply. "I don't have any-place else to go."

"Then get yourself a good lawyer and let him nail this title down for you. You're from England, I take it?"

"Yes, sir, I am."

"I can tell you're used to the better things in life," Camrose said, squinting at her. He spat juice expertly into a brass spittoon and did not bother to wipe his mouth. The amber fluid stained the corners and ran down slightly, adding to the residue already there. "It's a big country, miss, and wild. I wouldn't advise you to go there unless you have to."

"Well, I have to. Do you know any lawyers in that area whom you might recommend?"

"No, miss, I don't. Sorry about that. But there's plenty of lawyers there like there is everywhere else. Just be sure you get a good 'un."

Sabrina nodded and turned, saying, "Thank you very much, Mr. Camrose."

"Watch out for your scalp, lady."

Sabrina nodded at his advice and left the office. When she got outside, she found Sion in a conversation with a man, and the two turned to her.

"Sion, we'll have to find someplace to stay tonight."

"This is Mr. Sam Satterfield, miss. He knows this town very well. Do you want to go to an inn?"

"Yes," Sabrina replied firmly. "Hurry up and load the luggage. I'm tired."

Sion and the driver quickly loaded the baggage, and Satterfield said, "Bossy, ain't she?"

"I suppose she is."

"You're not married to that filly, are ya?"

"Not likely." Sion grinned.

Sion went to help Sabrina into the carriage and then got into the front seat next to the driver.

"You want a fine place or a cheap place?"

"We'll only be staying one night, I think," Sabrina answered, "and it shouldn't be too expensive."

"I've got a cousin who runs a place. It ain't the finest in the world, but it's clean and only two dollars a night, including breakfast in the mornin'."

"That will be fine," Sabrina said. She leaned back and watched the stream of people as the carriage made its way down the street. She was thinking of what Camrose had said, and it discouraged her. Her thoughts were interrupted with Satterfield's description of the Tennessee Country, as the driver said some folks called it.

"It's thick as fleas with Indians. That's what I hear. I was in General Washington's army from Bunker Hill clear up to Yorktown. We seen some rough days from you English soldiers, but I don't reckon I'd want to tangle with them redskins. From what I hear, they'll skin a man just for fun after they catch him."

"Literally?" Sion asked.

"Of course I mean literally! Take the skin right off the meat."

Sion continued to question the man until they pulled up in front of a plain building. "I'll go in and make sure my cousin has a room available," Satterfield said.

When the driver was gone, Sion turned and asked, "Did you find out anything, miss, about the place we're going to?"

"Not much. We're going to have to go there, Sion." She

hesitated, then said, "I can't afford two rooms. You understand that."

"Don't worry about it. I'll find a place."

Satterfield returned to the carriage. "You're all set. Here, lady, I'll help you down."

As Sabrina stepped down, she felt the hardness of the man's hands and his curious eyes upon her as well. She waited until the two men had unloaded the baggage and started for the building. She followed them carrying the wicker cage. Once inside she was introduced to Satterfield's cousin, whose name was Fredrickson. He was a small, decently dressed man with clean white hair. He spoke in a different manner than the two drivers she had spoken with, and she wondered if he came from a different part of the Colonies.

"Just one room, Miss Fairfax?"

"Yes, I don't know how long we'll be staying. Probably only one night. We need to get a coach to Tennessee."

"I can take care of that for you, miss," Satterfield said, putting down the luggage. "I've got another cousin who drives the stagecoach."

"That would be very kind of you."

Sabrina followed the two men as they carried the luggage to a room on the second floor. When the baggage was outside, she asked Satterfield, "How much do I owe you?"

"Oh, maybe a dollar."

"How many dollars in a pound?"

"Don't rightly know," Satterfield said cheerfully. "If I was you, I'd get all that English money changed. People would rather have American money, for the most part, unless it's gold coins. That'll spend anywhere."

Sabrina negotiated the fare, and Satterfield promised to find out about the stagecoach. When he left, she gave Sion a coin, saying, "Buy something to eat and find a place to sleep."

"Right enough," Sion said cheerfully.

"I don't have money to stay in this place any longer than necessary. We'll leave as soon as we can find transportation."

"I think Satterfield's a good man. He seems to be, anyway. I'll say good-night, now. If you want me, I'll probably be sleeping in the loft at the stables. All of these inns have stables, it sounds like."

"Be here early, Sion."

As soon as Sion left, Sabrina went over and looked out the window. The street was busy, and she marveled at the people as they moved busily by. Her land seemed a million miles away, and she said aloud, "I mustn't think of it. We'll get there. I know we will."

Sion wandered the streets for some time, listening to the strangeness of the speech. He knew his own brand of English would identify him instantly. Some of the voices spoke almost harshly, cutting off their words before they were even finished. Others spoke with a slurred speech, rather languidly, and he knew soon enough he would discover which areas of this new country they came from. He grew hungry finally and entered an inn.

A black-eyed young woman, full-bodied and with a bold manner, put her eyes on him as he came in. She smiled as he stood in the middle of the floor and said, "Come and have a seat. You just in from off a ship?"

"That's right. How could you tell that?"

"Can always tell newcomers. My name's Frannie."

Sion wondered if it was customary for tavern women to introduce themselves and decided that perhaps it was. He had already discovered there was a freeness in the mannerisms of Americans, and he followed the woman to a table.

"We have roast beef or venison."

"Venison? What's that?"

"Why, it's deer!" Frannie said. "You *are* green, aren't you?"

"That I am. I'd like to try the venison. I've tried roast beef."

She laughed at him. "Where are you from, handsome?"

"From Wales. It's next to England."

"I see. Better be careful. There're still lots of men around who would cut any Englishman's throat."

"I'll try to avoid such a situation."

Frannie smiled and winked. "I'll be right back. And I'll bring you some good ale, too."

The room was only half filled, and while he waited for his meal, Sion listened and studied the men. There was a similarity to them somehow. They all talked rather loudly and without inhibition. Most of them cursed rather fluently, and few of them were dressed in finery. The inn was evidently for workingmen.

Sion became aware that the man at the table next to him was watching him carefully. He was a tall man with gray eyes, and Sion nodded pleasantly and said, "How do you do, sir?"

"Hello. Welcome to America. Why don't you join me? I hate to eat alone."

"It would be a pleasure, sir."

Sion rose from his seat, and when he moved to take his seat, the man reached across the table. "My name's Nate Strother."

"Sion Kenyon."

"Zion? That's a Bible name, ain't it?"

"No, it's S-I-O-N. That's Welsh for John."

Strother was a well-set-up individual with broad shoulders and a neck that was thickly corded with muscle. He appeared to be in his late thirties, and there was a wearied look about him. He seemed to be an outdoorsman for he looked a bit out of place inside. Now he said, "If you stay here long, you might as well call yourself John or else you'll be explaining that name to everybody you meet."

"I may have to do that."

"Just got off the boat, I heard you say?"

"Yes. We're headed west."

"You married?"

"Oh no. I'm a servant to an English lady. She's inherited some land in a place they call Tennessee Country."

"That's my part of the world."

"Do you tell me that!" Sion said eagerly. "Maybe you can tell me a little bit about the area. I've heard some stories, but you Americans are—"

Strother smiled. "We're a little bit given to embroidering the truth. Is that what you're telling me?"

"Maybe I'll change my mind later on."

"No. It's true enough. But I can tell you a bit about it."

"Can you tell me how to get there?" Sion asked. "That's the first problem. A driver told me we could go by stagecoach."

"I reckon he told you right. I just came from there. You can take the stage, but sooner or later it runs out."

"How do we get the rest of the way?"

"Well, you'll have to buy wagons and animals and follow the trails."

"That might be hard for me, Mr. Strother."

"We're not much on the *misters* around here. Just Nate's good enough."

"Well, I suppose I could get a map."

"You can do that, but most of the trails ain't marked. How many of you are going?"

"Just me and the lady I work for."

"Well, it's a big country and not entirely friendly," Strother said. "I'd advise you to hire somebody to take you in."

"Because of the Indians?"

"Always danger of Indians. Your best bet would be to buy a wagon, some animals, get in with a bunch on the way. The more wagons the better."

The two men talked until the meal came, and they ate their first few bites in silence. Frannie managed to push against his shoulder with her hip, giving him a rather obvious invitation, and when he made no response, she gave him a disgusted look and left.

"She's lookin' for companionship, Sion."

"She'll have to find it somewhere else."

"You don't like women?"

"Not that kind," Sion said.

"Well, that's a man's choice. Listen, it may get too rough for you out on the trail. You might want to quit this woman you're workin' for."

"I can't do that."

"Why not?"

"I'm an indentured servant for five years."

"Like I say, it's a big land." Nate shrugged. "Once you get out of civilization, you could just take off."

"I don't think I could do that, Nate."

Nate Strother studied Sion. "No, I can see you're not the

runnin' kind. Well, have you got a place to sleep?"

"No. I thought I'd find a place in the stable."

"You can stay with me tonight. I've got an extra bed."

"Thanks. I'll take you up on that. I hope I don't snore."

"Won't matter. I do." They laughed, and the two got up and left the inn.

No sooner had they stepped onto the street than they practically stumbled over Satterfield. "Say there, I've been looking for you."

"I'm glad you found me. Did you find out when the post leaves?"

"Tomorrow morning at ten o'clock, and my cousin says there's still room on it."

"I'll let Miss Sabrina know, and we'll see what she decides. Thanks for looking into it for us."

"You're welcome. Well, if I don't see you in the morning, I wish you good luck."

"Thanks. You've been a great help."

The men parted ways—Sion and Nate in one direction and Satterfield back to his rig. Tomorrow would be quite a day.

A Fork in the Road

Ten

*T*he sound of voices brought Sabrina out of a fitful sleep. She had tossed and turned for hours and several times drifted off only to awaken as her mind flooded with doubts concerning the future. Now she sat bolt upright, startled by voices that seemed to be in the room with her. Ulysses, who had been sleeping with his head wedged against her, growled deep in his throat and tried to settle down to sleep again.

A thin gray light was filtering through the single window, barely able to pierce the dirty panes, and her back ached from the sagging mattress. She had examined it carefully for bugs and found none, but the thought of sleeping in a bed previously occupied by someone else had not aided her comfort.

A man and a woman were on the other side of the thin wall, and their voices rose as they engaged in a bitter argument. Sabrina had little choice but to sit there and try not to listen. Obviously the two had reached the point where they weren't happy with each other, or at least so it seemed to her. Finally, after an indeterminable time, the woman said in a voice deadened by weariness and utterly devoid of hope, "All right, Ed, we'll have to go on."

"That's right," the man said in an angry tone. "We're stuck with each other, Edith, and we might as well make the best of it!"

Throwing back the cover, Sabrina moved over to the rickety washstand made of cheap raw lumber, poured the basin full of water, and washed as best as she could. She longed for a bath, but there was no chance of that today. After she dried herself she put on a fresh dress. Finally she did the best she could with her filthy hair, which hadn't had a good washing since she left England. Staring at her image in the small, cloudy mirror fastened to the wall, she shook her hair and then said rebelliously, "I'll have a bath and wash my hair soon, you can believe that!" She then turned to the cat, which was watching her lazily. "Well, Ulysses, how do you like America?"

The big cat watched her with its enormous eyes as it lay at the foot of the bed. Suddenly it yawned, revealing white teeth and a red mouth, then got up, stretched, and leaped off the bed. It came over to her and tapped at her calf, saying, "*Wow!*"

" 'Wow' yourself," Sabrina said. She picked the cat up, tucked it over her shoulder, and stroked its fur. "I haven't got time to fool with you today." She put the cat down, finished dressing, and left the room. The stairs creaked ominously and sagged as she went downstairs, and for a moment she was afraid the whole structure would collapse. But she reached the first floor of the inn safely and found the dining room, where she saw Sion eating his breakfast.

When he saw her, he rose and said, "Good morning. The food's good here, miss."

Sabrina sat down and thought, *This may be the first time I've ever sat down with a servant.* She gave Sion a brief good-morning, and when Mrs. Fredrickson brought her a plate, she began to eat hungrily. The breakfast consisted of thick slices of bacon with a strong flavor, spiced bread with a large bowl of butter, and battered eggs. The coffee was so strong it was bitter, but she had eaten little the day before and knew she needed all the strength she could get.

Sion spoke of America cheerfully as she ate. "The people here are rough, but some of them are helpful enough. I met a man last night named Nate Strother. He's been west."

Sabrina asked, "Did he tell you anything about the best way to get to my land?"

"He said the best way would be to take the stagecoach, but it doesn't go all the way. After Nate and I had dinner we ran into Mr. Satterfield—remember our driver from yesterday? He said the stage leaves at ten o'clock this morning, and there's still room on it. Nate says the thing to do when the stage gets to the end of the line is to buy a wagon and some horses."

"But we don't know how to get there."

"He said there'd be plenty of people headed that way, and the best thing would be to join ourselves to a group already going. That way," he added, "it would be more protection from Indians."

The two finished their meal, and as Sabrina tried to think of what to do next, a big man entered the room. He was wearing buckskins and had on a strange-looking cap with a ringed tail hanging down from the back. He had a full set of black whiskers and a pair of bold black eyes. He spotted Sabrina and came over to say, "Well, howdy. My name's Zeke Thomason."

Sabrina could not speak, she was so surprised. She gave the man one look, then coolly returned her gaze to Sion.

"Well, ain't you a pretty one," the man said. He moved around the table so she would have to face him, and at that instant Sion stood up. He was not as large as the American, and the loose clothes he wore disguised the muscular strength of his body.

"Best move on, I suppose, friend," he said quietly.

Thomason stared at him. "You tellin' me to leave?"

"I think it would be wise."

Thomason laughed. "You don't know who you're talkin' to. I'm Zeke Thomason. Half man, half alligator. Most men with half a brain wouldn't be talkin' to me like that. I reckon I'll just carve myself a steak out of you, fancy man!"

"All right, Zeke, that's enough."

Thomason turned to see the innkeeper, who was wiping his hands on his apron.

"Sit down and eat or git!"

Thomason seemed to be weighing the alternatives in his mind. Then he laughed. "Sure, Fredrickson. No problem. I just wanted to pass the time of day with these two limeys."

As the man left, Sabrina turned and smiled. "Thank you. He was beginning to be a bore."

"He's a rough one," Fredrickson said, "but he won't bother you anymore."

"The food was very good. Tell your wife I enjoyed it."

"I'll do that. You two are headed out, I take it?"

"We're thinking about it."

"You'll see lots of his kind out there if you head west. They're a pretty rough bunch, those hunters."

Fredrickson turned and left, and Sion took his seat again. As he sat down, Sabrina was thinking of what she would have done if he had not been there or if Fredrickson had not come.

Without meaning to, she blurted out, "I can't make up my mind."

"It's a hard choice for you."

"What if we get all the way out there and find out there's something wrong with the title and I can't get the land?"

Sion shrugged his shoulders. "Then we'll have to do something else."

"But I don't have much money, and I don't have a living soul there who cares for me."

Sion tilted his head to one side the way he sometimes did. "You will have two who care what happens to you, miss."

"Two? What do you mean? I don't know a soul."

"Well, you'll have God. He knows about you. And then, of course, you'll have me."

Sabrina felt strangely comforted by this. The sense of loneliness that had built up in her for weeks was a dark specter that always stood close. And now this kind man who was really a stranger to her had brought comfort simply with a few words. She looked across the table at him and considered his appearance as if seeing him for the first time. She guessed his height at six feet, and although rough and durable, he was very attractive and had a gentle face. He had brown eyes and he always kept his wavy light brown hair pulled back neatly behind his head. She remembered how smooth and strong his muscles had looked when he had been stripped for the fight in the ring. She sensed there was a strength in the inner man of Sion Kenyon, and it gave her comfort to know that she had chosen well when she had decided to help him.

"That's kind of you. You really believe that about God caring for each one of us, don't you, Sion?"

"Why, of course I do!"

"I'm glad you do. I hope you always will."

"Don't you believe it, Miss Fairfax?"

"I'd like to, but it's hard sometimes." She shook her head,

trying to shove away the doubts, and said, "Tell me more about Nate Strother and what he said."

Sion leaned forward and for the next ten minutes told her the essence of Strother's information. He finished by saying, "It's not my place to say so, but from what you've told me about yourself and your past, I'd say God's opened up a door for you. There's nothing for you in England, is there?"

"No. There isn't." Sabrina knew she was at a juncture in her life. It was as if she had come down a path and arrived at a fork in the road. Now she would need to choose the best way. She kept her eyes fixed on Sion. He seemed to be a good man, but who could tell? What would he be like when they were away from civilization?

Finally, in desperation, she made the decision. "All right, Sion, we'll go." But even as she spoke, fear came over her.

Sion said cheerfully with a nod, "That's fine. We'd better get ready. The stage leaves in two hours."

Sabrina didn't like making such an important decision so quickly, but she knew she couldn't delay making the choice. "All right," she said quietly, "I'll make sure there's still room on it."

"U.S. Territory South of the River Ohio. The name sounds pretty, doesn't it? I bet it'll be a pretty place, too." Sion smiled, and as always, the smile lightened his face. "I'm thinking you'll like it there, miss. It's a good, new land. It may be a little hard, but we'll make it."

Sabrina was encouraged by Sion's use of the word *we*. She knew it would have offended her back in England when she was a lady of property to have a servant enjoin himself with her, but now she took a deep breath and said, "I hope so, Sion—I surely hope so!"

New Acquaintances

Eleven

Whatever pleasant anticipation of the journey Sabrina had entertained did not last longer than an hour after the stagecoach left the station. The driver, a tall, taciturn man with a droopy mustache and a pair of sad-looking eyes, had watched as they all boarded. There were eight passengers, and when she got aboard, Sabrina found that the accommodations were of a spartan simplicity. Three benches without backs were fastened to the floor, and she chose the backseat so she could at least face forward. The other passengers quickly filled the seats, and a very fat man put himself down beside her, saying, "Good day for travel."

Sabrina murmured her agreement and noted that Sion had chosen a middle seat. His back was to her, and he seemed relaxed, which she was not.

No sooner had she gotten settled than she heard the stage driver call out to the horses, and the coach surged ahead. The three passengers on the middle seat were caught off guard so that they all tumbled backward. Sion tried to catch himself, she saw, but the start was too powerful, and he was thrown back against her knees. The other passengers on the middle seat sprawled backward also, and one of them, a short, muscular man, began to curse.

"Sorry, miss," Sion said. He laughed and winked at her. "A spirited beginning to our journey, isn't it?" Sabrina wedged herself against the side, for the large man was spilling over against her. It was not intentional, she knew, for the seat was barely long enough to accommodate three average-sized individuals. *I've got to spend at least two days, maybe three, in this awful coach.* The thought pressed against her and was so depressing that she simply sat there looking out the window for the next two hours.

The scenery that flowed by was not spectacular and soon became very boring. The coach was passing through mostly farmland, where the fields stretched away on either side, broken only by farmhouses and barns and fields fenced in for cattle.

It had been a dry spring, evidently, for the horses and the wheels of the coach stirred up dust, which boiled around the coach. She leaned out the window just enough to see that the wheels were lifting the dust in ropy, dripping sheets that rolled up into gauze clouds that finally settled over the trees that lined the road. Most of it was left behind, but the residue from the horses ahead drifted in through the open windows, leaving a fine but gritty dust on all the passengers and everything inside the coach. From time to time Sabrina tried to clean her face with her handkerchief, but it was almost a hopeless task.

There was only one other woman on the coach, who sat in the front seat facing backward. She appeared to be in her sixties and must have been a workingwoman, for the discomfort of the journey did not seem to trouble her. She chatted amiably with her husband, who sat beside her, the two often laughing. Once, she saw the man reach over and hold her hand. *How nice. I hope when I've been married as long as they have, my husband will still want to hold my hand.* She smiled at the thought, and at that moment Sion turned around and caught her smile. He turned to see what she was smiling at, and when he saw the couple holding hands, he twisted in his seat and leaned backward to whisper, "There's still a little romance in the world, isn't there."

At that moment the coach hit a deep hole, throwing all the passengers roughly to the left. The fat man's weight nearly crushed Sabrina, and he shook his head and apologized. "Sorry about that. These roads are terrible."

The horses pulled the coach steadily, and as the morning wore on, Sabrina was beginning to think she could not stand much more of this. Her legs were stiff, and her seat was numb from the pounding of the unpadded bench. Even though it wasn't hot outside—it was actually quite comfortable—the sun was beating down on the carriage, and she was absolutely miserable. In despair she wiped her face and blew her nose, for the fine dust crept into her nostrils and lungs. There was no avoiding the rolling of the stage. It seemed almost as bad as being on board the ship. The stage rolled along, striking holes and occasionally the rocky bottom of a creek, which tilted upward, throwing the passengers violently around. By noon everyone's face was slick with oil, and the smell of the coach had become rank as the odors of stale sweat mingled in the small space. She steeled herself and tried to ignore the discomfort.

Finally the coach slowed, and Sion looked out the window. "A station," he said. "It looks like we're going to make a stop."

The coach did pull up, and the driver called out, "Thirty-minute stop!"

The passengers disembarked, and Sion was there to help her to the ground. They were at an abandoned house, but there was a well, and Sion went at once to it and primed it. He filled a tin cup with water and offered it to Sabrina. "Wash a little of the dust down," he said gently.

Taking the cup, Sabrina drank thirstily. She drained the contents of the cup twice and then handed it back, saying, "I've never felt so grimy in all my life."

"It's rough going. We'll just have to hold on." He drank a cup himself and then handed the cup to the big man. He turned to Sabrina and said, "Let's get a little exercise. It may be night before we stop again."

Sabrina nodded, and the two walked alongside the back of the house. A large grove of trees banked the small field, but there was no stock grazing. They walked silently along the edge of the field. Sion finally said, "This is a little rough right now, but I think it's a little exciting."

Sabrina laughed without joy. "Exciting! I don't know how you can say that. It's miserable and uncomfortable."

"It is for you, miss. You're used to the finer things." He reached down and picked a small flower. "This is pretty, isn't it?" He studied it as if it had some great meaning before letting it fall to the earth. "It's not so bad on me. After being down in a coal mine, anything is comfortable."

"I suppose you've had a very hard life."

"Not as bad as some, but I'm glad to be out of the mines. And I'm glad not to be fighting anymore."

"You say you did that to help some friends of yours who were in trouble?"

"Yes. Very good friends."

"What are their names? How did you meet them?"

Sion glanced at her with surprise, then quickly told her of how he had met the Grufydds. As he spoke, the sun was putting fingers of light through the trees. The taller trees were shouldering the sun out of the way, and a breeze was blowing, which was refreshing after the heat of the coach. A bird with a blue back, white belly, and pointed head appeared before them, and they both turned to watch it. "What kind of bird is that, I wonder? We don't have those in Wales."

"I'm not sure. I don't know much about birds."

Finally they stopped and looked back and realized that they had walked quite a distance; the coach and the houses seemed to have shrunk. The passengers were all walking around stretching their legs. As they started back, Sabrina asked, "Do you have any good memories, Sion?"

"Why, of course I do. Lots of them. Mostly my head's stocked with good little things. It's kind of like a picture gallery. When I want to think of something pleasant, I go into the gallery, and I take out a picture and look at it."

Sabrina was intrigued at his poetic imagination. "I've never heard anything like that. Can you really do that?"

Sion turned to her and lifted one brow. "Aye, that I can. For example, I remember once when I was passing by a confectionery store with candy and pies and things like that in the window. There was a little girl standing there staring at the candy trays, and I stopped and looked with her. The look on her face touched me, maybe because I'd stood in front of windows myself and wanted something very badly."

"What did you do?"

"Oh, I went inside and bought a sack of candy and gave it to her. She was very shy, but I pressed it on her. She smiled at me and held the candy to her breast as if it were some great treasure of diamonds or gold." A smile turned the corners of his lips upward. "The candy only cost a few pence, but every time I think of that I get my money's worth again."

"That's nice," Sabrina murmured.

After a moment of quiet, Sion said, "I wish you wouldn't worry so much, miss. I know it's troubled, you are. Things will be all right."

Sabrina turned to glance at him. He was a very intuitive man, she had learned. A small gust of expression crossed her face as she said, "I've had things too easy."

"Well, I've had things too hard, so I suppose we make a good average, don't we?"

Sabrina laughed, and some of the weight lifted from her. "My mother told me that when I was a baby she would take me outside at night when the moon was full and lay me on my back on the grass. She said I always reached for the moon, as if I could reach up and get it. That I never learned any better." She shook her head and added quietly, "I've learned that you can't reach out and get things like that."

"Sometimes you can. I know life gets hard, but things work out sometimes. Why, look at me. I was headed to jail for ten years of misery, but along came Miss Sabrina Fairfax. And now I'm in America, where a man has a chance. I'm strong and healthy, and I've got the most agreeable, attractive employer I've ever had in my life. You should have seen some of the ugly ones I had."

Sabrina quickly glanced at him to see if he was flirting, but there was only a pleasant smile on his face, and she knew it was merely his way. "I'm glad you feel like that, Sion. I'll try not to burden you with my gloomy ways."

"Not blaming you, I am," Sion said quickly. "I think you're learning to catch grace."

" 'Catch grace'? What does that mean?"

"Why, I think a man—or a woman—catches grace in the same way a man fills his cup under a waterfall. God's grace is all around us. We just have to hold our cups out to catch it."

The two returned to the coach and drank some more cold water from the well before the driver called out, "Time to move out!" As she took her seat, Sabrina thought, *What in the world would I do without Sion? I'd be lost.* She braced herself as the coach started and tried to forget about the hardship of the next few hours.

———————

The coach pulled into the station early in the evening, just as it was getting dark, and Sabrina was so numb and weary that she had to steel herself and make an effort to rise and get out. Her feet had gone to sleep, she discovered, and when she stepped out, she nearly collapsed. Sion was waiting for this, however, and he easily caught her. He steadied her with his arm around her back for just a moment and then said cheerfully, "I guess we're all pretty stiff after that ride, but it's over for today, at least."

The passengers made their way into the station, which consisted of a large room with a stove at one end and three tables with mismatched chairs. The smell of fresh-cooked meat laced the air, and despite her weariness, Sabrina felt a sharp pang of hunger. The woman who met them was no longer young, but she still had traces of attractiveness. She was wearing a brown vest, and her pinned-up brown hair showed glints of red.

"I'm Mrs. Tompkins. Supper's ready." Her eyes fell on Sabrina, and she guessed at her upbringing. "Perhaps you'd like to freshen up first."

"Yes, Mrs. Tompkins, I would."

"Come this way."

She led her to a room that had a single bed and a washstand in it. "There's fresh water in the pitcher and towels. Take all the time you need."

"Thank you."

Sabrina washed her face and longed, as she had all day, to get into a bathtub and simply soak. But she was hungry and quickly went back to join the group. Sion and several of the other men rose as she entered. She sat down and saw that the others had already started.

"This lady's a good cook," Sion said. The meal consisted of steaming mutton, freshly baked wheat bread with whipped butter, green beans, and steamed carrots. She tasted the beverage in her cup but did not recognize it.

"That's fresh cider," the fat man said. "Mighty good, too, ain't it, now?"

"Very good."

The passengers ate rapidly, and there was little talk around the table. When they were done, Sabrina went outside and sat in a rocker on the porch. The sun was down now, and the air had a chill to it, which was a welcome relief after the heat of the stuffy stagecoach.

She sat there for a long time, relaxing and almost dozing off. The men inside began to gamble, and she glanced inside and saw Sion looking on but not playing. She leaned her head back and enjoyed watching the stars. The moon was full and laid its silver beams down on the earth, and she thought how much more beautiful the land was bathed in silver than it was during the day.

Mrs. Tompkins came outside and sat down in a chair. "I expect you're pretty tired. It's a long trip from Portsmouth."

"Yes, I am tired. The meal was so good. I appreciate it."

"After a while I'll fix you some tea. I know how you English ladies love tea."

Sabrina liked the woman. "Yes, I do, but I don't want to be any trouble."

"I always have my tea before I go to bed."

As the women sat there, Sabrina felt the tension drain out of her. The two talked for half an hour, and somehow Sabrina found herself telling Alpha Tompkins her story. She was the kind of woman who made you feel like you could tell her anything. Finally Sabrina finished, saying, "So here I am in a strange country with little money and a great many fears."

"Don't be afraid, Miss Fairfax. God is in all we do. He wouldn't make us, would He, and then not care what happens?"

Sabrina turned to face the woman. She could see her face clearly in the moonlight and noted that there was a gentleness about her that had not been erased by hard work. "It sometimes seems He doesn't care."

"We make mistakes sometimes, but God can use even those." She hesitated, then said softly, "I married the wrong man, but God will bring something good out of it."

Sabrina wanted to ask about her husband but did not feel she had the right.

Alpha asked her, "What about this man who's with you?" She listened as Sabrina briefly outlined how she and Sion happened to be traveling together.

"He looks like a strong man, but I don't know if he's good. Strong and good don't always go together."

Sabrina did not answer for a time, and then she said, "I think he's a good man."

Mrs. Tompkins watched the younger woman's face and then said, "Let's fix tea. I think it would go down well."

After the two enjoyed their tea, Sabrina made her way to bed. She was exhausted and fell asleep as if she had been drugged.

———

By the time Sabrina had cleaned herself as well as she could with the fresh water from the basin and a sweet-smelling soap, she was ready to face the day. She put a protesting Ulysses into his cage, then left the room. When she got to the dining room she saw that Mrs. Tompkins had already started feeding the passengers.

"Good morning, Miss Fairfax. You need to have a good breakfast now."

Sabrina greeted her, then turned and saw a couple who had not been there the previous night. They were eating breakfast, and the only seats available were right opposite them. Sion was sitting across the room and gave her a smile but did not get up. When she sat down the man arose and said, "Good morning," and the woman nodded at her.

"Good morning," Sabrina said.

The man said, "We'll be traveling together, it seems. My name is Joshua Spencer, and this is my sister, Hannah."

"I'm Sabrina Fairfax." Sabrina studied the two. They were both young, perhaps nineteen or twenty. Joshua was a tall man with dark hair and dark eyes, rather handsome in a way. Hannah Spencer had honey brown hair, a heart-shaped face, and unusual green eyes.

She smiled and said, "It's good to meet you, Miss Fairfax.

Now, you'd better eat. I think we'll be leaving soon."

The breakfast consisted of eggs, ham, some sort of porridge or mush, and biscuits with jelly. The meal was delicious, and knowing that the next meal might not be as good as Mrs. Tompkins's, Sabrina ate everything she was served.

"Are you traveling far, Miss Fairfax?"

"I'm going to Tennessee Country, but I understand the coach doesn't go that far."

"Why, no, it doesn't," Hannah said. "We're going there ourselves."

"That's your home?"

"Yes, it is. We came to Virginia to see a relative who was ill, but we're on our way home now."

"What part of the territory are you from? I know so little about this country."

Joshua Spencer said, "We're near Holston."

The name meant nothing to Sabrina. "I wish I knew more about the geography of America."

"Well, that part of the country's a little confusing right now," Joshua said. He sipped his coffee, then added, "We've had a war, and some of the new states are arguing over claims."

"I'd be very interested in hearing about that, Mr. Spencer, because that's why I'm going to your part of the world." She went on to tell about the land she had inherited, and when she had finished, she said, "I'm told that I actually have to be there before I can discover much about the legality of the claim."

"Well, I think my brother could help you with that, Miss Fairfax," Hannah said. "He's studying to become an attorney and has had some experience dealing with claims like this."

Sabrina put her eyes on the young man. "I would very much appreciate any help you might give me."

"Well, I'm pretty new at this. I'm actually just getting started, but I'd be glad to help you all I can. Can you tell me the location? Perhaps when we stop to stretch our legs later today you can show me your papers, and I can tell you what I think."

"That would be so kind of you."

Sabrina felt better about her situation, for these two appeared very presentable. Joshua Spencer seemed young for an attorney, but since she had encountered him she had determined to accept his aid.

Breakfast was almost over when a man entered the room and called out, "I need some grub before that stage leaves." Everyone turned to look at him, for his voice was as loud and as rough as his appearance. He was a big man, wearing a coat that appeared strange, at least to Sabrina. It was made out of some sort of leather and there were strings attached to it. He wore the same sort of fur cap with an animal tail attached as she had seen on the previous day.

He was big enough to fill the room, it seemed, and wore a huge knife at his side. The rank odor he gave off reached even to where Sabrina sat. He turned to Alpha Tompkins and said, "You hear me, woman? Put some grub on the table!"

"Take your seat," Alpha said, "and lower your voice."

"You tell me what to do? I'm Jack Fry. I don't lower my voice for no woman!"

"Then get out."

Fry glared at her. "It's a good thing you're a woman," he said, "or I'd cut your gizzard out for that!" He sat down and everyone was very much aware of his presence. He seemed to enjoy their attention, and when his eyes fell on the two women, he said, "Good-lookin' fillies. Maybe I'll give you two a chance at a real man."

Alpha Tompkins set a plate filled with food down before him, but she did not remove her hand. "Jack Fry, you can take this plate outside. But you won't bother the passengers in my station."

"All right. Have it your own way. Bring me about a gallon of coffee."

"He's a rough-looking man, isn't he?" Sabrina said after Fry moved outside.

"I've seen him back in Tennessee Country," Hannah said. "He's not a nice man."

"He looks dangerous," Sabrina observed.

"He is," Josh said. "He's the kind that'll fight at the drop of a hat, and think nothing of gouging out a man's eyes or cutting him wide open."

"I don't look forward to sitting beside him," Hannah said.

"Let's all sit together," Sabrina said quickly. "If we get on early enough, we can take the backseat."

"Sounds good to me," Josh said.

When the three had finished their meal, Sion came over and said, "I'll see that the luggage is all on board, miss."

"Good, Sion."

After Sion left, Hannah asked, "Is he a friend of yours?"

"An indentured servant. His name is Sion Kenyon."

The two waited for her to say more, but she had no chance, for the driver outside called them to board the stage. The three got up and made their way outside. Sabrina watched as Sion carefully stowed the luggage and made sure it was tied down.

She was just about to enter the stage when she heard Fry's voice.

"Well, ain't you a pretty one, now."

She turned to see that Fry had approached and taken Hannah's arm. She saw the young woman struggle to get away, but the man merely laughed.

"Turn her loose!" Josh commanded.

Jack Fry did not even hesitate. He shoved Josh Spencer, who flew backward and barely managed not to fall. The strength of the man was enormous.

"You stay out of this, sonny, or I'll cut your gizzard out."

Sabrina was frightened, for the man was a brute. He kept his grip on Hannah's arm, and Hannah said nothing, although she still struggled to get away.

Suddenly a voice said, "I think you'll be taking the next stage—not this one."

Jack Fry turned, and his hand went to the knife in his belt. Sabrina saw him studying Sion, who had approached and stood watchfully. He appeared relaxed. His feet were spread slightly apart, and his arms were at his sides. There was a strange expression in his face that she had never seen before, watchful and somehow dangerous. His body did not look dangerous, however, for he appeared small beside the monstrous form of Jack Fry.

Fry cursed and drew the knife with his free hand. "Come on! I'll cut your throat with this and throw you out for the wolves to eat!"

Sion Kenyon moved so quickly that Sabrina had trouble following the movement. His hand shot out, and he grabbed the wrist of Jack Fry and repeated, "It would be better if we didn't have trouble. You're not taking this stage."

A silence had fallen over the onlookers. Sabrina saw the scene as if it were a painting. The stagecoach driver was leaning over, watching with alarm. Alpha Tompkins had come out the front door and paused there with a troubled expression. Josh stood still, his face pale and his jaw clenched.

Sion said no more, but suddenly Fry released Hannah's arm and tried to wrench his hand holding the knife away from Sion's grip. Sabrina saw Fry's huge muscle strain, but Sion hung on, and Fry's eyes opened with astonishment. He was obviously not accustomed to finding men stronger than he, and he shouted, "Why, I'll kill you!" He struck out with his left hand, but Sion simply ducked under the blow. Then he put his other hand on the right wrist and with a jerk began to throw the man in a circle. Everyone jumped back, and Sabrina saw Sion take a complete circle, heaving the man around as if he weighed nothing. He released him, and Fry sailed backward toward the station. He crashed into the wall, his head making a hollow, thumping sound, and the knife fell to the ground. The man was not unconscious, Sabrina saw, but his eyes were dull and he wasn't moving much.

Sion picked up the knife and stood over the fallen man. He turned to the others and said, "I think we'd better be on our way."

The passengers started to get on board as Fry staggered to his feet. "You can take the next coach, Fry," said Sion. "I'll drop this knife out a hundred yards down the road."

Fry's eyes were still unclear, and blood was running down his face from the spot where his head had struck the wall. He cursed at Sion, closing with, "I'll kill you! No man does that to me!"

Sion did not answer. He got into the coach, and at once the driver called to the horses, and the coach pulled out.

It was silent inside, and Sabrina found her heart was beating fast. The violence had exploded like a bomb, surprising everyone. She put her hand on Sion's shoulder, who was sitting in front of her. When he turned, she said, "If you ever see that man again, he'll try to kill you."

"Don't worry about things like that," Sion said. The other passengers were stunned with the outburst of violence, but he seemed unaffected by it. "We get so busy worrying about things that never happen, we don't have time to think about what's happening around us."

The fat man said, "I've heard of him—Jack Fry. He's a mean one. He killed two men that I know of. You should've kilt him."

"It wasn't a killing matter."

Hannah Spencer was sitting in the front seat, facing Sion. She had been frightened by the incident, and now she said, "Thank you, Mr. Kenyon."

Sion was surprised that she knew his name. "No trouble, miss. I didn't fancy riding on the same coach with him. He's not fit company for ladies like you and Miss Fairfax."

Josh Spencer said, "He'll try to kill you. Killing means nothing to men like him."

Sion smiled and winked at Hannah. "Well, now, he couldn't kill me but once, could he?" He apparently put the matter out of his mind and looked out the window as if he had already forgotten the incident.

Welcome to the Frontier

Twelve

There's Nashville." Josh smiled at Sabrina. "Not much like the big cities you're used to, I suppose."

"Not quite," Sabrina said. Indeed, she was disappointed in Nashville, which seemed to be nothing more than a collection of houses scattered haphazardly about. The main street was broad, and now as she looked at it, she realized how rough this country really was. She reflected on the journey she had made and once again was glad that Joshua and Hannah Spencer had been there to help.

"I don't think we could have made it without you, Joshua."

Josh turned to the woman who sat next to him on the wagon seat. "Why, of course you would."

"Well, perhaps, but you have been such a help. I don't know how to thank you." Sabrina smiled. Indeed, the Spencers had been sent from heaven, or at least that was the way Sion put it. They had traveled together as far as the coach went, and then it had been Josh who had supervised the purchase of a wagon and four animals and tools. Sabrina had been troubled about spending money for a project that might never be realized, but Josh had assured her, "Supplies are scarce in our territory. You can sell these for more than you paid for them. Don't worry about that."

They had joined with other wagons, a small train of six families, and had come through the South Pass with no trouble at all from Indians.

"Why don't you room with Hannah while we're getting the legal business done," Josh said. "Sion can room with me if he wants to."

"That would be wonderful."

She looked ahead to where Sion and Hannah had ridden on ahead of them on the two extra horses. "Your sister's such a fine young woman."

"Well, I think so," Josh said with a smile. "Come along. We'll get settled in, and then we'll go find my boss."

"You said his name is Andrew Jackson?"

"Yes. You'll find him a little rough, as far as manners are concerned, but he's the smartest man I know."

―――――――

The small party soon drove up to an inn, and the two women went inside to get cleaned up. As they were making themselves presentable, Hannah asked, "Have you known Sion long?"

"No, not very."

"He's an unusual man. His speech is so—musical."

"That's the Welsh strain in him," Sabrina said as she finished fixing her hair, then changed the subject. "Do you really think Josh can help me?"

"If he can't, then Andrew Jackson can. You'll find he's a very forceful man."

The two women left the room and found Sion and Josh standing outside the inn. "What are you going to do, Hannah, while Sabrina and I find out about the title?" Josh asked.

"Oh, I think I'll just show Sion around Nashville."

"We may be a long time," Josh warned. "You know how busy Andy gets at times."

"That's all right. We'll wait." Hannah waited until the two had started on their way and said, "Now, Sion, let me show you the town."

"That will be my pleasure, Miss Spencer."

"We don't stand on titles much around here. Hannah is fine."

"I'm not sure about that. Indentured servants are supposed to show respect."

"I don't think calling anyone by their first name shows a lack of respect. Come along."

For the next two hours Hannah and Sion roamed the

streets of Nashville. In truth, there was little enough to see, and Hannah remarked once, "After London this must seem like a wilderness to you."

"I like it," Sion responded. "It's a big country. A man can get some air into his lungs and not be crowded in by buildings."

"When you get out on Sabrina's property, you'll be longing for the sight of a building or two." Hannah smiled. She found herself liking Sion Kenyon a great deal. After she had shown him the town, the two of them went back to the inn where they took a table, and she ordered tea.

"Do Americans drink a great deal of tea?" Sion asked as he sipped from his cup.

"That and coffee. Tell me about yourself, Sion."

"About myself? Well, indeed, there's little to know, Miss Hannah."

"I don't believe that. Sabrina tells me you were a farmer and a coal miner and a pugilist."

Sion laughed and shook his head. "I hope I never again am either a miner or a pugilist."

"Well, tell me about it. I want to hear."

Hannah sat there listening as Sion began to talk. She did love the musical sound of his voice, and she drew the story from him. Finally she exclaimed, "So, you rescued Sabrina and nearly went to prison for it, and then she rescued you from prison!"

"You make it sound like a fairy tale or a storybook of some kind." Sion smiled. "It didn't seem quite that romantic at the time."

Hannah laughed. "It does sound almost like a novel, doesn't it?"

"What about you, Miss Hannah? Tell me about your family and about yourself."

"Well, my father and mother are the finest people I know. My father has been called Hawk Spencer for a long time. That's his Indian name. My mother's name is Elizabeth. She's very beautiful, and my father's very handsome. My father married when he was very young, but his first wife died. He has a son named Jacob, who is now married to a fine young woman named Amanda."

Sion listened, sipping his tea from time to time, and then finally he said, "It sounds like you're very close to your parents and your brothers."

"Yes, I am. As a matter of fact, out here on the frontier we have to be very close. We depend on one another."

"I'm surprised you've not married."

Hannah suddenly colored. "Why should you be surprised?"

"Well, not to be forward, but you're such an attractive young lady. Back in Wales you would have been snapped up before you were seventeen years old. I'll warrant you've had many gentlemen callers, though."

Hannah hesitated, and Sion did not miss it. "There must be a young man you're interested in." He laughed and said, "I don't mean to pry."

"It's all right. There is one young man I've gotten close to. His name is Nathanael Carter, but his Indian name is Fox. He's half Cherokee."

"Do you tell me that!" Sion exclaimed. "I'm surprised."

Hannah shook her head. "I know you've heard stories about how terrible the Indians are, but they are not all that way. You'll meet a man named Sequatchie when you get to our house. He's Fox's uncle. He's married to a fine lady named Iris Taylor. You will like him a great deal. He's my father's closest friend. Sequatchie taught my father how to live in the woods when he was a young man."

As Sion listened to Hannah, he became more aware of how attractive she was. Her lips curved in an attractive line, and her green eyes were pools of emotion. Her honey brown hair was piled on top of her head with feminine ringlets framing her face. He admired the smooth roundness of her shoulders and the womanly lines of her body. Her face was a mirror that changed as her feelings changed. She was a woman, he had learned, capable of robust emotion, and when she smiled a small dimple appeared at the left of her mouth, and the light danced in her eyes. He wanted to ask more about the man that she was interested in, but he felt it would be out of place.

He said, "Tell me about the land where we'll be going."

For a long time she talked about the land, and then a troubled look crossed her face as she said, "It's so rough I'm afraid Sabrina will be out of her element."

"Maybe at first, but she has no other choice. Is there a church near our land?"

"We have a fine church. The pastor's name is Paul Anderson. I hope you'll come."

"That I will."

Sabrina and Josh stepped into the inn at that moment, and Sabrina stopped abruptly. Her eyes fell on the two, and a frown came to her forehead. As the two advanced to the table, Sion stood up, and there was a moment's awkwardness. Sion understood it at once for what it was. Back in Sabrina's old world she would never sit at a table with a servant, but this new land was making the old ways difficult.

———————

Sabrina had come outside for one last look at the night sky before she went to bed. Josh and Hannah had already gone, and now she went to the stable, where she found Sion rubbing the soft nose of one of the horses. He turned and said in surprise, "I thought you'd be tired and in bed, miss."

"I am tired."

"God blessed us by bringing the Spencers our way. It would have been a hard thing without them. Do you really think the title is good?"

"I hope so, Sion. Mr. Jackson wouldn't say definitely. He says things are too upside down right now."

Sion left the horse, patting the animal on the shoulder, and the two walked outside. "Sion, I must warn you about something."

"What's that?"

"I don't mean that anything's wrong, but when I came in I saw you and Hannah talking. . . ."

"She's a fine young lady."

Sabrina blurted, "I don't think you should get too friendly with her, Sion."

Sion turned to face her. The moonlight was full, and he saw

the marks of strain on her. "I had no idea of doing anything unseemly."

Sabrina felt she had made a fool of herself, but she said, "You're my servant for five years, Sion. It would be difficult if you . . ."

"I think you need not worry about that, miss."

Sabrina bit her lip. She felt she had handled the matter badly. Her whole world had changed, and what was appropriate in England was completely out of place in this new land. She knew there had always been a basic selfishness in her, and she did not want to share Sion Kenyon with anyone else. He was her security. She wanted to express these feelings but wasn't sure how to go about it.

"I suppose I sound like a fool."

"No you don't. Not in the least. We have a hard way to go to carve a home out of the wilderness. I understand that very well."

Sabrina turned to face him and saw again the lean strength that was in him and the honesty in his eyes and felt a surge of gratitude that this man was here. "You always know how to lift me up, Sion."

He put out his hand, and Sabrina took it. She felt the strength of it, and he said, "As long as this hand has strength, I'll use it for you, Miss Fairfax."

Sabrina was moved by his words and the touch of his hand. His hand was strong and warm, and it gave her a comfort.

Sion released her hand and gave her a good smile. "God has brought you here, Miss Sabrina Fairfax—He won't abandon you."

PART IV

The Earth Breakers

April – October 1792

Learning New Ways

Thirteen

The sun was high in the sky as Josh pointed forward and said, "Well, there it is. There's our home, Sabrina."

Sabrina had been riding beside Josh in the front seat of the wagon. Sion and Hannah had preferred to ride the extra horses they had bought and had trailed behind for most of the way through the winding trail that made a serpentine pathway between the towering trees. Sabrina followed the direction of Josh's gesture and exclaimed, "Why, it's so pretty, Josh!"

"It is, isn't it? My folks have put a lot of work into this place."

The cabin that Sabrina looked at was much more attractive than most she had seen on her journey. For one thing it had been painted rather recently, it seemed, and the white gleamed against the background of the fields and the green trees. It was situated high on a rise of ground that overlooked its surroundings, and there was an air of serenity and permanence about it. As Josh urged the team forward, Sabrina said, "That's the prettiest cabin I've seen since we left Nashville."

"Be sure you mention that to my folks. As I say, they worked hard on it."

A pack of dogs came boiling out as they approached, and Sabrina smiled. "Every house we've passed has had dogs. I believe you Americans have more dogs than anyone I've ever heard of."

"Dogs are good companions, and they make good watchers for keeping track of the Indians too."

Sabrina turned with wide eyes. "Were you ever attacked by Indians?"

"No, there's been trouble enough, but it's passed over us for the most part. Of course, we have to go out when the militia's called to fight them, but that war is pretty well over now."

"That's good. I'd hate to think of being attacked by Indians."

"It could happen even now," Josh said. "A lot of the Cherokee and the other tribes, too, are pretty angry at the way they've been treated. They feel like white men have robbed them of their land."

"Have they?"

"I guess they have. I'm not proud of it. One of my best friends is half Cherokee; his name is Fox Carter—his real name's Nathanael. His uncle Sequatchie is Pa's best friend."

The conversation ended when Josh pulled the wagon up near the front porch. He leaped down as Hannah and Sion rode up and lifted his hand to help Sabrina to the ground. As he did, the door opened, and he turned to smile. "Folks, this is Miss Sabrina Fairfax. She's coming to settle on that tract of land over to the north of us."

"Why, how nice!" Elizabeth said as she crossed the porch.

Sabrina was not surprised to find Josh and Hannah's mother an attractive woman. She was in her midfifties, Sabrina guessed, with blond hair and green eyes. "Your son and daughter have been such a help to us. I don't think I could have made it here at all if it hadn't been for them."

"Well, now, I'm glad to learn that those young'uns of mine have learned a little manners."

"Welcome to the territory, Miss Fairfax."

Mr. Spencer's hand was hard and strong, and she could see where Josh got his good looks. Hawk Spencer was tall and broad-shouldered with black hair showing streaks of gray, and he looked about the same age as his wife. He had the darkest blue eyes she had ever seen—so dark they were almost black.

"Come into the house," he invited. "We want to hear all about this."

Hannah and Sion, by that time, had approached and waited until the introductions were over. "This is Sion Kenyon. These are my parents, Sion."

"It's happy I am to meet you," Sion said. He bowed slightly

toward Elizabeth, then took the hand that Hawk extended.

"Come inside." Elizabeth said. "You must be worn out, Miss Fairfax."

Sabrina entered the house and noted that the floor was made of a beautiful wood. She had learned that many cabins in the area had dirt floors, but the home of the Spencers was much more ornate. It was built of logs, but the room she entered was wide, and overhead peeled logs made girders that held up the attic. A ladder went up at one end of the room, and two doors led to other rooms.

"Here, won't you sit down, Miss Fairfax?" Elizabeth said.

"Oh, I think it would be nice if you called me Sabrina— and I believe I'd rather stand. Sitting in a wagon isn't the most comfortable thing in the world."

"That's a nice name—Sabrina. I don't believe I've heard it before," Hawk said. "How is it that an Englishwoman such as yourself comes to settle in the Colonies?"

Hannah explained how she had found the deed after her father died and described their journey on the ship.

"You know the tract, Pa," Josh cut in. "It's over the side of Cain Ridge, where the big bluff is on the river."

"Yes, I know it well. I'm afraid I shot quite a few deer over on your land, Miss Fairfax."

"There's some sort of question about the title," Josh said, "but I've got Andy Jackson looking into it. He'll get it straight in no time."

Elizabeth and Hannah were bringing water to a boil as Hawk talked with the visitors. The two started to serve the tea, and Sabrina was impressed at the Spencer family. They were all fine looking, and Elizabeth Spencer had something of an aristocrat in her. She moved and spoke with such assurance and yet such grace that Sabrina took to her at once.

"As soon as you get rested up," Josh said, "we'll take you over to see the land."

"Oh, could we go today?" Sabrina asked quickly.

"I think it would be a little much for you. It's not too far from here, but I know you're tired," Josh said. "Why don't we go first thing in the morning."

Sabrina agreed, for she was tired. "All right. First thing in the morning, then."

————

The next morning Josh and Hannah waited only long enough for breakfast to be served before they offered to take Sabrina to see the land. She was happy to go, and they left as soon as the meal was over. Once again Sion and Hannah rode the horses while Josh and Sabrina rode in the wagon.

As Hannah rode beside Sion, she found herself asking him all sorts of questions about his native land. She found he was better spoken than most of the young men she knew. There was a quickness about him and a sense of humor, she discovered. After a time she asked him, "What has impressed you most about America, Sion?"

Sion's eyes danced with mischief. "I expect," he said without hesitation, "it's the spitting."

"The spitting!" Hannah stared at him. "Whatever do you mean?"

"I mean Americans spit a lot. Almost everyone chews tobacco. I noticed that on the ship coming over with some Americans we met. And ever since we've been here it's been something I've paid attention to." He glanced slyly at her and smiled. "It's a good thing spit evaporates or America would be flooded."

Hannah laughed aloud and moved her horse closer to his. "You're teasing me. Tell me, what really has impressed you?"

"I suppose two things. Everything is so big. You have to remember, Miss Spencer, that in England and in Wales everything is much smaller." He gestured toward the west and said, "That seems to go on forever. I've never seen such huge tracts of land and forest. It numbs the eye, almost, and the spirit to think of it. The other thing is how free people are."

"Free? What do you mean, free?"

"I mean the English are a fairly reserved nation. They take a long time to get acquainted with each other, but Americans seem to be born to be close together."

Hannah thought about Sion's words, then said, "I suppose that's true. Here people have to learn to serve one another."

She was thoughtful and did not speak for a time as her mind toyed with this idea. "Out here we live on credit, balances of little favors that we have to give and ask to have returned. In a country with as few people as we have, 'Love thy neighbor' is less a pious injunction than a rule for survival. If you meet someone in trouble, you stop, because another time you may need him to stop for you."

She continued to press him, wanting to know more about what he was really like. Finally she said, "Does it trouble you to leave your old home and come to a new place where everything is different?"

"Not at all. I'm very excited about being in America. Life is like a tree. It gets new branches, and some of the old dead branches have to go. Old things pass away and new things come."

"I think Sabrina's worried about the title of the land."

"Aye, she is."

"But you're not?"

"No, I think God will take care of her and of me, of course. Sometimes my heart counts all the moments that come like a bank teller. It's more than the rustling of paper and the ringing of gold. Life is more than that, I think."

Hannah liked his poetic way of speaking, and she drew him out as they made their way around the twisting road.

Josh drew up the wagon beside a bluff, and the two on horseback moved close to the wagon and stopped.

"Well, you're right in the middle of your own land, Sabrina."

Sabrina looked around. Below the bluff she could see clear water running in a creek, and overhead the sky was blue. She took a deep breath of the glorious April air. "You know what I notice most about this country, Josh?"

"What's that?"

"It smells so clean. You can't imagine how bad London smells. Nearly a million people burning coal fires, and then the fog comes in, and you're breathing air that's loaded down with evil-smelling things. But here it's so clear and pure and beautiful."

"I think so too. I'd hate to live anywhere else."

"Isn't there a house anywhere on this place? Didn't the former owner build something?"

"He did build a small cabin, but it burned down. Some say the Indians set it on fire."

Sabrina felt a touch of apprehension. "Are there still Indians around?"

"Oh yes, they come and go. They don't view land like we do."

"How's that, Josh?"

"They see land as belonging to the whole tribe, not to an individual. It's hard to get into their heads that once they sell a place they can't come back. It's a sad situation, Sabrina. I feel sorry for the Indians."

"Let's go show them the big meadow," Hannah said. "Come on, Sion, I'll race you." She kicked her heels into the mare and went flying off. Sion bounced along after her, for he was not an expert rider.

"That sister of mine will wear Sion to death. She's got more energy than any ten women I ever saw."

"She's quite a woman."

"Well, I think so too. Come along. I'll show you where the wild raspberries grow."

––––––––

The first week Sabrina spent with the Spencers had flown by. Every day had been busy, and she had gone back twice to view the land, once with Hannah and once with Josh. She had discovered some cleared ground, and Sion was anxious to break it and get a crop in. She herself knew nothing of planting crops, but she was grateful for Sion's interest. He had begun the work under the direction of Hawk, while she had spent a great deal of time with Elizabeth and Hannah finding out what women did in America. She was shocked at the amount of hard work that was necessary to keep a household going. Things she had always taken for granted had to be done the hard way. The only time she'd ever had to do any household work was when she'd lived with her aunt.

On Sunday there was no spoken invitation to attend

church services, but the Spencers just assumed she would go. She made no protest, for she was anxious to meet more of her neighbors.

She dressed carefully for the occasion, wearing what she considered one of her simpler dresses. It was a linen dress of royal blue with a square neck and long sleeves and a snug bodice decorated with a single green ribbon bow.

Both Hannah and her mother wore even plainer dresses, and when they got into the wagon she was not surprised to see Sion wearing what he always wore, a pair of lightweight gray trousers and a white shirt. He had acquired a hat from either Hawk or Josh, and now it was pulled forward on his head. Sabrina smiled at him, and he nodded in return.

They made the trip into the town and found the church surrounded by wagons, carriages, and horses. People were talking and shaking hands as they made their way into the church. The building was made of logs, as was every other building in the village.

As Sion got out of the saddle, Hannah said, "Come along. I'll introduce you to the pastor, Sion."

Sion followed her into the building, noticing that everyone's eyes were upon him and Sabrina. "Everyone's looking at us," he whispered.

"We don't get too many strangers here. Come along. There's Rev. Anderson."

The two went up to a man of middle size whose brown hair was turning gray, but his eyes were young. "Rev. Anderson, this is Sion Kenyon. He's Miss Fairfax's servant. He's been anxious to come and hear you preach. He's from Wales."

"From Wales, is it?" Paul Anderson smiled. "Well, I understand they have great preachers there. I doubt you'll hear anything that eloquent from me."

"Glad I am to know you, Reverend."

They had no time for talk, for it was time for the service. Sion found himself guided to one of the pews near the front by Hannah, and they were joined by her parents.

Sabrina took in the interior of the church, which was rough indeed. The seats were all split logs with the flat side turned upward and supported by legs made of saplings. The log walls were unpainted, and there were only four windows in the entire structure. They were, as a matter of fact, the first real glass windows she had seen in any building, save the Spencers' house. She had discovered that glass windows were a mark of extreme prosperity. Even now before the service, the room was filled with talk, and many of the men were smoking. She even saw one old woman puffing away at a corncob pipe.

"We're fortunate to have a regular pastor," Elizabeth said to Sabrina. "Some settlements have to wait for weeks or even months for an itinerant preacher to come by."

Even as she was speaking, a tall, thin man got up and said, "We're ready for the service to begin. We'll start by singing 'Old Hundredth.' "

Sabrina did not know the hymn, and she was surprised to see that there was no musical accompaniment whatsoever. Everyone sang loudly, and as the service progressed, she was surprised at how hymns were sung. The song leader would sing the first line, and then the congregation would join him in singing it together. Then he would sing the second line, which would then be sung.

"That's called 'lining out' the hymns," Elizabeth whispered to her. "I'd never seen it done before I came here."

The song service went on for a considerable length of time. An offering was taken, and numerous announcements were made. Finally Rev. Anderson got up and began to speak. From time to time during the sermon Sabrina would glance at Sion, who appeared to be drinking in the man's words. As for Sabrina herself, she had not paid attention to a sermon in years. She had sat through the high church services out of habit, but something about Anderson's preaching held her. He was talking about the woman taken in adultery, and when he spoke of the compassion of Jesus, his voice almost broke.

Why, he's almost ready to weep! Sabrina saw with astonishment. She had never been so affected by the Scriptures, but as she sat there, she became aware that there was a reality to the religion of this man of God that she was not accustomed to. Glancing around, she saw that the worshipers were drinking in his words. Many times there were shouts of "Amen" or "Hallelujah" or "Praise God," which startled her at first, but gradually she became accustomed to it. Finally the pastor invited those who were not saved to come forward, and she was surprised to see six people stand and leave their seats. They were greeted by the pastor and then several of the men—leaders of the church evidently—began to pray with them. This went on for some time, and finally one woman who had gone forward began to shout.

"What's wrong with her, Elizabeth?" Sabrina whispered.

"Nothing is wrong. She's just come through. That's Hetty Sanders. She's been seeking now for nearly six months."

"Seeking what?"

Elizabeth turned with surprise in her eyes. "Why, seeking God, of course. Haven't you ever seen that before?"

Sabrina did not answer, for this was far outside of her experience. After the service was over she went outside and met a great many people, most of them whose names she could not remember. The majority of them were rather poorly dressed farmers, but she met one young man who was different.

"Miss Fairfax, may I introduce Mr. Drake Hammond."

Drake Hammond was a tall man in his midtwenties with light blond hair and gray eyes. He was better dressed than most of the worshipers, and his manners displayed at least some culture.

"I'm happy to know you, Miss Fairfax, and to welcome you to Tennessee Country."

"It's good to meet you, sir," Sabrina said. She extended her hand, and he took it and bent over it. "I hope we may expect you to become a settled member of the community."

"I trust so."

She had no more time to continue the conversation, for others were crowding in to meet her, but on the way home she mentioned him to Elizabeth and Hawk, who sat beside her on the wagon seat. "Who is Drake Hammond?"

Hawk laughed. "I thought he might catch your eye, but be careful. He's a ladies' man."

"Be quiet, Hawk. He's the son of a wealthy man." She smiled, adding, "He *is* quite a ladies' man."

"I reckon he is." Hawk grinned. "Mothers lock their girls

up when he comes around. You be careful, Miss Fairfax."

Sabrina smiled. "I don't think I have to worry about that."

"How did you like the preacher?" Hawk asked.

"I have never heard anyone like him. He's so earnest."

"He's that, all right. We're lucky to have a man of God like that for our pastor."

Sabrina could not forget the sermon nor the way it had affected her. She had always thought religion was a set of rules to be kept, and she had kept most of them on a fairly regular basis. But something in her was whispering that this was not all there was to it, and it troubled her.

One of the chores Sion set himself to was splitting logs. Hawk Spencer had told him that it would be necessary to fence in the horses to keep the bears and even the panthers away from them. He had watched Hawk and Josh split a few logs one morning, and that afternoon he decided to split some himself. He borrowed an ax, went into the woods, and cut down a tree. When he had sawed it off to the proper length, he took the wedge and began trying to split the log. He soon discovered that splitting logs was not as easy as it looked. He struggled all morning and made pretty much a wreck of the wedge and the maul.

Hawk Spencer came in from the fields and took one look at him. "It looks like you bit off more than you can chew, Sion."

Sion shook his head and flexed his hands. "I thought it was a matter of strength, but this wood just won't split."

"You got the wrong kind. It's a sweet gum. It'll never split. Come along. I've got a white oak here. Let me show you."

Sion followed Hawk to where a tree had been cut down and sawed off. Hawk took the iron wedge and set it in the large end of the log. With a few blows it sank in, and suddenly with a ripping sound the log fell into two pieces.

"White oak is easy to split. Here, you try splitting these halves up."

Sion took the wedge and the maul, and after getting it started he was gratified to see the halves split open.

"It's all in knowing what to do, isn't it? I've got a lot to learn in this country."

"You'll make it. You just have to have a little education. Here, let's see how many rails we can make out of this tree."

In less than two hours the two had finished between forty and fifty rails. Sion said, "You're right, sir, it's knowing what to do," shaking his head.

They were loading the split logs when a man rode into the clearing. Sion was startled to see that the newcomer was an Indian.

"This is Sequatchie," Hawk said as the man came off his horse and moved forward. "Sequatchie, this is our new neighbor, Sion Kenyon."

"I'm glad to know you," Sequatchie said and put his hand forward.

"I'm happy to know you," Sion said with a nod. The tall stranger wore a pair of simple trousers and a gray chambray shirt. His hair was black without a tinge of gray or white, but he was an older man, Sion could see. This was the first Indian he had ever come in contact with, but he had heard from Hawk what a good friend Sequatchie had been to him in his younger days. "Hawk is teaching me how to split logs. I'm afraid I must be the most ignorant man in Tennessee Country."

Sequatchie's eyes glinted. "There's hope for a man who knows his ignorance. What did you do back in your home country?"

"I was a farmer and a coal miner."

"You dug coal out of the earth?" Hawk said with interest. "That's a job I'd hate to have. I can't stand to be cooped up."

"It's not a job I wanted to do for a lifetime, but I had little choice."

The men talked for a while, and Sequatchie finally smiled, and a glad light came to his eyes. "Fox is on his way home."

"He is? Well, it's about time." Hawk turned to Sion and said, "He's talking about his nephew, his sister's son. Nathanael Carter is his American name, but his Indian name is Fox."

"I'll be glad to see him," Sequatchie said.

"Do you suppose he settled that business of his plantation back in Virginia?"

"He was anxious to do something with it. It's been a trouble to him for years now."

Sion did not understand a great deal of this, but when Sequatchie left, he asked Hawk, "So Fox is half Indian and half American?"

"Yes."

Hawk did not speak for a time, and then he shrugged. "Elizabeth and I have thought that Hannah might marry Fox one day."

"Will that be a problem having an Indian in the family?"

"No. Not in the least. He's a fine man."

———————

Sabrina was getting an education, just as Sion was. She had never taken thought in her life to such a thing as a broom. To her, brooms were something to be bought at a store—or something that a servant might buy. But Hannah had been engaged in making a broom, which fascinated Sabrina. She watched as Hannah took a hickory sapling and split thin pieces down the outside of the trunk with a jackknife. She bent them back and held them down with her other hand, and when there was no more flexible wood, she sawed off the central part of the trunk. The splits then turned back to their original places and were tied to the toe string. Hannah smoothed the handle down and said with a smile, "Behold, a broom!"

"I'm afraid I'd cut my fingers off if I tried that."

"Oh, not likely. Come along. We're going to make soap today."

"Make soap! Does everyone do that?"

"Yes, of course. It doesn't grow on trees, you know. It'll be inconvenient for you, but you'll learn."

The soapmaking was a tedious chore, but Sabrina was determined to learn all she could. She discovered that Hannah and her family had been saving meat scraps of all kinds during the year to be used for soap. She learned also that the lye was obtained by leaching ashes. She watched as Hannah poured water over a hopper made out of boards forming a V-shaped receptacle with a crack at the bottom. When the water dripped through the ashes down into the trough, it soaked the alkali from the ashes, and this brown liquid was strong enough to make soap. It was poured over the grease and gently boiled until it reached a ropy consistency.

"I always put something sweet in it to make it smell good," Hannah said. "I saved a little perfume that my folks gave me for my birthday two years ago." She found the small bottle, poured it into the bubbling mass, and stirred it zealously.

Finally Hannah poured the soap into a pan, and when it was cool she cut it into squares as if it were a cake. She carefully took out one square with the blade of her knife and said, "Now, when we get ready to wash our hair we'll have some nice sweet-smelling soap."

During this whole process Hannah had asked many questions about Sabrina's life in England but many more about Sion. She had heard some of the story but insisted on hearing it again. Finally she gave Sabrina a curious look and said, "That's a romantic story—just like a novel."

"I suppose it is."

Hannah chewed her lip thoughtfully, as she often did. "Maybe you'll marry him. That would really be like a novel."

Sabrina straightened up and fastened her eyes on Hannah with surprise. "Me, marry a servant! Don't be foolish, Hannah, of course I won't!"

This outburst took Hannah off guard, and she shook her head slightly but said no more about it.

Joshua came running into the cabin, and Sabrina looked up with surprise. "What's wrong, Josh? When did you get in?" Josh had been gone for over two weeks.

"Just now. Andy Jackson is with me. Let me tell you what happened. Mr. Jackson is serving as circuit court judge in Jonesboro," he said, his eyes sparkling. "There was a man called Russell Bean who had beaten a man badly. He got indicted, and the officers went to arrest him, but they couldn't."

"Why not?"

"Because when they went to get him he was standing in front of his house with a rifle and a pistol. He said he'd kill the first man who approached his house."

Sabrina had never heard of such a thing. "Well, what happened?"

"The sheriff went to tell Jackson about it, and Jackson, right off, ordered the sheriff to bring Bean in dead or alive if he had to summon every man in the courthouse." He laughed, saying, "The sheriff said, 'Then I summon your honor first.'"

"What did Mr. Jackson do?"

"Why, he said, 'By the eternal, I'll bring him!' He grabbed his pistol, and a bunch went with him just to see what he'd do."

"Well, what did he do?"

"Do? What did Andy Jackson do? Why, you'd better believe he arrested Bean. But I asked him to come out here and talk to you about your land. Come on. I want you to meet him."

Sabrina followed Josh outside to where she saw a tall, very thin man with a bushy head of hair and a long, craggy face getting off his horse.

"Andrew, this is our new neighbor, Miss Sabrina Fairfax. Miss Fairfax, Mr. Andrew Jackson. He's teaching me about the law."

Jackson had a rather hard-looking face, but his eyes were kind enough. He bowed gallantly and spoke in a high-pitched voice. "I'm happy to make your acquaintance. Josh here has told me a lot about you."

"Come inside, sir. There's some fresh milk, I believe."

"Any buttermilk? I'm downright partial to buttermilk."

"I believe so," Sabrina said. She went inside, followed by the two men, and when they sat down at the table she brought them both glasses of buttermilk.

Jackson drank the milk, wiped his lips with his sleeve, and plunged right away into an explanation of the situation concerning Sabrina's land.

"I've done some work on the title, and I've got some letters out that I'm waiting for responses to. That'll take a while. What bothers me most is Caleb Files."

"Who is he, sir?"

"He's a man who's made quite a name for himself for grabbing land. He's out to get all he can. He's bought a lot of people out, and some he tied up in court until they had to sell."

"Well, what does that have to do with me, Mr. Jackson?"

"Well, he's filed a claim on your land. I don't think it'll stand up, but he has enough money to wait people out."

"I have no other choice, sir. That land is my only hope. I hope you can help me."

Andy Jackson leaned back in his chair, and when his coat fell away she saw the pistol stuck in his belt. "I'll do the best I can for you. This young fellow here"—he waved toward Josh—"has told me you need help, and by the eternal I'll give it to you. We'll see Caleb Files in purgatory before he gets a foot of your land."

Suddenly Sabrina was very glad that her fate lay in the hands of Andrew Jackson. There was a roughness in him but also a strength, and she needed a strong man to help.

Cabin Raising

Fourteen

The question of a place to live had troubled Sabrina ever since she had come to the frontier. No one could have been more warm and hospitable than the Spencers, but a restlessness had overtaken Sabrina, and finally it had been Hawk Spencer who had approached her, saying, "About time to raise a cabin for you, I think, Sabrina."

Sabrina had been at a total loss. Her funds were low, and she had said as much to Hawk, who had simply responded, "We don't spend money on cabins around here. We'll have a cabin raising."

"I don't think I could ask people to do that."

"You don't have to ask. It's just something we do for each other."

Sabrina had been hard to convince, hating to accept charity, but Hawk had told her, "You'll find out we have to depend on each other. First we'll have a logrolling, and then we'll have a cabin raising, and then we'll have a housewarming."

"But where will we build it? There's still that claim that Caleb Files has on my land."

"I'd say the best thing to do is to build you a cabin right in the middle of your land, and we'll worry about Files when the time comes."

Sabrina had agreed, since she didn't want to impose on the Spencers any longer than necessary.

Both Sabrina and Sion were intrigued as the process was set in motion. The logrolling was the hardest work. Sion worked diligently with a team of men to gather and cut the logs. As soon as the logs were down, Hawk showed him how to cut notches in the top of the large logs about every ten feet and start a fire on each notch. When the fire was well started, a dry limb was laid across the burning notch, which would direct the fire to burn straight through the log, cutting it into the appropriate length quickly. Sion quickly caught on to this, and morning and evening he fed the fires until the logs were burned into lengths. After about a week this work was done and had saved chopping or sawing logs into carrying lengths. It did leave them so sooty that Sion's hands and face were blackened as the logs were moved.

The next step was to carry the logs to the building site with handspikes. These were stout dogwood sticks about five feet long and three inches through at the center. The men worked together to pry at a long log and place several handspikes under it. Then with one man on each side of each handspike, they would lift the log and carry it to the log heap.

When the logs were ready, the next step was the cabin raising. But this was interrupted when Nathanael Carter rode into the clearing one day on a fine gelding. Sion had been working hard along with the Spencers, who had stayed over another day. Sion's first indication of the new arrival was when Hannah cried out, "Fox!" and ran to meet the rider, who pulled the horse up, slipped out of his saddle, and greeted the young woman.

"Hello, Hannah. I'm back."

Sion watched from a distance as the Spencers surrounded the young man about whom both Sion and Sabrina had heard a great deal. Sabrina came to stand beside Sion and said, "So that's the famous Fox. A fine-looking man, isn't he?"

"Indeed he is."

Fox Carter was a strong-looking individual. His Indian blood showed in the high cheekbones, but his skin was no darker than many of the settlers, although it did have a slight coppery tinge. He was wearing a pair of deerskin pants with a blue calico shirt. He pulled off a broad-brimmed gray hat and shook hands all around. Sion and Sabrina moved in closer so they could hear the conversation.

"I'm so glad you're back," said Hannah. "It seems like you've been gone forever."

"I think I see a little romance in that pair," Sabrina whispered.

"Her father told me he and Elizabeth thought they might marry someday."

They had no chance to say more, for Hannah brought Fox over, her face alight. "These are our new friends, Sabrina Fairfax and Sion Kenyon. This is Nathanael Carter."

"I'm glad to know you. Just call me Fox."

"We've heard a great deal about you, sir," Sabrina smiled.

"Good things, I hope."

"Oh, very good."

"You're from England, I've heard."

"Yes, and Sion here is from Wales."

The two men shook hands, and Hannah said, "Tell us all about your trip."

"No, that'll be later. I want to pitch in and help all I can here, but I need to go see Sequatchie first."

Fox Carter spoke to a few of the others before he rode off. Sabrina moved to Hannah's side and said, "You two are old friends."

"Oh, yes! We've known each other forever, it seems."

"He certainly is a fine-looking man."

"Oh, yes, Fox is good-looking. And he's a great hunter. And he knows every tree in the forest, I do think."

"You're very fond of him." Sabrina smiled.

Hannah flushed and dropped her eyes. "I suppose so." Changing the subject abruptly, she said, "Well, the cabin raising will be tomorrow. You'll have a place of your own to live in. I'll miss you. It's been so good to have another young woman around to do things with."

"We won't be very far apart. I'll be very lonesome out here. I'm not used to this solitude."

"We'll visit every day."

The work had started soon after sunrise, and both Sabrina and Sion were amazed at how quickly the work went, and also at the fun that accompanied this work. The children were delighted to have a day with no chores, and they chased one another in and out of the woods, alternately screaming and laughing. Nearly everyone enlivened the occasion by bringing food and whiskey. The favorite dish, Sabrina discovered, was burgoo—a stew made from a mixture of vegetables of all kinds and meats such as squirrel, turkey, and venison, all highly seasoned and cooked in a big iron kettle.

Sion watched carefully and followed the instructions of the other men as the building progressed. At the proper time the window was cut, the fireplace constructed, and the roof covered.

Sion went once to get a drink of water from Sabrina, who was dipping it out for the thirsty workers. "I never saw anything like this, miss," he murmured as she lowered the dipper. "That cabin is going up as if by magic."

"It's wonderful, isn't it?" She looked at Sion, and a question nudged at her. Finally she said, "I don't know what you'll do, Sion, for a place to sleep. You can't stay in the house with me, of course."

"That's already settled. We're going to build a lean-to on the back. I don't need much, you know."

Sabrina did not answer. She was afraid the difference between mistress and servant was disappearing fast. Back in England it had all been a simple matter, but here in America the lines were not at all clear. "Be sure you make it as comfortable as you can."

"Of course. Well, I'd better get back to work."

The cabin was up by late afternoon. All that remained to finish was the roof, and that would be done the next day by a special crew. A group of the men had been splitting shakes so that they would be ready, but at about four o'clock Hawk Spencer called the operation to a halt. "It'll be time to eat in an hour or two. Let's see who's the best man."

"Come along, Sion," Joshua said. "Time for games."

Sion found himself admiring the men. He was tired, and he knew the others had to be too. But in the hour that followed he found out that these were tough individuals he had come to live with. Josh entered the first race, but Sion declined. "I'm slow as molasses, Josh," he said. "I'd just embarrass everybody."

The race was for a distance of half a mile over an agreed-on route. Sion stood beside Hannah as the men lined up. "Do you think Josh will win?" he asked.

"Oh, no, Fox will win. He always does."

Sion watched as Carter leaped forward. There was never any question about the winner. Fox Carter simply pulled away right at the start and left the others in a group. Josh came in third, but Fox was fifty yards ahead of all the others.

"He was always the fastest," Hannah said with a smile. She waved and said, "Fox, come and get a drink!"

"Congratulations." Sion smiled. "I wish I could run that fast."

"Well, it's not something I had to learn. I guess God just put it in me." Fox drank thirstily and then looked at Sion's sturdy frame. "You ought to do well at the wrestling or maybe the boxing."

Sion shook his head. "I think I'll just watch."

They all stood there watching as the strongest of the young men tried to throw each other in wrestling matches.

"That's Rufus Gaines. He always wins at wrestling and boxing," Fox noted. "He's strong as a bull."

Indeed, the young Gaines, who was no more than twenty, had no trouble with the local challengers.

Finally Gaines looked over and smiled. "What about you, Kenyon?"

"I think I'd better just watch."

Gaines was insistent. "You look stout enough. Let's just try a short bout."

Sion shook his head. "It wouldn't be fair," he said.

"Well, I know I'm larger than you, but I'll go easy on you." Gaines grinned.

"It's not that," Sion said. He hesitated, then shrugged. "I was a professional boxer in England."

A murmur went over the crowd, and several began urging Sion on. He stubbornly refused, but finally Sabrina, to her own surprise, said, "Go ahead, Sion. Just don't hurt him."

Her words insulted Gaines, and he frowned. "Hurt me! I reckon not! Are you comin' or not?"

Reluctantly Sion went forward, and the spectators formed a circle around the two men. Gaines was a big man, about six feet two inches tall and weighed about 220. Sion looked rather frail beside him, for his looks were deceptive. He had a muscular build, but his muscles were smooth and not bulky like those of Rufus Gaines.

The crowd began to call out encouragement to the two—most of them, of course, feeling that Sion was entirely outmatched. Still, since he had proclaimed himself a professional, they were eager to see what he could do.

Sion lifted his hands and moved lightly around and saw that Gaines was watching him cautiously. He knew Gaines's pride had been hurt. He could not believe a smaller man could give him any problems. *He's probably never been beaten by any of the men around here,* Sion thought. *I'd hate to make an enemy of him. That would be a bad way to start a new life.*

Suddenly Gaines lunged forward and threw a long, looping right, which Sion easily avoided. He saw that Gaines was very strong but not particularly fast. For the next few minutes Sion simply circled, dodging most of the blows and catching the others on his forearms. Several times he could have struck hard, for Gaines had little idea of self-defense.

"Come on, limey, let's see a little action! You can't run forever," the voices began to cry.

Sion dodged blow after blow with ease, and finally Gaines's face was red. He stopped and put his hands down. "What's the matter with you? Are you a coward?"

Sion did not answer. He simply kept his hands up, but he knew he would have to display something other than defense. He let Rufus throw another blow, but as he blocked it with his left, he pivoted and drove a hard right into the pit of Gaines's stomach. He heard the breath whoosh out as the blow drove Gaines backward. The big man did not lose his footing, but he was struggling to regain his breath. Sion said, "That's about enough of this, isn't it?"

In Gaines's humiliation, he threw himself forward, raining blows furiously. A few of them struck Sion despite his attempts to avoid them. Finally seeing that there was no other answer, Sion waited until Gaines had worn himself out, then planted his feet and struck with a hard right. It caught Gaines on the point of the chin and drove his head back, and he fell loosely to the earth.

"He's out!" someone exclaimed in the shocked silence. Several of Gaines's friends rushed forward, and one of them held his head up.

Sabrina came to stand beside Sion. "I wish you hadn't hit him that hard."

"I know. I didn't mean to either, but he's a strong man."

Josh was standing on the other side of Sion with his father. The two men looked at each other, and it was Hawk who said, "Well, I don't guess you'll get many challenges after that."

Sion went over and knelt beside Gaines. He waited until the light came back into the man's eyes and said, "I'm sorry about that. I didn't mean to hit you so hard."

Rufus Gaines was a proud man, but as his senses returned to him, he was more shocked than hurt. He felt his jaw and clambered to his feet with Sion's help. "A professional fighter, you say."

"It wasn't a thing I liked. I had no other way to make a living."

Rufus Gaines suddenly laughed with good humor. "Well, you learned it well. Maybe you could teach me how to hit like that."

———

After the boxing match the people gathered for a meal that included bear meat, salt pork, bacon, and ham. Sabrina and Sion tasted bear meat for their first time, and Sion liked it very much, although Sabrina found it rather rank. There was also sweet potatoes, white potatoes, string beans, and cherry pies.

Hannah found herself seated with Fox, and she was eager to hear about his trip. "What did you do about your place in Virginia?" She spoke of the plantation that Fox had gone to settle. There had been disputes about the title, and some of his distant family had been determined to claim a share of it.

Fox told her a little of the story and then said, "I don't have many good memories of that place, so I decided to sell it."

"I thought you might go back there and take it over."

"No, there's nothing for me there, Hannah." He put down the cup of water he was holding, then turned to her. "I thought about you a lot while I was there."

Hannah colored and did not know what to say. Her eyes went across the clearing to where she saw a pretty young woman sitting with Sion Kenyon.

Fox followed her eyes and straightened up. "I said I thought about you a lot while I was there, Hannah. Didn't you hear me?"

"Oh, I'm sorry! Well, I thought about you too, Fox, but I was pretty sure you would decide to go back there and stay."

"You didn't think like that when I left," Fox said stiffly. He glanced across to where Sion Kenyon sat, then got up and left, which surprised Hannah.

"What's wrong with Fox?" Elizabeth had seen Fox leave and came over to question her daughter.

"I don't know. We were just talking, and he got up and walked away. He sold his plantation in Virginia."

"I'll bet you were glad to hear that," Elizabeth said with a smile.

"I suppose so."

Elizabeth was a very astute woman, and she knew this daughter of hers very well. She saw that Hannah could not keep from watching young Sion Kenyon, and a question came to her. She almost asked it but knew it was too soon. The question troubled her, and later on, when she was alone with Hawk, she told him what had happened.

Hawk stared at her. "Why, she couldn't be interested in him! She's only known him a few weeks."

"You don't know much about women, Hawk."

"I know *everything* about women," Hawk declared with a hurt look. "Just ask me."

Elizabeth laid her hand on his arm. "I know we both thought she was interested in Fox, but it looks like things have changed now."

"Well, they'll have to work it out for themselves, I suppose.

But I don't see how she could work that out. I think she likes him because he's different."

"He is that, all right. Women are drawn to that sometimes."

Sabrina had enjoyed the meal, and she enjoyed the dancing as well. Most of the men were rather poor dancers, but one young man danced with all the ease in the world. Drake Hammond, the man she had met at church, had simply cut in on her dance with another young man. "I suppose this is pretty rough in your eyes, Miss Fairfax, after the balls you must have attended in England."

"It's different, but I do appreciate so much all the help I've been given by all of you."

"That's the way it is here on the frontier. It's a very close-knit community. Do you really intend to stay here?"

"Why, of course. Why would you ask that?"

"You seem to be made for finer things than a log cabin out in the wilderness." Hammond was a handsome man with smooth features. His hands were not as rough as Sabrina's other dance partners' had been. He was better dressed, and the quality of his clothes was much higher than his neighbors'.

"Why, you live here, don't you?"

"I do for now, but someday I'd like to go east. Perhaps New York or Washington. I'm not much of a frontiersman, I'm afraid."

"Well, I'm afraid I'm not much of a frontier lady, but I have little choice."

Hammond's hand pressed against her back, and she was aware of his magnetism. "I don't think you'll stay here," he said.

Sabrina looked up and smiled into his eyes. "We all do things we don't particularly want to do."

"Not me. I do what I want to."

"Sometimes you do, but sometimes you can't."

"You're right about that. My father's a little tight with the purse strings. One day, though, I'll be able to do exactly as I please."

Sabrina knew quite a bit from that simple statement. He evidently had a rich father who was rather tight on his son.

She said no more to him but threw herself into enjoying the dance.

The music and the dancing went on, then finally everyone piled into wagons or got on horses and rode away. Sion and Sabrina went back to the Spencer house, for the new cabin had no roof. As Sabrina rode back, she felt a sense of security. *Tomorrow I'll have a roof over my head and a house of my own.*

———————

The next morning Sabrina and Hannah were washing the breakfast dishes at the Spencers'. Fox had come over early and was out back showing Sion how to load and shoot a musket. Fox was an expert shot, of course, and as Sion shot, Fox was able to give him a lot of help. "You're a natural good shot. You have steady hands," he said. "What you need is practice."

"You've had lots of that, I suppose."

"All my life. There were times when if I didn't shoot straight, we didn't eat."

The two men shot for some time, and finally Fox said in an offhand manner, "You've gotten to know the Spencers very well, haven't you?"

"They're fine people. I've never known better."

"Aye, they are." He hesitated, then said, "I didn't have anything to offer Hannah before, but now that I've sold my place, I do."

Sion suddenly turned, his eyes open wide. "Oh, is that right! Are you engaged to her?"

"No, nothing like that, but we've always liked each other."

"She's a fine woman. I don't know as I've known a nicer one."

His answer brought little comfort to Fox. He yearned to ask Sion what his intentions were but did not know the man well enough for that. He looked up as two men rode in and said, "There's Caleb Files."

"Caleb Files . . . Isn't he the man who has an interest in Sabrina's land?"

"I guess I hadn't heard that. He's not too particular about how he gets his land. He's a big landowner to the east of us here. I don't care much for him. I don't know who that man is with him, though."

Sion suddenly straightened up and narrowed his eyes. "I know him. His name is Jack Fry."

Fox stared at him. "How could you know that?"

"I had a little trouble with him on the way out here."

Fox did not ask any more questions. On the frontier a man didn't ask those questions unless they were better friends than he was with Sion. But he determined to find out about it. He watched as the two men dismounted and then shook his head. "Miss Fairfax better watch her step dealing with him."

Caleb Files nodded to the two women as they rode up. "Hello, Miss Spencer."

"Hello, Mr. Files," Hannah said coolly.

"I don't believe you know Jack Fry."

Fry pulled off his hat. His hair was shaggy, and he grinned, showing yellow teeth. "Howdy," he said. "Seems to me we've met before."

"Is this Miss Fairfax?" Caleb Files asked.

"Yes."

"I came out to have a little business talk with you, miss, if you have the time."

"Why, certainly."

"I'll be in the house if you need me, Sabrina," Hannah said as she turned to go. Sion and Fox watched from a distance in case there was trouble.

"I'll make this brief. I'm buying up land, and I'd like to make an offer on yours."

Sabrina remembered what Jackson had said about this man and was cautious. "I'd rather you wouldn't right now. I just had a house built, and we've already planted some crops."

"Ma'am, a woman can't make it out here by herself."

"I'm not alone. I have a servant."

"You need more than that," Files said. "Besides that, I don't know if you know it, but I think I've got a claim prior to yours."

"You'll have to talk to Mr. Jackson about that," Sabrina

said. She did not like the man and saw that her answer fronted him.

"Now, look, Miss Fairfax, let's get this over with easy. What's the use of going to court and paying the lawyers a lot of money, and then after it's over you'll have nothing and owe them to boot. I'll make you a good offer on the land, and we can avoid all that."

"I'm sorry. I can't speak about it right now."

Files stared at her for a moment and then made himself smile. "Ma'am, I'll get that land. I wish you'd make it easy on yourself."

"Talk to Mr. Jackson."

Sabrina turned and left the two men standing there. Files glared after her and then went back to his horse. The two men mounted and rode out.

Too Many Suitors

Fifteen

*T*he water of the creek was almost as clear as air. As Sabrina eased herself into it, she saw a school of silver minnows hanging suspended as if frozen. The water was so clear that they seemed to be hovering in air, but as the ripples she made reached them, they turned as one body and darted away toward the center of the stream.

I wonder how they do that? It's like all of them have different bodies but only one brain.

She heard a noise in the woods behind her, and she turned quickly, her eyes wide with alarm. She had come down to the creek to bathe, being tired of dirt and grime that could not be washed off in a basin. She had left her clothes on a nearby tree stump and was enjoying the warmth of the sun as it filtered down through the leaves of the sweet gums that lined the bank. She almost ran back to get her clothes, but then a large bird, the likes of which she had never seen, came down a tree upside down. It had ladder-like stripes on its back, a red head, and an enormous beak—sharp and pointed like a chisel. She watched it for a minute, the anxiety flowing out of her.

Sabrina reached for the small jar of soap she had left on the bank and scooped out a handful of the soft soap. Putting the top on awkwardly, she tossed it back to the bank, then holding her hand up over her in the air she submerged herself. The water was deliciously cool. The first three weeks of June had been very hot and humid, and the refreshing water seemed to go down into her very bones. She lay there on the sandy bottom of the stream, holding the soft soap up, savoring the coolness and the comfort of the water. Then she rose and lathered herself all over. Hannah had made the soap, and it had a sweet smell of some kind of perfume. It lathered well, and soon she had covered herself, almost like an ointment, with the fragrant soap. Finally she lay down in the water and let the stream rinse away the suds. She watched them as they were carried downstream swirling around a bend, and her eyes stopped on a turtle she had not seen. He had crawled out on a stub of a log extending over the water and was sunning himself. His wise old eyes regarded her, and she said, "Hello, turtle," then felt foolish and laughed. "I'm going crazy out here in the woods—talking to turtles."

Reluctantly she removed the last of the soap and then waded out of the water and back to where she had put her clothes. She dried off, dressed, and gave one last look at the creek, wondering what she would do in the wintertime when it was too cold for such bathing.

Making her way along the serpentine path that twisted its way through the woods, she stepped out into the clearing and saw that Hannah's mare was tied to a sapling. She hurried forward and as she approached the cabin, Hannah stepped out.

"Hello, Sabrina. I've been waiting for you."

"I went down to the creek to have a bath. I couldn't stand being dirty any longer."

"You're lucky to have a nice creek like that so close." Hannah smiled. "I have to go nearly three miles to find a sheltered place."

"You're welcome to use my creek," Sabrina said. "Come on in. We'll see if we can make something to eat."

"I've come over to give you a cooking lesson."

"Well, I can use it," Sabrina said ruefully. The two entered the cabin, which seemed dark and dreary after the bright sunshine. "I miss windows," she said suddenly. "If I ever build a house—a real house, I mean—I'm going to put ten windows in it. One in every room, at least. This one window doesn't let in nearly enough light."

Hannah opened the cotton sack she'd brought and showed Sabrina the contents. "This was part of our corn crop."

"How did you grind it up?" Sabrina asked, letting some of the fine meal run through her fingers. "Is there a mill here?"

"Oh, no, we have to grind corn in a hominy block. . . ." She went on to explain how to make a mortar and pestle from a section of a large hardwood tree. A hole was burned in the top of the log, then corn was placed in the hole that was created, then a huge pestle made of hardwood would be used to crush the corn.

"It must be very hard, lifting that pestle and dropping it."

"No, you attach it to a long sapling with a rope. When the sapling bends, the pestle hits the corn in the hole, then the sapling pulls it up again. I'm sure Sion will make a good one for you." She broke off and said, "Someone's coming."

"You have good hearing."

"I think you get cautious living out here."

The two women went to the door, and Sabrina groaned, "Oh, no, it's another one!"

"Another what? It's just Silas Bone."

"It doesn't matter what his name is. I know why he's come."

Hannah stared with surprise at her friend. "Silas lives about ten miles down the river. Do you know him?"

"Not yet," Sabrina said grimly, "but I will. He's come courting."

The two women waited until the man wearing buckskins stepped off of his horse. He pulled off his floppy hat and grinned at the two. "Howdy, ladies. How are you, Miss Spencer?"

"Oh, I'm fine. I don't believe you know Miss Fairfax here."

"No, I don't believe I've had that pleasure." Bone came forward. He was a weather-beaten individual showing the effects of a lifetime of labor. He had shaved recently, for his face glowed, and his hair was cut rather roughly.

"I'm might proud to know you, Miss Fairfax. I've heard a lot about you."

"I'm glad to know you, Mr. Bone. Won't you come in? I think we have some tea."

"That'd go down right well." As he entered the cabin, Bone said, "I come lookin' for a horse that strayed away. Got a bay with three stockin' feet. I don't reckon you've seen her?"

"No, I haven't, Mr. Bone," Sabrina said. As she prepared

the tea, she listened as Hannah talked to the man about the affairs of the community. When she brought the tea, Bone picked his up and drank it without stopping, even though it was boiling. "That's right good sassafras." He nodded with approval. "Well, Miss Fairfax, I'm not a feller to waste time. I heard you was here and you didn't have no man. So I've come to tell you that I'd like to join all them fellers been comin' to make you an offer."

Bone reached into his greasy shirt pocket and pulled out a paper. "I got here a list of my ownin's, and I know you'd be interested in that. I got four hundred acres, over a hundred of it cleared, the rest in good timber. I got three milk cows, four beef critters, a fine flock of dominiquer chickens . . ."

Sabrina glanced over at Hannah, who was trying to cover up a smile while the two women listened to Bone's voice drone on.

Finally he finished his list, saying, "I lost my woman two years ago, and I got three young'uns—one boy twelve and two girls younger. I'd be mighty happy if you'd consider my offer."

Sabrina cleared her throat and kept her face straight as she said, "It's very kind of you, Mr. Bone. I certainly will keep you in mind."

"Well, I'll be moseyin' along. Good to see you, Miss Spencer, and good to meet up with you, Miss Fairfax. I hope we'll be seein' lots of each other. I think we'd team up together right nice."

The two women went to the door and watched as Bone jammed the hat on his head, mounted his horse, and rode off with a cheerful wave.

"These men are going to drive me absolutely crazy!" Sabrina said, gritting her teeth. She crossed her arms across her chest and shook her head as she stared at the retreating man. "They show up at all hours of the day and night. All of them have got an excuse for coming. Some of them to bring a gift— more than a pound of butter or a quarter of a deer."

"Are all of them as businesslike as Silas?"

"No. Some of them are very shy. One of them came two days ago and stayed half a day. I finally had to just say that I had work to do, and he blurted out, 'I'd like to marry up with you if you're willing,' and then ran as if I had pulled a gun on him."

Hannah laughed. She had a good, deep laugh that made her eyes crinkle shut. "Too many suitors! That ought to make you happy and proud."

"Well, it doesn't! I wish they'd leave me alone. I have no intention of getting married."

Hannah shook her head. "It's hard on a single woman out here. As a matter of fact, most of them don't stay single long. When a woman becomes a widow, the unmarried men come flocking to her. Women are so scarce out here."

"Well, I'm going to lock myself in the cabin the next time one shows up."

"Let me help you," Hannah said, a smile on her lips.

"Help me how?" Sabrina asked as she sat down on the front step.

Hannah sat down next to her. "I can give you some advice on which man you need."

Sabrina could not help smiling. "I suppose you've been besieged like this also?"

"Oh, yes. You get used to it. Let's see, now. Who would be a good man. . . ? There's Ben Scroggins. He's the best looking. Oh, he's a handsome man! But he's flighty. Here today and gone tomorrow. You don't need him."

"Cross out Ben Scroggins."

"Yes. Let's see. Well, there's Daniel Ellencourt. He has a real good claim of over eight hundred acres and buying more. He lost his wife, May, over a year ago. He came courting me right away."

"You recommend him?"

"No, he's got three children who are devils."

"All right. I won't have him, then. Who else?"

"Jude Hellings. Now, there'd be a good man. He's got lots of money, but he's tight."

"How many children does he have?"

"Only two. Nice, well-behaved children. Jude might be a good man for you."

"Is he handsome?"

"Oh, no! Mercy no! He's downright homely. But he's a good man."

"I won't have him. The man I get will have to be handsome, dashing, and charming, have a sack full of money, and have a beautiful house all built ready for me to become mistress of it."

"I don't think you're going to find anybody like that around here. You'll have to go east for that. New York or Boston."

"Then I'll just stay single." Hearing a rustle, the women looked up to see Sion coming out of the woods. He had a rifle over his shoulder and he was carrying a leather bag. "Sion went hunting early this morning. I hope he got something good to eat."

The two women waited until Sion was close, then he shifted his rifle and said, "Well, I shot something. If you can cook it, I can eat it."

He leaned his rifle against the wall of the cabin, opened the bag, and dumped out the contents. "Six squirrels!" Hannah exclaimed. "Why, that's great, Sion!"

"The woods are full of the creatures. I won't tell you how many I missed, though; I can't hit them in the head like Josh or Hawk can. And I don't know how to clean them very well."

"I'll show you how to do that. I've cleaned a thousand of them, I suppose. Do you have a sharp knife?"

Sion pulled the folding knife from his pocket, then loaded the squirrels back into the bag.

"All right, then. Come along."

The two went to the stump that had been sawed off at waist height to make a worktable. Sion put the first squirrel on the stump, and Hannah went straight to work. Sabrina stayed in front of the cabin, but she kept her eye on them. She noted that the two of them always seemed to enjoy being together, and for a moment felt a pang that she had no one herself she felt that free with.

Finally the squirrels were cleaned, and Hannah said, "Do you know how to cook squirrel, Sabrina?"

"I suppose I could fry them in grease."

"Let me show you how to make squirrel and dumplings."

"Well, there's more than enough for all of us. You stay and show me how, and we'll have a good supper tonight."

———

The day had gone quickly. Hannah had taught Sabrina how to make squirrel and dumplings, and as the three sat down at the table, there was a moment's pause. Sabrina said, "I suppose you'd better ask the blessing." She smiled at Hannah. "He makes me feel like a heathen. We never said anything like blessings while I was growing up."

"It's a good thing to give thanks unto the Lord, especially for a good dinner of squirrel and dumplings."

The three bowed their heads, and Sion prayed, "Lord, we thank you for this food, and for every blessing. You're the giver of every good gift, and I thank you for this home and for Miss Spencer and her family. Watch over us and guide us. In Jesus' name, amen."

"Amen," Hannah said. She dipped into the large bowl of dumplings, helping herself, and then passed it to Sabrina. Sabrina took out a sizable portion and then Sion did the same. She had made fire bread, which was simply cakes baked in front of the fireplace.

"What's that?" Sabrina asked curiously as Hannah took something out of the pot.

"Why, it's squirrel brains."

Sabrina stared at Hannah. "You're going to eat the brains?"

"Best part of the squirrel. You have to crack the skulls to get 'em." Hannah grabbed the hammer she had found earlier and cracked the skull to extract the gray matter. "Help yourself, Sabrina."

"I don't know what I'd do if I had to eat a thing like that!" she shuddered.

"How about you, Sion?"

"Well, I'll try almost anything once."

Sabrina watched as the two seemed to enjoy the feast. She had learned to eat many things she had never heard of before coming to America, but squirrel brains were a bit too much. She knew that the settlers treasured pork brains and she'd also heard of eating the tongues of beef cattle and buffalo.

As they ate, they talked, and Hannah mentioned the creek being handy. "Sabrina's lucky," she said to Sion, "to have a creek to bathe in so close."

Sabrina glanced at Sion, who was watching her. "I guess you miss city life a lot."

"Well, I do miss having a bath. My father had a copper bathtub made for me at our home. The servants would fill it up with hot water every day in the wintertime, and I'd just soak it up. Oh, that was delicious!"

"I don't think there's a bathtub in this whole territory," Hannah said. "We need too many other things worse."

"I suppose," Sabrina said. "Still it would be nice." She changed the subject and saw that Sion was looking at her in a strange way with a smile on his face. "What are you smiling about, Sion?"

"Just feeling good after a fine meal of squirrel brains with two fine ladies."

————————

Sabrina returned from a morning visit with Hannah four days after the squirrel feast. She had grown very fond of the young woman. The two had become fast friends. They were nearly the same age, and although their backgrounds were different, they found a great deal to talk about. Hannah knew much about frontier living, and Sabrina felt grateful to her for the lessons she gave. As she approached the cabin, she saw Sion sitting outside whittling on a piece of cedar. He kept his knife sharp and liked to peel shavings almost as thin as air. A pile of the curls of wood was at his feet, but he got up and folded the knife and stuck it in his pocket as she approached.

"Did you have a good visit with the Spencers?"

"Oh, yes. What have you been doing?"

She waited for Sion to answer but saw that he was smiling. "What are you smiling about?" She suddenly remembered he had been gone a great deal during the past few days, and now she tilted her head to one side and studied him. "You are absolutely smirking, Sion."

"I got your Christmas present."

"Christmas! But it's June!"

"I know, but I thought you could use it now."

"You are a strange man. Christmas presents in June. Well, what is it? And remember, I don't give presents until Christmas comes."

"Come along. I'll show you. It's in the cabin." Sion stepped back, and Sabrina walked inside. The light slanted through the one window, and she stopped dead still, for it fell upon an object that had not been there.

"Why, Sion, what is it, a trough?"

"I'm insulted!" Sion said. He moved over toward the object that was set against one side of the cabin. "Can't you guess?"

Sabrina moved closer and saw what appeared to be a rectangular box. It was about two feet wide and at least six feet long. She reached down and saw that it was made of wood that had been smoothly planed until it was almost as smooth as glass. She saw a hole in the bottom of it that had a round peg of wood stuffed into it. Suddenly enlightenment came to her, and she exclaimed, "Why, it's a *bathtub!*"

"That's what it is, all right. Not made out of metal. I couldn't get any of that, but it's made out of cypress. I got the boards from John Miller. They make boats out of it in some parts of this country. The water just swells the joints up and makes it watertight. That hole there is a drain so you don't have to haul the water out in buckets. Just pull that plug out, and the water will drain right out."

Sabrina was stunned. She had known that Sion was a hard worker, but this caught her by surprise. She turned to him, her eyes sparkling, and a rush of gratitude filled her. "I could almost kiss you!"

Sion laughed and reached forward, and putting his arms around her, kissed her firmly on the lips. "I take that as an invitation," he grinned and stepped back.

Sabrina felt a shock at the touch of his lips. The kiss had sent an unfamiliar sensation through her. She was flustered and embarrassed. "Well," she laughed haltingly, "I guess I can't fault you for that. Sion, it was so thoughtful. I'm going to try it right away."

"I'll help you fill it up."

The two hauled water in from the shallow well that several

of the men had helped Sion dig after they had built the cabin. It produced clear, cold water. Sabrina did not heat it, for the cool water would feel wonderful on this hot day. She shooed Sion out and ten minutes later was basking in the water. She thought about what kind of man would go to this much trouble for an employer, and then she thought about the kiss.

I ought to rebuke him for that, but I just can't. He is a strange sort of man. . . .

A Serious Suitor

Sixteen

*H*awk Spencer moved the razor down his lean cheek, wiped the lather off on a cloth in his left hand, and then carefully removed the excess lather from his face. He was standing at a cherry washstand with a small mirror fastened to the wall over it. He studied himself carefully, then finally, without taking his eyes off of his face, he said, "Wife, you are blessed."

Elizabeth Spencer was getting dressed. The two had just risen, and now she paused long enough to look with surprise at her husband. "Well, I know I am, but in what particular way?"

Spencer turned and grinned at her, his eyes dancing. "In having such a handsome husband."

Elizabeth could not help laughing, although she shook her head. "You are a fool, Hawk Spencer!"

"I suppose—" Hawk continued looking in the mirror, examining his features—"but what a handsome fool." He suddenly turned and put his arms around her. "It's a good thing you're a handsome woman. Otherwise we wouldn't be the best-looking couple in the territory."

The two stood there, and Elizabeth Spencer felt content. She had had a good first marriage, but her second was even better, if that were possible. This man loved her, she knew, with all of his heart, and she felt the same about him. She rested against him and said, "We're too old for this sort of thing."

"I'll be romancing you when we're a hundred and don't have any teeth."

Elizabeth laughed. "All right. I know you're trying to get something out of me."

"A cherry pie would be nice. We haven't had a cherry pie for a long time now."

"No, not for three days!" Elizabeth slapped him on the chest and moved away. "I'll go fix breakfast while you milk."

"Why don't you let me fix breakfast and you milk?"

"I'd hate to see the mess you'd make cooking," Elizabeth sniffed.

The two went about their chores and shortly were seated at the table. Hawk was eating the battered eggs and fried ham with gusto. He lifted a biscuit and said, "I will say this. You are still the best biscuit maker in the world—or anywhere else, for that matter."

The conversation gradually turned to Hawk's plans for improving the place, and then it turned again to their daughter. "What do you think about Hannah?"

Hawk glanced at her with surprise. "About Hannah? Why, what do you mean? In what way?"

"I mean about her and Fox."

Hawk scratched his chin thoughtfully and then shook his head. "I haven't thought much about it."

"Men!" Elizabeth snorted and shook her head with disgust. "Don't you care who your own daughter marries?"

"She hasn't said anything about getting married, has she?"

"No, she hasn't *said* anything, but she thinks about it. What young girl wouldn't?"

"That's another difference between men and women. If women would just come out and say what they mean, it'd make life a lot simpler. Now, you take men—"

"I don't want to hear about that!" Elizabeth picked up the cup of coffee before her and took a sip. "You think Fox would make a good husband for her?"

"Why, of course he would. He's a fine young man."

"There are lots of fine young men around, but she needs exactly the right one."

"Well, how does a woman decide that? Now, you didn't have any trouble." Hawk's eyes sparkled. "You took one look at me and knew that no other man would be as good as I am for you."

Elizabeth could not keep from smiling. "Well, not every woman has my good fortune to find just exactly the right man. Sometimes they have to go through two or three."

"You make finding a husband sound like trying on a hat. I don't like this one. This one's too big. This one costs too much. It ought to be simpler than that, wife."

Elizabeth said in a serious tone, "This is important. You know how many bad marriages we've seen. I think they all turn out bad because people didn't choose rightly."

"We've been praying for Hannah and Josh since they were born, Elizabeth."

"I know we have, but it troubles me sometimes. I'm not sure how Fox feels about her." She looked up suddenly and asked, "Would it bother you having a half-Indian son-in-law?"

Her remark genuinely surprised Hawk Spencer. "Why, of course not! There's not a finer man in the world than Sequatchie. He's the best friend I've got in the world. And Fox is of his blood. If the two love each other, then I'd say amen."

Elizabeth did not answer for a while. She sighed and said, "I don't know about Hannah. She's not very outgoing about things like this."

"Why don't you just ask her how she feels."

"No, that's the sort of thing that would have to start with her." Elizabeth rose and said no more.

As Hawk Spencer went about his work that day, he thought long and hard about the daughter who was so dear to him. He had seen bad marriages many times, and the thought that Hannah might not have a good man or a good marriage troubled him. More than once as he worked, he prayed, "God, I'll have to ask you to help my daughter. She needs to get just the man you have for her and no other."

———

"My horse is gone!"

Fox was standing to one side and laughing silently. "Of course he's gone. What'd you expect?"

Sion turned in surprise. The two of them had tied their

horses deep in the woods while they were hunting for deer. "Well, I didn't expect him to be *gone*. You think somebody's stolen him?"

"No, you tied him up wrong."

"I tied him firmly. He couldn't have gotten loose."

"There's his bridle still tied to that tree." Fox motioned toward a sturdy young tree. The bridle had dropped to the ground, and Fox leaned over and picked it up. "I could have told you this would happen."

Sion blinked with surprise. "Well, why didn't you?"

"You'll remember longer this way. Look, see how my horse is tied?" He motioned toward his own horse, a clay-colored stallion. "You tie your horse up to a branch that will give. That way he can pull at it, but it'll spring back. When you tie one to a solid tree, you see what can happen."

Sion stared at the bridle in his hand, then laughed. "You're a hard teacher, Fox."

"I learned the same way. But the difference was I had to walk home, and I was fifteen miles away. The horse was there when I got there. He had more sense than I did. Come on. He won't have gone far. Let's see if you can track him."

Sion and Fox had become good friends. Fox knew the woods like he knew his favorite knife, and he was imparting his wisdom and knowledge as fast as he thought Sion could absorb it.

As for Sion, he felt like a child. He knew so little about living in this strange country, but he was a willing learner and had a truly humble spirit. He laughed at his own mistakes as quickly as anyone, which made others more willing to teach him. Now as he followed the tracks of the strayed horse, he was pleased to see that he had at least learned how to track a little bit.

"I'm getting better."

Fox smiled and shook his head. "A six-year-old could follow this trail. The ground is wet and soft, and you couldn't miss it. Try tracking one on rock sometime."

"Can you do that?"

"My uncle can. He's the best tracker I ever saw."

"Did Sequatchie teach you what you know about the woods?"

"Yes, he and Hawk, and I've learned from staying with the Indians. They're the best trackers, of course, except for Hawk."

The two found the horse not more than two hundred yards away cropping at the grass, and Sion walked right up to him and patted him on the neck. "I hope you enjoyed yourself, horse," he said. "You won't get away anymore." They went back and packed up their equipment and were soon on their way.

As the two made their way back toward the settlements, Fox pointed out different trees and plants and signs of animals. To Sion it was almost a miracle. He shook his head. "You know the names of every tree in the woods and every flower too, I think."

"You'll pick it up. You'll know most of it, too, after you've been here a year or two."

"I feel more at home farming or in a coal mine."

"Did you like coal mining?"

"I hated it more than anything I've ever done." Sion went on to tell of the hardships and mentioned his friend Rees. "I sent money to support him and his family for several months, but I trust he's well by now. Wales is so far away. I don't know if I'll ever see him again."

"That's the way life is," Fox observed. "Every time I see a man I wonder if he will be a good friend or an enemy."

Sion glanced at Fox with surprise. "I never think like that. Why should I think a man will be my enemy?"

"I think it's different here in this country, especially with the conflict between the Indians and the white men."

"It must be difficult for you being caught in the middle."

Fox did not speak for a time. "Yes, it is. I thought for a while about going and living with the Cherokee, but that way of life is passing." A spirit of gloom seemed to possess him. "The Indians will be forced out."

"Can't they learn to farm and take up the white man's ways?"

"I think I can, but I'm half white. It'll be hard for the old ones. Suppose you had to learn to live like the Indians. Think how hard that would be."

Sion pondered the words of Fox and finally said, "I believe you're right, but it's a sad thing."

"Yes, it is, and it's going to get worse."

The two rode together except when the trail narrowed to accommodate only one horse. Fox was curious about Sion and Sabrina. He knew the basics of their story but wondered how Sion felt about being a bond servant. Finally he asked him, "You've got five years to serve until you're a free man?"

"That's right."

Fox hesitated and then said, "That's almost like being a slave."

"It's better than being in a prison in England."

"I suppose that's true."

"I owe a lot to Miss Fairfax. If she hadn't gotten me out of that prison, I don't think I could have lasted my ten years there. That's how long my original sentence was. No, this is all right, Fox. Five years isn't forever."

"It would bother me a great deal. It's like you're being put in a box. You have to do what she says for five whole years. What if you wanted to marry?"

"Bond servants get married, but what woman would want to be married to a man who isn't free? I'll just have to put that off for a time."

"I don't think Sabrina will."

Sion turned in the saddle. "What do you mean by that?"

Surprised by Sion's sharp tone, Fox said, "I mean she's a beautiful woman, and she has property. And there are a lot of unmarried men in these parts. As a matter of fact, Hannah was telling me there's been a regular parade of fellows coming by offering to marry her."

"She's right about that," Sion said. "They're driving her crazy."

"It happens all the time out here. Women are so scarce. I think she'll marry Drake Hammond."

Indeed, Drake Hammond had become a frequent visitor to Sabrina's house. He had taken her to a celebration in town, and Sabrina had appeared to enjoy his company.

Fox noted that Sion had little to say about this. "How do you feel about Sabrina?"

"She's a good woman."

"Have you ever thought of marrying her yourself?"

Sion stared at Fox with surprise. "I'm her servant, Fox. She would never marry a servant."

Fox did not answer, and he noted that the conversation seemed to trouble Sion, so he changed the subject. "We'll stop on the way back and see if we can't get us a deer or maybe a turkey. I'd fancy a bit of that for a change."

Sion and Sabrina stood together looking out over the field of corn. A sense of pride came to both of them, especially to Sion. He had put in long hours working in this field, and now he felt a sense of possession, of ownership. He turned to Sabrina and said, "I don't know as I've ever seen a healthier crop. Those rains we had, they're so good for crops like this."

"I never noticed crops growing before, Sion—not at home, that is. They were there, I suppose, but I was interested in other things. But this is beautiful." She turned to him and smiled. "You worked very hard on it."

"I can do better next year. You learn from doing. The land is good here. Fox told me that his people catch small fish and fertilize the ground with them, but it would take a lot of fish to do a field this big."

"What will we do with all this corn? Sell it?"

"Keep some for seed corn. A lot of people make whiskey out of it."

"Do you know how to do that?"

"No, not really."

Sion had learned that corn could be traded for almost anything. He had also learned that by turning corn into whiskey, a farmer could have a product that was worth up to two dollars per gallon—whereas a bushel of good corn was valued at fifty cents.

The two walked around the field, lost in admiration, and from time to time Sabrina stopped to finger one of the strong stalks and note the tiny beginnings of ears. "We'll have fresh corn. That'll be good."

"Aye, and we'll have all kinds of fresh vegetables from the garden. The ground is richer here than in England. You just plant a seed and then jump back out of the way," Sion said with a smile.

The two continued their walk until finally Sion lifted his head. "Someone's coming at a run." The two turned, and Sion narrowed his eyes. "That's Josh. There must be something wrong. He wouldn't punish a horse like that." The two hurried forward to meet Josh, who slid off his horse in one easy motion.

"Bad news," he said. His eyes were troubled, and he shook his head. "There's been a raid on a family named Johnson. You don't know them, but they live about twelve miles from here."

"Indians?" Sabrina asked fearfully.

"Yes."

"Was it bad, Josh?" Sion asked.

"Very bad! The whole family butchered. The man and the woman and four children all dead and scalped and the cabin burned. I came to get you, Sion. A militia's being formed, and you ought to go along with the rest of us."

"Is that all right, miss?" Sion asked quickly.

"Of course, if it's what the men are doing."

"Will it be all right, Josh, to leave Miss Fairfax alone here?"

He turned to Sabrina and said, "I think you'd be all right here, but I'd feel better if you'd go stay with my mom and sister until we got back. Dad will be going, but you three women will be all right there. It was a small party, and they were headed north. They won't come this way. I wish they would," he said grimly. "They'd be easier to catch up with."

"I'll get my horse and gun."

"Bring some extra powder and balls if you've got them," Josh said.

————

Sabrina had attended the funeral of the family killed in the raid. They had been buried on their own place, and the six graves there made a distinct impression on Sabrina. She had stood beside the grave as Rev. Paul Anderson had read from the Scriptures, and the thinness of the line between life and death in this country had become clear to Sabrina. It was the custom in the country to wait until the graves were filled in, and she had stood there along with the others until they heard the dirt strike the caskets. It made a terrible sound to her, and she had had bad dreams about it.

After the funeral she had been more silent than usual, and Sion, who had come back from the fruitless chase after the raiders, had noticed it. He had said nothing for a few days until finally one evening as they were eating supper together, she pushed her plate back and said, "I'll never get used to this country, Sion."

Sion hesitated, not knowing exactly how to answer that. "You're bothered about the Indians, aren't you?"

"Yes. It could just as easily have been us, Sion."

"I know, but it's no different than in England. Every time you went for a carriage, you could have had an accident or the plague could have come. Death is always part of life. It will never change, miss."

"Doesn't it bother you, Sion?"

"Why, I don't think it does."

"I don't see how you can put it away from you like that."

"Well, I didn't always. When I was a younger man working in the mines, it was all I could do sometimes to make myself go down in the cage. You can't imagine how bad it is when the cage just falls away into utter darkness. You feel like it will never stop. I never ceased to be afraid of it. And then when you get out of the cage, it's just as bad. At any moment the roof could fall in. It did more than once when I was working. It killed my father, and I knew it could kill me, too."

Sabrina listened as he described the terrible life that coal miners led. It was all foreign to her, for she had led a sheltered life. Since coming to America her world had been shaken, and she felt vulnerable. When he finished speaking, a silence fell between the two, and he said finally, "I hate to see you troubled."

"I get discouraged. And that poor family! They had their lives before them, Sion. Those two girls could have married and had their own families. And the boys, they could have found wives. And the couple, their parents, will never see their grandchildren grow up about them. They got up in the morning, and I doubt if they thought about dying. They went about their work, they laughed, they cried, they had arguments, they lived, and that night they were all dead. It all seems so—so useless!"

"God knows all about that family. I think they're with Him right now. They were a fine Christian family, I understand."

This was cold enough comfort to Sabrina. She knew there was something lacking in her life, but she didn't know what it was, nor could she express her emptiness to Sion. She envied his calmness and his certainty, and she knew that his beliefs were sincere—that he was not afraid of life nor of death. Finally she shook her head. "I'll never get used to this country, and I'll never get used to death. I'm afraid of it."

Sion clamped his lips together in thought, then said gently, "God loves us. When bad things happen, He knows about that."

"I don't see how that family being butchered by Indians could please God!" she said sharply. "Don't talk about it any more!"

———

Drake Hammond had arrived early in the afternoon to take Sabrina to town, and she had been glad to see him. Hammond was the one man she had found in her new world who brought back a trace of what she had known in England. He was always well dressed, his father was wealthy, and one day Hammond would inherit all of the property. He lived in a fine house—one of the few, Sabrina understood, that was in the least like the fine home she had grown up in. Hannah had been there for a party and had told Sabrina about the carpets on the floor, the paintings on the wall, and the fine furniture.

Drake obviously liked Sabrina, and as the two made their way toward town, he teased her about her suitors. "Well, how many men seeking your fair hand came by this week, Sabrina?"

"Don't even talk about it, Drake!"

"I thought you'd be pleased. Most women would."

"Most of them are just looking for someone to keep their house and raise their children. Almost all of them are widowers."

"Robert Southland isn't. He told me he had come by to court you, and you just about ran him off with a shotgun."

"Why, I did no such thing! I just—" Sabrina saw that Drake was laughing at her and found herself joining in. "I suppose I was a little harsh. He's a nice enough man, but I'm sick of suitors."

"That's the way it is out here," Drake said, echoing the words Sabrina had heard before. "Women are scarce."

The two pulled into town as he uttered these words, and as Drake parked the buggy, he turned to her and said, "Well, I suppose it's time for me to join the ranks. What about me, Sabrina? You think I'd make a proper husband?"

Sabrina studied Drake for a moment. She could not tell if he was serious or not. "You'd make a terrible husband."

Hammond was surprised. "Well, that's speaking right out. How did you arrive at that evaluation of my quality?"

"Gossip. They say you're a gambler, a womanizer, and as unsteady as the wind."

"So are half the men in the world. What would you want— a dull person who never tasted life?"

Sabrina could not answer. She was drawn to Drake Hammond. He was entertaining, and she knew he had ambitions. It would be simple enough for her to marry him, to go live in his fine home and think that she would never have to make grits or scrub dishes again. Still, she was troubled by the rumors she had heard of his gambling. She had had enough of this with her father. Now she put him off by saying, "You don't want a wife. You're having too much fun as a bachelor."

Drake jumped out, and when he came around and helped her down, he said, "I've had my good times, but sooner or later that has to come to an end and a man has to marry."

Sabrina laughed. "You make it sound like a jail sentence. Don't trouble me with your foolishness, Drake."

Drake was holding her hand, and now he turned her around, and for a moment he was serious. "I'm not sure it's all foolishness, Sabrina. You're a lovely woman, and you'd make any man a fine wife."

The two were silent for a moment as Sabrina studied him. Her life seemed to lie before her, and all she could think of was living in a rude log cabin and how little she liked it. Still, the wreckage of her father's gambling had scarred her heart and her emotions, and she knew it wouldn't be wise to marry a gambler.

Shaking the unpleasant thoughts away, she determined to enjoy the evening. She smiled and said, "Let's go see the show."

The entertainment was a drama troupe consisting of three men and two women. They had set up a theatre of sorts in the one available empty building, a half-finished structure destined to be a general store. A stage of rough lumber had been thrown up, but there was no curtain. The seats consisted of narrow ten-inch boards with no backs. The admission was a dollar, but since there was no other entertainment available, the building was packed.

Sabrina was vastly amused at the troupe. They put on scenes from *Hamlet, Romeo and Juliet, Macbeth,* and other plays, all thrown together and mixed up like stew! During one scene Sabrina commented to Drake, "Juliet was about fourteen in Shakespeare's play. That actress playing her role must be at least forty!"

But despite the crude attempts of the actors and actresses, Sabrina enjoyed the evening. As they left the makeshift theatre, she thought of the ornate dramas she'd attended in London— and was surprised to discover that she'd enjoyed this drama more than any she could remember!

Drake jumped out of the buggy and jogged around to the other side. Sabrina took his hand, and he led her to the door. "I haven't been up this late in a long time." She turned to face him and smiled up at him. "It was a lovely evening. I had such a good time, Drake."

Drake Hammond was amazed, indeed, at the good time he had enjoyed. He was a man who liked to be pleased and knew how to please women. He had found most of the young women of marriageable age in the settlement—and there were few enough of them—were simple women knowing only the life they had been born into. They were good workers and knew how to keep a house, but this woman was different.

Drake suddenly realized there was something in Sabrina Fairfax that he desired in a woman, something that had been missing. He had traveled more than most men, spending considerable time in New York and Boston, but he had not realized how limited the women were until this evening with Sabrina.

Sabrina was watching Drake and was about to say goodnight when suddenly he moved forward. She knew he was going to kiss her and could have moved away, but she did not. Perhaps it was curiosity, or perhaps there was a little of the temptress in her, but now as he lowered his head, she took his kiss. Her arms went around his neck, and she held him tightly, surprising even herself. She liked Drake Hammond, and there was a loneliness, a vacuum, in her life that grieved her. Now he held her tightly and she returned his kiss fully and without reservation.

Then suddenly, as if coming to her senses, she turned her head aside and whispered, "Good night, Drake. Thank you for taking me."

Inside the cabin Sabrina undressed quickly and got into bed. She did not sleep, for the day had excited her. She could not shake the memory of Drake Hammond's kiss and wondered if what she felt was the beginnings of love or just her loneliness. She lay there for a long time, the moonlight streaming in through the single window. She thought about all the men who had come calling with their proposals of marriage and tried to imagine life with each of them. She saved Drake for last and allowed herself to relive their good-night kiss one more time. . . .

Housewarming

Seventeen

The Spencers had told Sabrina that a housewarming always followed a cabin raising, but the people were so busy hunting and farming during the summer months that they waited until September to have it. The Spencers arrived soon after Sabrina had finished her breakfast, loaded down with food, and soon the fire was roaring in the fireplace, and the cooking had begun.

By midmorning the yard was full, as was the cabin. Most of the visitors had brought gifts, all useful things that a new-comer could use. One family brought a powder horn for carrying gunpowder, she learned, scraped thin and polished, another a leather-shot pouch, another a tinderbox. Soon Sabrina sat in a pile that included a spider, trenchers, gourd vessels, and a host of other items. She was shocked when tears came to her eyes, and she whispered to Hannah, "I didn't know people could be so kind! How can I ever repay them?"

"You can give at the next housewarming," Hannah answered with a smile. "We have good people here."

The day ended with a dance that went on long into the night. Sabrina danced until she could hardly stand! Finally when all the visitors had left, she turned to Sion and exclaimed, "I'm so tired! I don't think I could dance one more dance."

"It's kind, they are," Sion smiled. "They work hard and they play hard. Best get your rest. You need it!"

Sabrina slept late the day after the housewarming. She had heard Sion stirring earlier, but he had told her the night before that he was going over to help a family that was raising a cabin.

She hated those days she spent alone but knew that such co-operation among neighbors was necessary. The endless list of daily chores had finally become routine to her, but now she decided she deserved a day off. She set out to spend the day reading a book instead of working. She cooked and ate breakfast, then went outside and sat down in the shade of a tree. She had brought this book all the way from England, the only one she had not read at least half a dozen times. It was a novel by Henry Fielding, *Tom Jones*.

She read until noon, then rose, stretched, and went inside. For a time she thought on the book, but often her mind strayed to Drake Hammond. Since he had taken her to town he had been by twice, and each time there had been something in his eyes as well as something in his manner that alerted her. He had said nothing more about marriage, but he was so serious lately, as if he were preoccupied with his thoughts. As she fixed a quick lunch for herself, she thought suddenly, *He's going to ask me to marry him.* The thought startled her, and as she sat down to eat the lunch she had prepared, she wondered, *What will I tell him?*

She was pondering her answer and finding none when suddenly the door opened, and Sabrina's blood froze as two Indians burst into the room. They were both wearing white men's clothes, but their hair was braided, and there was a bold look in their eyes.

"What do you want?" she said. "Get out!"

One of the Indians laughed and said, "Want whiskey."

"There's no whiskey here," Sabrina said. "Now get out!" She had seen Indians before in the village and more than once at the Spencer house, but these two were different. There was a boldness in their manner, and fear clutched at her. She thought for a moment of the gun that was over the fireplace but knew it was not loaded, and even if it were, she could not possibly get to it. Both Indians moved forward, and one of them suddenly reached down and grabbed the food that was on her plate and began eating it. The other man, who was short and muscular, stood watching her, his eyes glittering.

The Indian who had eaten her food began wandering around. He pulled the can holding sugar off the shelf fastened to the wall, opened it, and began eating it with his fingers. The sugar covered his mouth, giving him a more sinister appearance.

When the shorter of the two came forward, Hannah backed away, and he laughed at the fear in her eyes. She backed up until she touched the wall and cried out, "Stay away from me!" She could smell the rank odor of his body, and he reached for her, but then suddenly whirled at the sound of a voice speaking his own language in the doorway. She glanced quickly at the door, and relief washed through her when she saw Fox standing there with a musket in his hands. He spoke shortly and curtly, and one of the Indians reached for the knife in his belt. Fox raised his rifle, and his voice was cold as he spoke again in the Indian language.

For one moment it seemed to Sabrina that the two would ignore the rifle, but then Fox pulled the hammer back and leveled it at the short, squatty Indian. He spoke one word, and Sabrina could see his finger tighten on the trigger.

The muscular Indian grunted, cast a glance of hatred at Fox, and then moved quickly out the door. His companion followed him. Fox moved to watch as they left, and Sabrina stepped to the door. She saw the two look back, and one of them called something in a taunting voice.

Fox did not answer, but when the two disappeared into the woods, he turned and said, "Probably a good thing I stopped by."

"Fox, I was frightened to death."

"I don't think they would have harmed you. Is Sion at the cabin raising?"

"Yes, he left early this morning."

"I'm going there myself. Are you all right, Miss Fairfax?"

"I don't know. I was so frightened," she repeated.

"Might be a good idea for you to keep a loaded gun around when Sion isn't here. I'll warn him that he needs to. Those two aren't vicious. Just pesky."

"Are they Cherokee?"

"Yes." Fox's voice was short. "They're no good—a disgrace to their people."

"Would you mind if I accompanied you to the cabin

raising? I'd rather not be by myself right now."

"That's a good idea. Come along."

Sabrina quickly got her bonnet and put on a light coat. She pulled the door shut and said, "There's no way to lock this door."

Fox laughed. "People don't believe in locks around here. There was a man named Porter who lived here a while back. He put a lock on his door, and all the neighbors didn't like him. Said he didn't trust them."

Sabrina forced herself to smile, but she was still troubled. She mounted her horse, and Fox rode beside her. He tried to take her mind off of the scene by talking about the pleasant weather. Finally he said, "Sion's done a good job making this land into a farm. He's learned a lot in a short while. I think his crops are as good as anybody's."

"He's a wonderful farmer. He has a green thumb, and I've got a brown one."

Fox continued to speak about the progress that had been made on Sabrina's land. He asked, "Is there any word about the title to your land, Miss Fairfax?"

"You can call me Sabrina, and I'll call you Fox."

"That sounds good."

"I haven't heard anything, but Mr. Jackson is working on it."

"He's a good man. He'll get to the bottom of it, I'm sure."

The two spoke of titles and land, and Fox apparently knew a great deal about them. He knew about all the treaties the white men had made with the Indians and mentioned that most of them had been violated.

Fox fell silent for a time, then finally he turned and said, "What do you think about Sion and Hannah?"

The question surprised Sabrina. "What do you mean?"

"Surely you must have noticed she favors him."

"Why, I hadn't noticed. He never mentions her."

"Well, she mentions him," Fox said rather grimly. "She talks about him a lot. I think she's interested in him."

Sabrina had picked up enough to know that Hannah and Fox had been interested in each other at one time. Now she turned to study the young man and saw that he looked sad.

"Why, I don't think there's anything to that. You know he's bound to me for five years—a little less now."

"That wouldn't matter to Hannah."

Sabrina found herself troubled by this. She knew that if Sion would marry, his loyalty would lie with his wife and not with her. She had become accustomed to his care, and the thought of losing him was not pleasant. She shook her head. "He's never said a word about her."

"Why, he wouldn't to you," Fox said. "I think it's a bad thing for Hannah."

"That's because you're interested in her yourself, isn't it, Fox?"

"Yes, I am," he said simply.

Later that afternoon while they were getting a drink of water at the cabin raising, Fox found himself telling his uncle what was troubling him. Sequatchie listened, and Fox's remark did not come as a surprise. "You must tell Hannah how you feel."

"Well, I'm not sure myself."

"I think you are. You wouldn't be so troubled if you didn't care for her. She's a wonderful young woman. You couldn't do better."

Fox did not reply, but he carried the words of Sequatchie in his mind all afternoon. During the evening meal Fox managed to sit with Hannah after she had finished serving. He said, "This is good. You're a fine cook, Hannah."

"My mother is. I suppose I've learned a little from her."

The two spoke about unimportant things for a time, and finally, after the others at their table had stood and started to gather for the evening's festivities, Fox turned to her. "Hannah, I want to tell you something."

Hannah's mind had been far away. She had been only half paying attention to their conversation, but now she saw the seriousness on Fox's face. "What is it?" she asked. But even before he answered, she knew. She was young in years but had a great deal of discernment. She remembered how before Fox had left to go back east and settle the matter of his plantation he had told her that he had a special feeling for her. She had not responded except to say that she was glad he liked her. Now, however, she saw that his face was drawn and tight, and she knew what he was going to say.

"I settled all of my affairs when I sold the plantation. I want to buy land, and I want to build a house." He hesitated for a moment and then put his hand over hers. "And I'd like for you to think about marrying me, Hannah. You know I care for you, don't you?"

"Why, Fox . . ." His declaration did not exactly catch Hannah off guard, yet it had come sooner than she had expected. She could not answer for a moment as she thought rapidly. Finally she said, "I'm honored you think of me like that, but I'm not sure it would be a good match."

"It would be for me. You'd be a good wife for any man." When she did not answer, he said, "You're different, Hannah. You've changed."

"Changed? Why, I don't think so."

"You have. I think you cared for me, or were beginning to, before I left. But now you're interested in another man."

Hannah flushed, for he had touched on a nerve. "I don't know why you should say that," she said defensively.

"Because it's true. You're in love with Sion Kenyon!"

"Why, he's never courted me."

"But you've hoped that he would."

Hannah knew his statement was true, but at the same time she wasn't at all sure how she felt. She was confused, for she found Sion one of the most attractive men she had ever known. She had thought, perhaps, it was simply that he was different. His language was different, and he was entertaining. He was also a fine Christian, which she admired. She had watched him carefully for any signs of weakness and had found none. Now, however, she found herself defensively saying, "There's nothing between Sion and me. Why, he's never even tried to court me."

"That's because he's indentured, and that makes it a little more complicated."

"Yes, I suppose you're right."

For a while, neither of them spoke, then suddenly Fox burst out, "If I weren't half Indian, you would feel differently!"

"That's not true!" Hannah responded. "It never has been true and it never will be."

"Yes it is!" Fox said breathlessly. He got up and walked away with his back stiff.

Hannah sat there confused and angry. She was confused by Fox's sudden declaration, for she had not expected it, and she was angry that he had accused her of something that had never entered her mind. Not once had she been put off by Fox's Indian blood. She had found him an attractive young man and had thought that someday he might come courting. She was a sensitive young woman, and Fox's words had hurt her. Now she looked over to where Sion was sitting talking with Hawk and went over at once to sit down beside him. In her hurt it felt good to make him hurt a little too. She saw that Fox was watching them and made herself smile and give her full attention to Sion.

When the young men began to have their usual after-dinner frolic, Fox was still angry. He entered the running race and won, as usual, but when it came time for wrestling and boxing, he shocked everyone when he walked over to Sion and said, "I think I can whip you, Sion. I know you're a fighter and all that, but I don't care."

"Why, Fox!" Sion said, astonishment sweeping over his face. "What are you talking about?"

"I don't think you're as tough as everybody else says. Now, come on!"

Fox squared away, and Sion blinked with astonishment. He looked around and saw that everyone was as surprised as he was. "I don't want to fight you, Fox."

"You're going to have to!" Fox knew he was behaving like a fool, but his anger overrode his common sense. He stepped forward and struck Sion in the mouth, and instantly blood seeped out.

Sion, taken completely off guard, automatically lifted his hands, but he still protested. "This is foolishness, Fox!"

But Fox was determined to finish what he had started. He

threw himself forward, raining blows upon Sion. Hannah cried out, "Stop it, Fox!" But her words only drove Fox on.

Sion caught his balance and managed to block most of the blows, but he did take several, including one in the forehead that stunned him. After defending himself for several minutes, he finally threw a hard right, which caught Fox directly on the jaw. Sion's superior weight and his strength, combined with Fox's forward motion, caught Fox with a solid, meaty blow. It drove Fox backward, and he lay there still, except for his legs, which were twitching.

"I didn't mean to do that," Sion said as he bent over to help Fox up. "Come on, Fox. Let's forget all this nonsense."

But Fox wouldn't acknowledge him. He shook his head and looked around, his eyes falling on Hannah, who was standing stiffly next to Sabrina. "Let me alone, Sion!" he said as he whirled and walked away.

Harvesttime

Eighteen

The courtroom was nothing more than a rough country store, but Andy Jackson held court wherever he could find some space. He had persuaded Judge Thomas Johnson to set up the courtroom in the middle of a mixture of canned food, harnesses, and bolts of cloth. Judge Johnson was a scrawny man with a wispy beard and a pair of sharp eyes that missed very little. He leaned back in a cane-bottomed chair from time to time, taking a bite out of the enormous pickle he had fished out of a barrel and paid for with a few pennies. His mouth puckered with the sourness of the delicacy, and it seemed to irritate him.

"If you two gentlemen will get down to business, I'd appreciate it. I've got to be over at Raven Hill before dark."

Caleb Files spoke up immediately. "Judge, this is a very simple matter. I have a prior claim to this land in question, and all we need is a simple decision on your part to settle it."

Judge Johnson took another bite of the pickle, pursed his lips, and swallowed it before saying, "What say you to that, Mr. Jackson?"

Andy Jackson leaned over and snorted. "I say it's a bunch of fool nonsense! That paper he's got isn't worth the paper it's written on. It was never notarized, and the date has been added in a different hand with a different kind of ink. Now, *my* client's claim is solid, Judge. This deed was made out to Sir Roger Fairfax, and the date's plain and clear. Not tampered with at all. This woman I'm representing is Sir Roger Fairfax's daughter and only heir."

"Are you claiming that I've doctored that paper, Jackson?"

Files said, his face growing red. "That's the same as callin' me a liar!"

"I haven't gotten quite that far yet, Mr. Files," Jackson said, turning his lean face toward his opponent. "You'll know it when I call you a liar. I don't mince words. All I'm saying is that the paper you've got lacks legality."

Judge Johnson listened as the two men argued back and forth. He had been introduced to the case before, and finally in lieu of a gavel he struck his fist down into his open hand. "All right, I've heard enough of this! We'll send these conflicting claims in and let the Continental Congress settle it."

"Fine with me, Judge," Jackson said. He smiled at Files and said, "Unless you'd care to give up your claim right now, Mr. Files."

"I'll see you in Hades first, which is where you're going, Mr. Jackson!"

"Both of us, maybe." Jackson grinned with a wolfish expression. "You take exception to the remark?"

Caleb Files clamped his lips together and turned away and left the courtroom without saying another word.

"I reckon you got him all riled up, Jackson," Judge Johnson said. "Now, listen. Don't you go shootin' him, you hear me?"

"Not unless he provokes me more than he has already, Judge. You know what a patient man I am."

Johnson laughed, took another bite of the pickle, and then extended it to Jackson. "Have a bite," he said.

"Thanks, but I'll pass. I don't see how you eat that mess."

Outside the general store Files fumed as he walked down the main street of Nashville. When he got to his room at the inn, he found Jack Fry sitting beside the window, staring out. He had a whiskey bottle in one hand and extended it.

"Have a snort, Files."

Files took the bottle and drank three quick swallows. He took a deep breath as the alcohol hit him and then handed the bottle back. "You win your case?" Fry asked.

Files cursed vividly and said, "That blasted fool of a judge is sending the titles to the Congress. Now I'll have to hire somebody to look after the case or go myself."

"It seems like a slow way of doin' business. Why don't you just run 'em off?"

Ordinarily Files would have ignored Fry's suggestion, for brute force was always the man's preference. The brutal Fry only understood one method of persuasion. The whiskey had hit Files hard, and he said little but took several more drinks. Fry watched him, meeting him drink for drink, noting that his employer was simmering with anger. "Why don't you just let me run 'em off. It wouldn't be hard. It's just that greenhorn and that dame."

Ordinarily Files would have been more cautious, but now he was fuming over Jackson's cavalier treatment, and he said, "All right, Fry, you can have a try at it."

"You want me to kill 'em? I wouldn't mind that—especially that Welshman."

"They'd hang you for that, Fry. Scare 'em off, but don't shoot 'em."

"I'll find a way."

"Make it look good. I don't want you involved with it. They'd trace you right to me. You know what Jackson's like. He's a fox, and he never lets go."

Fry laughed and said, "I'll get some Indians to do it. Give me some money to buy whiskey for 'em and some beads."

"I got this letter from Mr. Jackson, Hannah," Sabrina said. She took the letter out and began to read it:

"My dear Miss Fairfax,

I have good news. I met with Judge Johnson and our opponent, Mr. Files. Judge Johnson took the right view of the case. Obviously Files's deed had been altered, so Judge Johnson has sent both claims to the Continental Congress. I don't think we'll have any trouble with them. Files, of course, may hire another slick lawyer to argue the case, but I'm hopeful that we'll get this matter settled. It will take at least a month, perhaps a little longer, but things are looking better than I expected.

Your obedient servant,
Andrew Jackson"

"That sounds very good, Sabrina!" Hannah exclaimed. "I know you'll be relieved to get this title settled."

"Yes, I will," Sabrina sighed. Folding the letter up, she put it back in her pocket. Hannah had come over for one of her frequent visits, and the two women had spent the morning putting up the fruits of the harvest. Hannah had been teaching Sabrina how to dry some foods and pickle others. They stored the potatoes, turnips, and onions in the root cellar that Sion had dug. Now they went outside, and Hannah looked over at the garden, which was laden with vegetables of all kinds. "You have a good harvest here."

"I wish you'd take some of it home with you, Hannah. Sion and I can't possibly eat it all."

"I could take some of it for the Herrington family. With all those children they need all the help they can get."

"That's fine. Let's pick an assortment for them."

The two women talked as they moved through the garden picking vegetables for the Herringtons. After a time Sabrina asked cautiously, "Have you seen Fox since the fight?"

"No," Hannah said shortly. "He hasn't been around."

"I was sorry to see it."

Hannah had been embarrassed by the scene, and now she turned to Sabrina and shook her head. "It was all foolishness."

"Everybody thought it was because Fox was jealous of Sion."

Hannah did not answer, and for a time the two women were silent. Finally Hannah looked at Sabrina and said, "He had no cause to pick a fight with Sion."

"Are you sure about that?" Sabrina said, and her voice was sharper than she intended. "Everyone knows you favor Sion."

"Do you think that?"

"Yes, I do. You two get together every chance you have, and you're always laughing and having fun together."

"Everyone likes Sion."

"It seems Fox doesn't—at least not anymore."

Hannah flushed as she continued picking green beans. "I was surprised at Fox. He hardly ever gets angry."

"A man in love is likely to be angry when someone tries to steal his woman."

"I'm not his woman! We've never had an understanding."

"That's not what I heard. Everyone says you favored him."

Hannah could not answer, and finally Sabrina added, "I hate when people give advice unasked, but if I were you, I'd talk to Fox."

"Talk to him! He won't even come around."

"You can find him if you want to."

"And what would I say to him?" Hannah was disturbed.

Sabrina said, "Just tell him you're not interested in Sion— and you shouldn't be."

Hannah straightened up. "What do you mean by that?" she said, her voice sharper than it had been.

Sabrina knew she had touched a nerve. "I mean he's a bound servant for four and a half more years. He can't be thinking about marriage."

"He's got a right to get married if he wants to!"

"Hannah, don't even think of it. What kind of a life would you have? He'd be working for me full time. He wouldn't have time to build his own cabin."

Hannah stared at Sabrina. "You know what I think? You're a jealous woman!"

Both women had said more than they intended to, and Sabrina said, "I think it's better we not talk about this anymore."

"You're right," Hannah said. There was a silence while Sabrina squatted to pick some squash, then she said, "I'm sorry. I didn't mean to speak so sharply."

"I'm sorry too. You've been such a friend to me, Hannah. Let's not quarrel."

Even though the two women had apologized, there was still an awkwardness between them, and Sabrina was relieved when Hannah went home. She continued working with the vegetables for a good part of the day and was nearly finished when Sion came in for a midafternoon snack.

"Did Hannah stop by?" Sion said. "I thought I saw her horse."

"Yes, she was here."

"Why did she leave early? She usually stays all day."

"I suppose she had things to do."

Sion was sensitive to the moods of his employer. He watched her covertly as he ate a big hunk of bread, and when she said nothing else about Hannah, he went outside to enjoy the fresh air and began whittling on a stick. Ulysses came up and gave him a curious look. "You're a curious cat, Ulysses. Don't you know curiosity killed the cat?"

"Yeow!" Ulysses said and rubbed against his leg. Sion picked up the big cat. "You're getting fat," he said. He stroked the animal and enjoyed listening to the purr. "You're a spoiled fellow. I wish someone would spoil me that way."

After a time Sabrina came out and threw the dishwater out on the ground. "Don't spoil that cat," she said. "There are rats in the house."

"They're not rats. They're mice. I think they're rather cute. There'll be even more coming in as it gets colder. You ought to feel sorry for them. They're harmless fellows."

"I hate mice."

"One comes to my lean-to every night, and I feed him crumbs. Or *her*, rather. She's a mother. I haven't seen any of her pups yet."

"I don't like mice or rats. Now put that cat down."

Surprised at her tone, Sion put the cat down and then stood up. "Something bothering you?"

"I don't like it that you're courting Hannah Spencer."

"Me? I'm not courting anyone!"

"You're giving a pretty good imitation of it. Enough that you and Fox had a fight over her."

"That was all his doing," Sion said defensively. "I hate it worse than anyone. He's a good friend of mine. He just got tangled up in his own harness."

"Well, I think you should stay away from Hannah."

Sion Kenyon was an easygoing man, but her words rubbed against him. "Miss, I'll do the work, but I'll see whomever I like."

It was the first time Sion had ever spoken to her sharply, and Sabrina seemed surprised. She put her hands on her waist and said, "Don't forget you're working for me for the next four and a half years!"

"No question about that. If you find fault with my work, let me know."

"You know I don't find fault with that. You've been a hard worker, and I'm pleased. But you're going to hurt Hannah."

"That's between her and me."

"And Fox. He's a fine man and he loves Hannah. Do you?"

Sion stared at her. "Miss Fairfax," he said formally, "have I asked you if you love Drake Hammond?"

"No, and you'd better not."

Sion couldn't help himself from laughing. "I think you're as mixed up as Fox is. Everyone says you're going to marry him."

"I probably will."

"You'd better not," Sion said quietly.

"Why not?" she said with a challenging look flashing in her eyes.

"Because you don't love him."

The simple statement seemed to catch Sabrina off guard and anger her. "How would you know about a thing like that? Are you an expert in love?"

Sion knew he had gone too far. He was silent for a moment and looked down at the ground studying Ulysses. Then he lifted his head and said quietly, "It's all written in your eyes, miss," then turned and walked away.

The conversation with Sabrina had troubled Sion greatly. He knew that both of them had spoken out of turn, and he was sorry for his own part in it. "You talk like a fool, man," he said aloud as he walked down to the creek where he knew deer sometimes came to water. He had taken his rifle and used hunting as an excuse to get away from the cabin. "What business is it of yours if she marries Drake Hammond? But on the other hand, what business is it of hers if I find Hannah Spencer attractive?"

He shook his head in disgust and tried to push the matter out of his mind. He examined the sand along the creek for signs of deer but found no fresh tracks. His stomach told him it was close to suppertime, so he headed back toward the cabin. He was still preoccupied with the confrontation with Sabrina and went back over their conversation in his head.

Just then he felt something strike him in the back and thought it must have been a rock, for he felt no pain. He looked down and saw with a sudden cold shock that an arrow-head had penetrated his body and was sticking out of his chest. He stood in disbelief for a moment, and then the pain struck. He turned to see where the arrow had come from and saw an Indian laughing and crying out in his own tongue. Sion raised his musket and squeezed off one shot, which hit the Indian in the shoulder.

Sion saw the Indian turn and run just before Sion fell to the ground on his side. The pain was worse now, and he looked down to study the arrow. It was stuck high in his chest, and the end of the arrow was covered with blood. There was more rich blood leaking out of his shirt around the arrow. The pain grew worse, but he knew he had to get help. He slowly got up, feeling the blood running down his back, and began walking unsteadily toward the cabin. He had gone no more than a hundred feet when he grew dizzy, and he felt himself falling. He was able to direct his fall sideways, trying to avoid striking the arrow. A red curtain fell across his eyes, but he couldn't stop now. He pulled himself to his knees and began to crawl to the cabin.

Got to get—to the cabin.

The red curtain was blinding him, and he was conscious only of the terrible pain and the weakness that was draining the life out of him.

A Horrifying Injury

Nineteen

$\mathscr{S}$abrina put the bowls on the table and went over to the fire, where she tested the meat with a fork, finding it tender. She was making stew, and the odor of the meal filled the cabin. She placed the fresh bread on a plate and covered it with a cloth to keep it warm.

Going to the window, she scanned the area, but Sion was nowhere in sight. She had gone out twice to call him, but he had not come in nor had he answered her call. She knew his musket was gone and assumed he had gone hunting as he often did late in the afternoon. She poured herself a cup of hot coffee and sat down at the table wondering if she should go ahead and eat without him. Darkness was falling quickly, and the lamp threw its amber glow over the cabin. After peering out the window once more, she sat in the chair Sion had made and covered with a deer hide cushion stuffed with grass. She picked up her book and tried to read but could not concentrate. Ever since the Indians had come to trouble her she had been nervous about being alone, and now she wished Sion would come back. She thought of the quarrel they had had and muttered, "I shouldn't have spoken to him like that. It was none of my business."

She tried again to read, forcing herself to move her lips, but the words meant little. Finally she straightened, for she thought she had heard something. "Sion?" she said nervously. She picked her musket off of the pegs and moved cautiously to the door. She opened the door slowly and stepped outside, whispering, "Sion—?" There was no answer for a moment, and then she heard a tiny noise—unmistakably a voice. She moved forward, puzzled, and said, "Who's there?" She waited again and this time the voice whispered her name.

Sabrina moved forward in the dark and almost stumbled over Sion. She cried out and laid the rifle down. "Sion, what's wrong?" He was lying on his side, and when she tried to turn him over, her hand encountered something unrecognizable at first. As she realized what it was, she stifled a scream. Quickly she felt his back and found the shaft and the feathered tip. Cold fear seemed to paralyze her, and she cried out, "Sion! You've got to get inside the cabin. Can you walk?"

"Don't—think so" came the faint words.

Using all of her strength and encouraging him to help, Sabrina managed to get him to his hands and knees. "Put your arm around me," she commanded, and somehow she managed to get him into the cabin. They had gone no farther than just inside the door when he slipped and began to fall. Fearful that he would injure himself worse with the arrow, she caught him and lowered him gently to the floor. The arrow had entered his back high up on the left side and penetrated his entire body. His shirt was soaked with blood. She had no idea what to do, but she knew she had to stop the bleeding. Quickly she ran to the table and grabbed the scissors and cut his shirt off. The sight of the arrow going through his body was terrible, but she saw the blood running from the entrance and the exit wounds and said, "Sion, I've got to stop the bleeding."

Sabrina could see that Sion was trying to speak, so she put her ear close to his lips and caught the words, "Pull the arrow out."

Sabrina had heard Hawk talk about his fight in the Indian wars. She remembered he had told about getting pierced by an arrow in the leg once and that Sequatchie had cut off the shaft containing the arrowhead and pulled it out. She knew there was no other way. She ran across the room, picked up her sharpest knife, and began to cut at the arrow just below the head. She knew it must be terribly painful and whispered, "I'm sorry, but I've got to do it."

The shaft of the arrow was slender and cut easily. By the time the head dropped off, her hands were wet with blood. She dried her hands on a cloth and then placed the cloth over the arrow and put her knee on Sion's back. Taking a deep breath, she gripped the arrow as hard as she could and gave a pull. The arrow came out much easier than she had expected, and she fell over backward. Scrambling to her feet, she reached under her dress to rip one of her petticoats. Tearing it into strips, then folding it quickly, she put a wad over the exit wound in front and another one on the wound at the back, both of which were bleeding freely. She held the bandages in place, wondering how to bind them. Finally she released the bloody wads long enough to tear several more strips of fabric. Working as fast as she could, she fastened long strips of fabric tightly around Sion's chest, then stuffed fresh pads of fabric under the strips to cover the wounds both front and back.

When they were firmly in place, Sabrina said, "Sion, you've got to get into the bed." She leaned over and saw that his face was paler than she had ever seen it. His eyes were closed, and when she placed her hand on his throat, she had difficulty finding his pulse. She knew she could not lift him into the bed, so she pulled the blankets off the bed and tried to make him comfortable on the dirt floor. She sat beside him and pulled his head and shoulders into her lap. Holding his limp body as she would a child, she rocked back and forth and began to pray. "God, don't let him die—please don't let him die!"

When Hannah slipped off her horse the next morning, she saw that the door was open. It was very early, barely half an hour after sunrise, and she had ridden over to get Sabrina to go into town with her. She tied her horse to an oak tree and stepped inside. "Sabrina, where—" She stopped abruptly, for there on the floor before her she saw Sabrina sitting beside a sleeping Sion. She took in the blood-stained bandages and with a cry she fell on her knees. "Sabrina, what happened?"

"It was an arrow. I pulled it out and got the bleeding stopped, but I can't move him. I'm afraid he's going to die."

Hannah quickly felt for Sion's pulse and looked at the wounds. "When did this happen?"

"Last night. I found him on the ground outside the cabin. I was afraid to leave him to go and get help."

"We've got to get him onto the bed."

Hannah waited while Sabrina stood and shook the feeling back into her numb legs, and then they worked together to drag Sion, who was totally limp, over to the bed. They eased him into it as carefully as they could.

"I've got to see how these wounds are," said Hannah as she began to remove the blood-soaked bandages. Sabrina, without a word, began to tear up her only other petticoat.

Hannah gently pulled the dried bandage from Sion's chest and examined the wound. It was clean but still bleeding slightly. She pressed the bandage back on his chest while checking his back. The back wound seemed to be bleeding slightly also. Sabrina placed the new bandages she had just folded firmly under the strips of fabric that were still encircling Sion's chest.

"We've got to make him drink something," said Hannah. "He's lost so much blood that he's probably dried out."

"He can't drink if he's unconscious."

"We'll have to try to wake him up."

The two women managed to pull Sion into a sitting position, and Hannah held a cup of water. She dribbled a few drops into Sion's partially open mouth, and he closed his lips.

"Sion, you've got to drink something," Hannah urged.

For some time it seemed hopeless, and then Sion coughed and opened his eyes, staring blankly out of them.

"Sion, try to swallow. You've got to drink all you can."

With much effort, the two women managed to get a cup of water down Sion, though he still stared at them with unseeing eyes.

"He feels like he's got a fever," Hannah said. "That often happens with a bad wound."

"We need to go get help."

"There's no doctor, but Dad could help him. He's good with wounds."

"Go get him."

"Are you all right?"

"I'll be all right. Go get help."

Hannah said, "He's lost a lot of blood, but I think he'll live."

"He's got to live. He can't die," Sabrina whispered.

Hannah left the cabin at once and spoke sharply to her horse. "Get up, Lady!" She drove the horse at a dead run out of the yard and kept the mare at that pace until she came to her own home. She saw her father out chopping wood and yelled, "Father, Sion's been shot by an arrow. He's in Sabrina's cabin." She watched as Hawk, without even a reply, ran for his horse, piled onto it, and drove out furiously. "He's got to be all right," Hannah said. "He can't die."

———————

Sabrina had lost track of the hours and had slept only in fitful stretches, but she knew it was the third day since Sion had been shot. Hawk had stayed the entire time and even now was outside the cabin attending to the horses. Hannah had gone home after taking her turn nursing, and now Sabrina sat beside the wounded man. She put her hand on his head and found it burning. The fever had come and gone over these last three days. When Hawk had first come they had stripped off Sion's outer clothing. Now Sabrina dipped a cloth into a bucket of cool water. She wrung it out and put it over his chest and then did the same for his lower body. Now she leaned forward and stared at Sion's face. His cheeks were sunken, and the fever had brought red marks to his cheeks. Otherwise he was as pale as he had been when she first found him. Sabrina had made a thin broth, and during his brief periods of consciousness had almost force-fed him.

"He's got to eat. It'll build the blood back," Hawk had said.

For a time Sabrina sat there filled with weariness. These last three days had been the hardest time of her life, and as she sat for hour after hour beside the wounded man, she found herself filled with hopelessness and doubts. He was so pale and weak. He had always been so strong, and now his strong body was useless to him.

She sat there in the quiet room watching Ulysses stretch and cross the room to jump up on the bed. "Go away, Ulysses," she whispered. She waited until the cat had strode across the room and curled up in front of the fireplace, then removed the wet cloths from Sion, noting how his body had heated them up. She dipped the cloths in the cool water and placed them on Sion again. There wasn't much else she could do for him except pray, which had quickly become a habit. She had never been a woman of prayer, but the words came to her even so. "Oh, God, don't let him die!"

The darkness seemed endless, and Sion felt as though he had been buried in some deep hole filled with a heat that was unimaginable. From time to time he would come to the surface of the dark hole and feel a coolness. He knew there were hands touching him, and once he had reached out and touched something soft and yielding. He thought he heard his name being whispered, but then he had sunk back down into the darkness again.

But now this was different; the darkness seemed to be gone. Sion opened his eyes and saw sunlight streaming through the window. A shadow was beside him, and he turned to see Sabrina. Her face was pale and her eyes were closed. He whispered her name and her eyes instantly flew open and her hands went to his face.

"Sion, you're awake!"

"Aye." Her hands were cool on his face, and he moved his head restlessly. "What's happened?" he murmured, and confusion filled his mind.

"You were wounded. You were shot by an arrow."

Sion suddenly remembered the pain and crawling back to the cabin. He looked down to see that he was wearing only his undergarments and his chest was bare except for a bandage on the upper part. "I've had a fever, haven't I?"

"You nearly died," Sabrina said. "Can you sit up and drink some water?"

"Aye." Sion felt her arm behind his back pulling him up to a sitting position. "How long have I been here?"

"Nearly three days. We've been forcing you to eat. Are you hungry now?"

"Aye," Sion said. "I am."

"I'll get you something."

Sion watched as Sabrina got up and went across the room.

She came back quickly with a bowl of grits and said, "Eat all you can of this."

Sion suddenly realized he was ravenous. He took the bowl and ate until the grits were all gone. "That was good," he said. He handed the bowl back and then took the water she handed him and drank thirstily.

"I don't remember getting here."

Sabrina bent over him and wiped his face with a damp cloth. "You crawled back to the door."

"But the arrow. It was all the way through me. I remember that. Who took it out?"

"I did."

"You did!" Sion stared at her. "How did you do that?"

"I cut the head off and pulled it out, and then I put some bandages on you to stop the bleeding."

"How did you get me into bed?"

"Hannah came by the next morning. The two of us have been nursing you, and Hawk, too. He's outside somewhere. I'd better go tell him you're all right."

He reached out and took her hand, and when she stopped, he fixed his eyes on her. "I feel so weak," he said, "but I'd be dead if it wasn't for you."

"I'm glad I was here to help, Sion."

He released her then and lay back, feeling weak. He heard her calling Hawk's name, and then he went to sleep again.

When Sion awakened, he heard voices, and he quickly opened his eyes. He saw Fox standing over him on one side and Hannah on the other. Then his eyes went across the room, and he saw Sabrina. "Hello, Fox," he said.

Fox looked down at him and said, "Well, you're going to live after all."

"Let me out of this bed."

"You stay right where you are," Hannah said firmly. "You're not about to get out of bed. Not for a few days."

"Well, I could at least sit up."

With Hannah and Fox both helping, Sion wriggled into a sitting position. Once he was sitting, he remembered he wasn't wearing much clothing. A coverlet was pulled up over his lower body, but he was still mostly naked.

"I'm not hurt that bad."

"Not hurt that bad," Fox said. "You get an arrow through your chest, and you say you're not hurt?"

Sion felt rather foolish. "I guess you're right."

"Did you see the Indian who put this arrow in you?" Fox said.

"Yes, I got a shot off with my musket. If I hadn't, I think he would have taken my scalp. He ran off into the woods."

"I wonder if he was a Seneca. But then again, a Seneca wouldn't usually come down this far—"

"You two can do your talking later," interrupted Sabrina. "He needs to eat."

Hannah moved to let Sabrina get closer. "I'll be going home now."

Sion said, "Hannah, you've been good to help take care of me. I feel like such a baby."

Hannah smiled. "I'm glad you're all right."

Fox put his hand on Sion's shoulder. "I made a fool out of myself at Sabrina's housewarming. I'm sorry."

"It's all right," Sion said. "I'd hate for you to know how many times I've made a fool out of myself."

Fox grinned and said, "We men do that. I'll be back to see you later." He turned and left with Hannah, and Sabrina came over and said, "Do you want to try something solid? How about a piece of this steak and some coffee?"

"I can get up and eat."

"No, you can't," Sabrina said. "You sit right there. Eat it all if you can."

Sabrina sat down and watched Sion eat. "Do you want sugar in your coffee?"

"Yes, all you can spare."

Sabrina took the coffee, sugared it liberally, and brought it back. She watched him while he drank it, and finally when he handed her the empty cup, he said, "I really would like to sit up in a chair."

Sabrina hesitated. "I suppose you are getting tired of that bed."

"Let me get my trousers on."

Sabrina pulled his trousers and his shirt off the hook on the wall. "Do you think you can get into them by yourself?"

"If you'll just get my feet into my trousers, maybe I can do the rest."

She did as she was asked, then turned her back while he finished getting dressed. He held on to her shoulders while he got slowly to his feet, then stood there for a moment swaying. He was surprised at his weakness. "Why, I'm as weak as a kitten!" he exclaimed.

"You lost a lot of blood. Take it easy, now. Let me help you to the chair."

"I'd like to look out the door."

"You'll sit down where the chair is," Sabrina said firmly. She maneuvered him to the chair, and when she got there, she turned to face him so she could lower him. Instead, he kept his hands on her shoulders and held her for a moment.

"I'm trying to think of some way to thank you, Sabrina." The realization hit him that this was the first time he had addressed her by her first name without a title of some sort. He had always called her *miss*, which was the proper way for a servant to address his mistress.

Sabrina didn't seem to notice as she looked into his eyes and said, "I'm glad I was around, Sion."

For a moment he just stood there, aware of her strength and beauty. He finally said simply, "You know, I never realized. We all have to have someone to hold on to."

Sabrina didn't answer for a while, then finally said, "Yes, you're right. Now, sit down." She eased him into the chair. "You'll have to be still. I'll fix you something good to eat. What would you like?"

"Blackberry cobbler," he said with a grin.

"All right." Sabrina returned the smile. "Blackberry cobbler it will be."

PART V

The
Captives

December 1792 – March 1793

A Time of Giving

Twenty

*F*ox had come to the Spencers' place to help smoke the venison, but his main motive was to make a final plea to Hannah. Ever since he had told her of his love, he had felt an uncertainty that had deepened into unhappiness. He had watched Hannah's actions, and at times it seemed to him that her feelings for Sion had changed, but at other times he could not be sure. Now finally the work was done, and Sion and Sabrina mounted their horses, preparing to leave.

"Thanks for your help," Hannah said with a smile.

"You're welcome. Come over and see us as soon as you can, both of you."

Fox and Hannah waved, watching the pair ride off, and Hannah commented to Fox, "It's been so good having Sabrina living so close. We've become very good friends."

"She's a good neighbor," Fox said briefly. He hesitated and then took a deep breath before saying, "Hannah, I've got to talk to you."

"Well, come along. Let's take a walk," Hannah said.

The two strolled under a sky gray as slate and unmarked by any clouds. It was the middle of December, and the air was frigid. From over the mountains came a cold breath warning of snow, which Fox mentioned as they walked along. "It's going to snow, but I don't mind that."

"Neither do I. I've always liked snow."

"Do you remember the snow fight we had three years ago?"

"Yes, that was a good time. We built a fort and divided up into teams and had a snow war. I remember you hit me in the ear with a hard snowball and made me cry." Hannah laughed.

"I know. I felt so bad about it. I offered to let you hit me with a stick."

"I should have taken you up on it. It didn't hurt nearly as bad as I made out, though. I just wanted to make you feel bad."

"You're a devious person," Fox said with a smirk.

They continued speaking of other Christmases and good times in the past, and Fox was trying to find the perfect opportunity to tell Hannah what she meant to him.

Finally the moment came. Fox reached out and took Hannah by the arm. "Hannah, I wish I knew how to tell you how I feel." He struggled for words and then grimaced, turning the corners of his mouth awry. "All the words in this language, and I can't think of the ones to say to make you know how I feel." He pulled himself together then and said simply, "I love you, Hannah. I have for a long time. But it was just a boy's love for a young girl. Now it's a man's for a woman."

Hannah seemed to be trying to think of a proper answer but nothing came, and finally she shook her head. "I'm confused, Fox."

"Well, tell me this. Do you love Sion Kenyon?"

The words hung in the air, and Fox felt as if he stood before a judge and jury, but his fate lay not in the hands of a group of men nor of a judge but of this woman who stood before him. He studied her face, noting again how beautiful she was. Her skin was as clear as any he had ever seen. Her eyes were bright and expressive, and now he noted that there was a depth to them that he hadn't noticed before. But it was not her physical attractiveness so much as what lay inside that drew Fox. This young woman was completely honest and fiercely loyal. The man she chose would get all of her. There would be nothing left for anyone else, and Fox yearned for this loyalty to be his.

Finally, after what seemed to be an inner struggle, Hannah whispered, "I don't know, Fox. I thought I was in love with Sion, but now I don't think so. I like him so much. He's such a good man, but I've always thought when I met the man I'd marry, there would be more than that. A woman has to respect that man she'll live with the rest of her life, but there has to be more."

"What does there have to be?" Fox demanded.

"I don't know how to put it into words. I'm like you, I guess. But there has to be something in a woman's heart that won't let her look at any other man. Something deep rooted that will never change."

"I hope you feel that for me."

Hannah answered quietly, "Maybe I do. Or maybe I will. You have to give me some time. I was wrong about what I thought I felt for Sion, but I have to be sure. You can see that, can't you, Fox?"

"Of course." He put his hands on her shoulders, and then simply put his arms around her and held her gently. Finally he released her and smiled, saying, "We'd better go on home. Your parents will be worried about you. I've got to stay on the good side of them. One day, Hannah, I'll be going to your father and asking for your hand."

"What will you do if he says no?"

"I'll run off with you like a wild Indian."

"You're not wild. You're the gentlest man I know, Fox." Hannah put her hand on his cheek and then laughed. "Come along. I'll race you home."

The next day Hannah rode over to see Sabrina, who was practicing some of the embroidery skills Elizabeth had taught her. Hannah watched Sabrina for a few moments, and finally she turned to her friend and said, "I know you've been worried that I might feel something for Sion."

"Well, yes, I have."

"You don't have to worry about that."

"What's happened? You changed your mind?"

"I think I had some sort of foolish attraction to him. He's so handsome, and he's such a wonderful storyteller. He sings beautifully, and he's such a fine Christian. He's everything I thought I'd ever want in a man, but he's not for me, Sabrina." Hannah smiled. "I told you once you were jealous of me, and I think I was right."

"Don't be foolish, Hannah!"

"What's foolish about it? You two have been together and alone for so long. I know he cares for you. I've seen his eyes follow you whenever you come into sight. But how do you feel about him?"

"I don't have time to think of things like that, Hannah." Sabrina was troubled by the conversation and shook her head almost fiercely. "Until this land issue is settled I have nothing. What if the Continental Congress gives it to Caleb Files? I won't have a place to lay my head. This will all belong to him."

"That's not going to happen. God won't let it happen."

"I wish I had your faith," Sabrina said as she finished another stitch. "I'll marry someday, but I don't know who my husband will be."

"I think you're in love with Sion."

"Don't say that. He's my servant."

"He wouldn't be if you married him. You'd have to release him then, wouldn't you?"

Sabrina laughed. "Of course I would. What man would marry a woman and then be her servant? A man like that I wouldn't have."

They said no more, but as Hannah went home later, she thought of the expression on Sabrina's face when the question of marrying Sion came up. "She loves him. I'm sure of it," Hannah said aloud. "She just hasn't realized it yet."

———

Christmas came quickly as the month passed. On Saturday, the twenty-fourth of December, Sabrina and Sion were sitting before the fireplace. He had been cleaning his gun and telling her stories of his days back in Wales during his boyhood. He told a story so well, better than anyone Sabrina knew. He knew all the old myths and fables of Wales, and she loved to hear his musical voice as he spoke of them. There was a poetic streak in him, and he had a way of putting things that pleased her.

Suddenly as Sabrina sat there, she thought, *Why, we're like an old married couple sitting here. I couldn't have done this when we first left England.*

The thought startled her, and Sion looked up at her and said, "What's wrong?"

"Nothing. Why do you ask?"

"You had an odd look on your face."

"Maybe I have an odd-looking face."

"That you do. None other like it," he said with a grin.

The two sat there talking for a time, and finally Sion replaced the rifle on a peg driven into the log wall of the cabin. He turned to her and smiled. "It's a present I have for you. Will you have it now or wait until tomorrow morning?"

Sabrina looked up and saw that he was smiling at her. "I'll have it now, and I have one for you, too."

"Wait here," he said. "I'll get your gift."

He disappeared outside the cabin, and Sabrina removed the chest from under her bed. She took out the package that had lain there for some time, and when she returned Sion was coming in the door. "Going to be snow tomorrow. It'll be a winter wonderland."

He had a package in his hand, but she handed him the one in her hand. "You first, Sion."

"Right you are." He took the package she handed him and untied the string. Putting it in his pocket carefully, he said, "I'm getting to be a miser. Always saving bits of string and nails that I would pay no heed to back home." He removed the paper and opened a box. He stood looking at it for a moment before looking up. "Goodness, woman, what have you done!"

"Do you like it?"

Sion removed the pistol and held it almost reverently. "What a beautiful thing it is! Feel the balance of it." But he did not surrender the weapon to her. He held it out at arm's length and ran his hand over the smooth coldness of the metal. He shook his head in wonder. "A finer weapon I have never seen. It's too fine a gift for you to give me."

"No it isn't. A peddler came by with it a month ago. I saw it and knew you had to have it. There's some powder and balls for it, too."

Sion could not get over his wonder at the beauty of the weapon. Sabrina did not think weapons were beautiful things, but she was pleased that he liked it so much.

"Tomorrow we'll have a shooting lesson. You'll have to learn to use it, too." He put the pistol back in the box and picked up the package he had brought. "Merry Christmas, Sabrina Fairfax."

Sabrina untied the string that held it and said with a smile, "I'm a miser, too. Put this with the other string." She unfolded the paper and then gasped. "Sion, what is this!"

"Something to keep you warm."

The gift was a beautiful fur hat with a flat top and a matching pair of mittens. Sabrina put the round hat on her head, and it fit her perfectly. "It's so beautiful!" she exclaimed. Then she slipped the mittens on and rubbed the fur against her cheeks. "I've never seen fur like this. Where did you get it? What is it?"

"It's ermine. Fox got it some time ago from his uncle, who got it from an Indian who trapped it. He said it's the rarest kind of fur. There were two of them, just enough to make this."

"You must have paid a lot of money for it."

"Not so much. Sequatchie made a good trade, and then he gave it to Fox. But Fox sold it to me."

"It's so soft but so warm. Feel the fur." Sabrina moved her mittened hand across his cheek. He reached up suddenly and caught her hand in his. "You look beautiful in it," Sion said simply.

Sabrina looked up at him and said, "Sion, are you ever sorry you met me at all?"

He stared at her with surprise. "Sorry? Why would I be sorry?"

"Because I got you into trouble. You were going to prison because of helping me, and now you're a bond servant."

Sion removed the mitten from Sabrina's hand and lifted her hand to his lips. He kissed the back of it gently and smiled fully. "Meeting you has been the best thing that has ever happened to me, Sabrina."

Sabrina was moved by his simple words. Her hand felt like it glowed where he kissed it, and when he released it, she could not meet his gaze. "That's a lovely thing to say, and it's a lovely present."

"Tomorrow we'll go to church, and then we'll have a shooting lesson when we get home."

"All right, Sion. If you say so."

———

The church was full as Rev. Paul Anderson announced his text. "If you have your Bibles, turn to the gospel of Matthew, chapter eleven, verses twenty-eight through thirty." Anderson waited until those with Bibles found the verse, then read aloud: " 'Come unto me, all ye that labour and are heavy laden, and I will give you rest. Take my yoke upon you, and learn of me; for I am meek and lowly in heart: and ye shall find rest unto your souls. For my yoke is easy, and my burden is light.' "

The minister's words echoed in the stillness of the room before he plunged into his sermon. "In one sense all of us have different needs—but one thing we all need—and that is *rest*. But where will we find it? Money can't buy it, for we all know that rich men and women often have terrible lives. And can you imagine any other human in history saying such a thing? Could Caesar have promised rest to anyone who came to him? You well know he couldn't!"

Anderson smiled and said firmly, "I don't know your burden, but I know that Jesus says to bring it to Him. He promises you will find rest for your souls. . . ."

Sabrina listened intently to the sermon. Usually the words of ministers had little meaning for her, but today the message seemed meant for her alone. She said little after the service was over as she smiled and greeted friends and neighbors. She thought of how close she had gotten to these simple people. England seemed a million miles away, and her life there lifetimes away.

———

That afternoon, after a simple noon meal, the two of them practiced with Sion's new pistol until they shot up all of the ammunition. Sabrina laughed at her own ineptness and was amazed at what a good shot Sion was. He shook off her praise, saying, "It's a true shooting weapon. Anyone could hit with this."

When they were chilled to the bone and out of ammunition, they went inside, and Sabrina fixed a nice meal of venison steaks, baked potatoes, and acorn squash while Sion warmed up and kept her company near the fire. They ate together, and afterward he read her the story of the birth of Jesus from the Bible. As she listened to the old, old story, she felt tears come to her eyes. She had thought so much lately about Jesus the man, and now the idea of God coming to earth as a baby, helpless and dependent on a woman's care, moved her.

Sion saw the tears in her eyes and whispered, "It's a good thing to weep over the Savior, Sabrina."

Sabrina just nodded and the two sat in comfortable silence as they watched the fire. Sabrina went to bed soon after that, but she lay awake thinking of Jesus, wondering what it would have been like to have seen Him, and found herself longing to know more about this One who had come as a child and had died on a cross to save those who had no care for Him. Finally she whispered, "I have such a burden—can you help me, God?" She waited in the darkness, but no answer came. *Maybe it's not for me. . . .* The thought troubled her, and she tossed and turned for a long time before falling into a fitful sleep.

Terror at Home

Twenty-One

$\mathcal{C}$aleb Files was accustomed to having his own way. Whenever he was opposed, his one impulse was to strike out and use brute force, if necessary, to take what he wanted. His technique had gotten him the things he had accumulated over the years and had bred in him a fiery impatience when things did not go well. He viewed anyone who stood in his way implacably as an enemy, and in the opening months of 1793 Files focused on Sabrina Fairfax as his enemy.

The legislature had been buried under a mountain of requests for title clarification. After the Revolution the Continental Congress had deeded land grants to almost all the officers who served in the Continental Army and smaller grants to those who served in the ranks. Many of these had to do with lands whose boundaries were vague and obscure. They were complicated by treaties with the Indians and conflicting claims by various states.

Caleb Files had waited impatiently. He had been successful in gobbling up almost all of the lands he had set his heart on, but Sabrina Fairfax was settled square in the middle of a large tract of land, and he lusted after a clear title to the whole enormous section. His failure to get his hands on it made him irritable, and inevitably he came to the conclusion that he was going to have to use stronger methods. His only confidant, Jack Fry, saw this coming, and late in February Files finally signaled the end of his patience.

"I've *got* to get that land the Fairfax dame is sitting on, Fry."

"I told you the government would never help you. You've

gotta be right in the middle of them lawyers and congressmen to get anything out of 'em."

"You're right. So, we're going to have to put some pressure on the girl. She's bound to be broke. I offered her a pretty fair price, but she turned me down."

"If the woman was dead, you wouldn't have any trouble, Files."

Files turned and stared silently at Fry. He knew Jack Fry to be a man of vicious temperament. He had killed before and seemed to have no more scruples than a wild animal. "That's right," he said. "But I told you, Fry, I'd be the first one they'd suspect if anything happened to her."

"Not if the Indians killed her."

"I don't want to know anything else about this," Caleb said quickly. But his voice was insincere, and he added, "Of course, I'd save a lot of money. I wouldn't mind spreading some of it around if something happened to the Fairfax woman."

"I need a little money in advance, Files."

Caleb Files hesitated for a moment. He had not sunk quite as low as Jack Fry, yet his greed took possession of him. He took some gold coins out of the safe and said, "I don't want to hear any of the details, Fry."

Fry did not answer. He fondled the gold, letting the coins ring in his hands as he rippled them, and he grinned wolfishly. "I'll see you later. I have some business."

Fire Cloud liked to think of himself as a war chief. But then, any warrior who could get a dozen braves to follow him called himself that. He would never be a mighty leader like Dragging Canoe or Tecumseh, but he had the ego of such men. Fire Cloud was not a big man, but he made up in meanness what he lacked in bulk. He was half drunk now, for Jack Fry had plied him with whiskey. He sat listening as Fry spoke, his obsidian eyes glittering, and from time to time he took another pull from the bottle. Whiskey was the Indians' worst enemy and Fire Cloud's best friend more often than not.

" . . . so this is what I want, and I got plenty of whiskey and guns for you and your warriors."

Fire Cloud studied the white man. He knew Jack Fry was a vicious killer. That did not trouble him in the least. "Five rifles, bullets, powder, and ten kegs of whiskey."

Fry knew he had his man then, and he bargained halfheartedly until they finally settled on a lesser price. He leaned forward and said harshly, "Let's go over this again so I'm sure you understand. You have to kill the woman, but leave the man— Sion Kenyon. Put some of your arrows in her that can be identified. Take her scalp."

Fire Cloud shrugged. "Yes. We will kill the woman. Now give me the guns and the whiskey. . . ."

"I never heard of hominy grits when I lived in England," Sabrina said. She smiled, and her laugh filled the cabin. "Maybe I can go back and get rich by teaching the English to love hominy grits like they love roast beef."

"I'll go with you," Hannah said. "You can introduce me to King George."

"I'm afraid I didn't travel in his circles."

The two women were having a lively conversation about the differences between England and America. They had already discussed some of the meats Sabrina had now grown accustomed to.

After a time Sabrina changed the subject, saying, "I haven't forgotten the sermon Rev. Anderson preached on Christmas morning. I don't know why, but I just can't get rid of it."

"You don't want to get rid of it. When a sermon stays with you like that, or even a single verse in the Bible, that's God speaking to you."

"Do you really believe that, Hannah?"

"Of course I do!"

"But with millions of people in the world, do you think God really cares about each one of us on an individual basis?"

"Why, certainly! He knows what each one of us is thinking and every single act we've ever done."

"I can't imagine that."

"Well, try to imagine this, Sabrina. You and I were born at a certain time and we'll die at a certain time. But God wasn't born. He always was, and He knows at this moment everything that everyone who ever lived said and did and thought. It's never out of His mind. So, if you prayed a prayer this morning, God heard it. He always hears our prayers."

Sabrina stared at Hannah. "I can't understand all that. It's too big for me."

Hannah laughed. "It's too big for me, too, but I think that's the way God is. I think that's the way we'll be in heaven. I think we'll always be living with what we did here—the good things, that is. We'll always remember finding Jesus and praising Him and singing to Him. It'll all come back to us. That's the reason we ought to spend as much time loving Him and serving Him as we can."

Sabrina grew quiet, and after a time Hannah changed the subject. "You never mention Drake Hammond anymore."

"There's nothing to mention."

"Everyone thought you'd marry him. Drake certainly thought so."

"He's a handsome man and he has money, but that's all he has."

"Most women would say that's enough."

"You know better than that, Hannah. Those things change. The handsomest men and the most beautiful women lose their looks. I've been thinking about that a lot. Will a man love me when I grow older, my skin toughens up, and I grow gray hairs and lose my teeth?"

"Some men would. Look at my parents. My dad practically worships my mother. He's always saying sweet things to her and touching her. Why, they hold hands half the time when they're walking along together."

"That's sweet, isn't it?"

"Yes, it is. And I want to be just like that with my husband." She turned and said, "Can you see yourself growing old with Sion? I think that's the test of whether you really love a man or not."

Sabrina answered, "You know, I think I really can, but—" Sabrina never finished her sentence, for the door suddenly shot open, and a group of Indians burst into the room. The man in front was small, not much larger than a boy, but his eyes glittered with fury. The two women, paralyzed with fear, backed up against the wall.

Two of the larger Indians started forward. One carried a knife and the other a tomahawk. They laughed drunkenly as they advanced toward the two women. One of them said something to the smaller man, who obviously was the leader. He had a tomahawk in his hand and murder in his eyes, but suddenly the leader seemed to change his mind. "We not kill these women."

One of the braves looked at him and said something in their native language, but the smaller Indian said, "No, we take captives."

Fire Cloud laughed and moved toward the two women. They shrank back from him, and he laughed again. He grabbed Sabrina by the hair and said, "You'll be good squaw." He looked over at Hannah and said, "And I trade you for many horses." He shouted something at the other Indians, and Sabrina guessed his command was, "Take what you want!"

Sabrina couldn't move under the small man's iron grip. She did not cry out, but when she looked at Hannah, she saw that her friend was as filled with fear as she was. But Hannah managed to say, "God will take care of us. The men, they'll come for us."

The Indian's face darkened and he let go of Sabrina's hair just long enough to slap Hannah across the mouth. When she fell backward, he snarled at her, "No, you will be a Cherokee's slave forever!" He grabbed Sabrina's hair again and held the edge of his tomahawk against her temple. "You will learn to please me. I always wanted white woman for squaw."

No One but God

Twenty-Two

The nightmare seemed to be never ending for Sabrina. Her hands had been left free, but Fire Cloud had tied a leather thong around her neck, and when she had stumbled or been unable to keep up with the men, he had jerked at her so that the rough rawhide had worn her neck raw and even caused it to bleed. The same fate had been dealt to Hannah, and the two women were practically dragged along as the Indians hurried through the woods.

They had walked nonstop for four hours, and then Fire Cloud, who led the line of warriors, closely followed by Hannah and her captor, who laughed harshly at Hannah's distress, suddenly stopped. He called out something to his followers and leered at Sabrina. "You rest."

Sabrina was totally exhausted, but she knew that the worst had not yet come. She sat down on the cold ground with her back to a tree and was joined by Hannah. The Indians milled around talking gutturally and examining their prizes. One of them amused himself by putting on one of Sabrina's dresses, which he had stolen. The others gloated over the booty they had taken, and if Sabrina had not been so frightened and shaken to the bottom of her emotional stamina by what had happened, she would have wept to see her possessions being handled by the savages.

She started to remove the rawhide noose from around her neck, but Fire Cloud, who was gnawing on a piece of the dried venison he had brought along from the cabin, reached down and struck her. "No!" he shouted. He glared at her, his eyes glittering, and then laughed at her fright. Going back to the pouches in the sack, he pulled out a bottle of whiskey. He drank it, and the other braves crowded around to join him. They shouted and sang and most of them came around to put their hands on the two women. The roughness of their touch was an abhorrence to both women, but neither of them opened their mouths to protest.

The warrior who had been leading Hannah—they had learned his name was Horse—brought some meat over in his bare hands and threw one chunk down at Hannah and another chunk at Sabrina. He said something in his native language, which they took to mean *eat.*

"We'd better eat all we can," Hannah said. "We're going to need our strength."

Sabrina forced herself to eat the meat, although it was gritty and the thought of it having been in Horse's filthy hand nearly sickened her. Still, she knew Hannah was right.

For a time Sabrina leaned back against the tree and closed her eyes. She was grateful for the coat that one of the Indians had thrust at her as they had forced the women from the cottage. She knew Hannah was praying, for she had seen her lips move, and as she sat there amid the raucous laughter and shouting of the drunken Indians, she found herself wishing she had followed her instinct during the Christmas message. She had felt an urge to simply call upon God in the name of Jesus. She had not done it, and now she wondered despondently why she had not. The thought came to her that she could do it now, but to her that somehow seemed cowardly. *I didn't let God into my life when things were going well, and now I can't go crawling to Him like a beggar.* The thought brought a sense of fresh despondency. She finally stopped thinking altogether and let her mind go blank, though she was conscious of the Indians' drunken voices and their rank smell as they came close. She suddenly came wide awake when a loud voice speaking in English penetrated her thoughts.

"What are these women doing here?"

Sabrina opened her eyes to see Jack Fry standing in front of her. She pleaded, "Get us out of this, please!"

Fry's eyes were as cold as polar ice, and he simply ignored her plea.

Both women were shocked when Fry turned to Fire Cloud and said, "I paid you to kill the woman. And where's the man?"

"He no there."

"Why didn't you kill this woman?"

"We carry them far off. They never be found," Fire Cloud said. His lips moved loosely, and his speech was slurred. His eyes were still bright, but they seemed to be covered with some sort of film.

He was crazy drunk, Sabrina saw. She glanced at Hannah and saw that she was staring at Fry. "He's the one that hired them," Hannah whispered. "He won't help us."

Fry was shouting now, and Sabrina and Hannah were sickened at what they heard. Sabrina well knew why Fry had hired the Indians to kill her. He was on Caleb Files's payroll—an instrument of death in the rich man's hand.

Fry was carried away in a fit of anger. He shouted wildly, "I paid you well, Fire Cloud, and you haven't done your job!"

Fire Cloud grew quieter, and his warriors watched warily from the circle where they had gathered. They knew that unlike some war chiefs, their leader was most dangerous when he was quiet.

Fry cursed and ranted, but Fire Cloud simply shook his head and said stubbornly, "We take women far off. No white man ever find them. Go away."

"I ain't goin' away till these women are dead!"

Fry suddenly pulled a pistol from his belt. He turned toward the two women, saying, "If you won't kill 'em, I will!"

Sabrina saw Fry raise his pistol, and she looked right down the barrel. *This is the end,* she thought dispassionately. She was somehow devoid of fear, and her only thought was, *I've missed so much, and Sion will be grieved.* She waited for the explosion as she watched Fry's finger tighten on the trigger, but suddenly there was a clunking sound, and she lifted her eyes to see Fry's eyes suddenly open wide with shock.

And then Sabrina saw the hatchet. It was buried in Jack Fry's skull clear to the handle. She heard Fire Cloud laugh his high-pitched drunken giggle while the other Indians cried out loudly and lifted their fists.

Jack Fry dropped the pistol and reached up to touch the hatchet in his head, but he was already falling and was dead before he hit the ground.

Both women stared in horror at the dead man, then Fire Cloud wrenched his hatchet from Fry's skull. He kicked the dead man in the face, laughed, and said, "We go now."

Grasping the rawhide, he jerked at it and it tightened around Sabrina's neck. She was half strangled as he dragged her out of the clearing. She did not look back, nor did Hannah, as they left the dead body of Jack Fry sprawled on the earth, his blood seeping into the ground.

——————

The two days that followed had been nightmarish for Sabrina. She had lost track of time, for time had ceased to have meaning for her. All she knew was to get up and keep from being strangled as Fire Cloud dragged her through the forest. She stumbled through thickets with the branches scratching her face and arms and the cold air biting at her. At times the whole group waded through the creeks that the Indians sometimes followed for what seemed to be miles, and it occurred to her that they were doing this to shake off pursuit.

During the first night she had been terrified when Fire Cloud had come to stand over her. The thought of rape preoccupied her, and she knew Hannah had the same terrible fear. Fire Cloud leaned down and roughly caressed her body, then laughed as she drew back.

"You be Fire Cloud's squaw. Soon we be with my tribe." He turned his attention to Hannah, his hands exploring her body, and he laughed again as she tried to draw back. "You bring many horses. Many warriors want white slave."

After Fire Cloud left, the two women huddled together for warmth. They were hungry and exhausted from the endless hike. The Indians had taken lots of meat from the cabin, but they had shared very little with the two women.

As they traveled the next day, the nightmare repeated itself. Sabrina tried to take refuge in thinking of more pleasant times. She thought of her home in England and of the happy days she had had there when she was growing up, but mostly she thought of the cabin and of the happiness she had found there. It shocked her to realize that she had indeed known some of her happiest days in that cabin. Her memories were filled with Sion as he sat cleaning his rifle before the fire, or following the horse plowing the earth, or coming in with a bag of game. She could see his face clearly, although everything else seemed vague and indistinct.

By the second night Sabrina was completely exhausted. She knew she could not stand much more of this, and she feared that if she could not keep up, Fire Cloud would kill her. She knew life meant nothing to the war chief nor to the other Indians.

On the second night the Indians were all drinking again. They danced awkwardly, flinging their hands to the sky and shouting their songs to the forest. They came over to jerk at the women's hair, put their hands on them, and taunt them, but the Indians were too drunk to be much of a threat, and besides, Fire Cloud knocked one of them down with the flat of his tomahawk, claiming ownership of both women.

One of the Indians had killed a deer, and they butchered it roughly, sticking chunks of meat on sticks and roasting it over the fire. They ate most of it half cooked and some of it raw. Hannah had cooked two pieces and brought one part of it to Sabrina, urging her to eat.

"I can't."

"You have to, Sabrina. The men will be after us."

"They can't follow these trails."

"My father can, and Sequatchie will be with him. He can follow any trail. God's going to get us out of all this."

Sabrina took the tough meat and forced herself to chew and swallow it.

She lay huddled against Hannah, and finally the savages settled down. Fire Cloud came over and lay down beside Sabrina. He pulled at her for a while, and she knew that he intended to have her. But he was completely drunk now, and he finally fell back, his mouth open, and began to snore.

It was there in the darkness, in the vile embrace of a drunken savage, that Sabrina Fairfax felt the presence of God in a way she never had before. She had been weeping silently when suddenly a silence seemed to fall on her spirit. She could still hear the snores and mutterings of the Indians and the crackling of the fire, but that seemed far away. This silence was pregnant with meaning. It was not simply the absence of sound, but there was something—holy about it. *Holy,* that was the word. She could think of no other word that might describe it, and she suddenly remembered the many times her Christian friends had spoken of being "in the presence of the Lord."

Those words had had no meaning to Sabrina. She had never had an experience like that, but now as she lay there, the silence seemed to wrap her in a mantle, as if someone had wrapped a blanket about her. The blanket was warm and comforting, and Sabrina knew that this was not a natural thing at all.

For a long time she simply lay there calmly, aware that all fear had left her. She was no longer afraid of what would happen to her body. She no longer held any fear of the Indians. Even the fear of death, which had been with her constantly, had ceased to exist for her.

She thought of what Hannah had said about the eternal God's consciousness of all people at all times. And in her mind a simple prayer began to form, just a reaching out in thought into the silence that surrounded her. It was almost like a conversation, except she did not hear her own voice and she certainly did not hear an audible voice in response. Nevertheless, she knew she was speaking out of her heart to God as she never had before.

I don't know you, God. I've heard other people talk about you as if you were real, and I've longed for that. But I haven't been able to find you. I've been lost for such a long time, and I've envied those who could call you Father. I can't call you that, but I do call out to you wherever you are and whoever you are. Right here I know you're listening to me.

Sabrina lay quietly, and she remembered the text of the sermon on Christmas Day. *"Come unto me, all ye that labour and are heavy laden, and I will give you rest."* The words echoed inside Sabrina's heart. They reminded her as she went over them again and again of the sound of silver bells, and they were more beautiful than any words she had ever heard.

I need rest. I'm so tired, Lord, and I know that Jesus is the only answer. I ask you, Lord, to come and forgive me of my sins. I don't deserve anything, but Sion says you are a God of mercy, so I ask you to have mercy right now. Forgive my sins in the name of Jesus.

Sabrina paused, and the silence seemed to swell. She still heard no sound, but there was a song in her heart. She did not know the words, and she did not know the tune, but nevertheless, it was there. And as the song went on, she was conscious of a great shock and surprise. There was no fear left, and she whispered, "Father, thank you for Jesus."

Sabrina slept soundly that night. As the sun came up in the morning, she wondered if it had all been real and waited for the peace to leave and for the fear to return. It did not, and a great feeling of gladness came to her. She reached over and touched Hannah's shoulder and pulled her closer. Hannah whispered, "What is it, Sabrina?"

"I called upon the Lord, and He's done something to me. I'm not afraid, Hannah. I'm not afraid!"

Hannah immediately turned over and put her arm around Sabrina. She held her tightly and whispered fiercely, "No matter what happens to us now, you're a handmaiden of the Lord, Sabrina!"

Pursuit

Twenty-Three

*T*he men who had gathered around the cabin were all armed and wore grim faces. Sion silently struggled with the emotions that made a tumult within his heart. When he had returned to the cabin from a hunting trip with Fox and found signs of the raid and Sabrina missing, it had been Fox who had taken charge. He had commanded Sion to remain at the cabin in case the women returned and had ridden off to alert the Spencers and other neighbors. His last words had been, "Don't give up, Sion. She's not dead. My uncle can track a bird across the sky. We'll get her back."

Sion had listened with part of his mind, but something in him practically screamed to go charging out to look—to do something!

He had forced himself to remain calm as he examined the cabin for clues. He found no signs of blood. The cabin had been ransacked, as had his own lean-to. Many things had been destroyed, and other lighter things had been carried away. Fox had said the Indians were probably renegade Cherokee, but how he knew that Sion could not tell.

For what seemed like a long time he moved around the cabin touching things that belonged to Sabrina, his mind crying out and his spirit struggling with sinking into despair. He had heard all the tales of the cruelty of Indians to their captives. He had heard of some women carried away who had dropped off the earth, it seemed. Some of them had been saved years later but had practically forgotten their native tongue and had become toothless crones—not at all the women that had disappeared.

But Fox had come back with a small party. Hawk Spencer was there, of course, with Joshua, and Andrew McNeal and Seth Donovan had joined them. Sequatchie had been visiting with Hawk, and he had come along too.

Sion was relieved when he saw the men ride into the yard, and he heard Hawk call out, "Sequatchie, you find their tracks out of here before we mess them up." Sequatchie covered the ground quickly. He went to the edge of the clearing, leaning over and moving back and forth like a dog on the scent. Joshua came over to say bitterly, "Hannah's gone, too. She had come over to visit Sabrina."

Hawk joined the two, saying, "I've got a man out raising more men. We'll have a hundred militia here, but we can't wait. We'll leave now. Are you going, Sion?"

"Aye." Sion's voice was flat.

"Get your weapons, then. We'll take any food we can. We won't have time to stop and hunt."

As the others prepared to leave, Hawk said, "They didn't kill them outright, Sion. That's good news. It means they want them as captives."

"They'll mistreat them, won't they?"

"Maybe not if we move fast enough. They know we'll be after them, so they'll be going as fast as they can. The harder we push them, the better the chance they'll be unharmed."

"Then let's go after them," Sion said grimly.

Sion joined the party with Sequatchie in the lead. Hawk was right behind him, and the rest of them followed in single file. They traveled hard, stopping just long enough to get a drink with their cupped hands from a creek.

"It's a good thing we've got Sequatchie here, Sion," Josh said as the two trotted along. "He's the best tracker among the Cherokees, which means he's the best there is, I think."

"I don't mind telling you that I'm worried sick."

"We have to put that aside. We can worry later. We've got some praying men here. You and me. Hawk, Sequatchie. All of us are praying men, as a matter of fact. I can't think of a better group to have out on a job like this."

Josh's words encouraged Sion, and he turned his attention to the task at hand. He was happy to find that he could keep pace with the rest of the men. He knew he could not have done this when he first arrived, but now he had become a woodsman himself, though not as skilled as many of the others in the party. They had been at it for a lifetime, while he'd only lived here for a few months. Still, he determined, *I'll die before I drop aside. If I need to, I'll run until my legs are run off at the knees.*

Sion's thoughts were interrupted when suddenly Sequatchie held up his hand and uttered a cry as he slid off his horse.

"Something's up," Josh said.

Sion moved forward with the rest of the men with fear in his heart. What he feared most was to find the body of one of the women. Sequatchie had indeed come upon a dead body, but it was clearly the body of a man with a horrifying wound to the back of his head. Sequatchie rolled the man over so they could see his face.

"It's Jack Fry!" Sion said aloud.

"Yes. He got a hatchet in his head," Sequatchie added.

"I don't think it was an accident," Sion said.

The men turned to look at him. "What do you mean by that?" Hawk asked.

"I think he was behind this raid. Everyone knows he worked for Caleb Files."

"You may be right. Caleb's a shrewd man. He wouldn't be connected with it, but he'd send Fry to do his dirty work."

"Well, he didn't get it done," Fox said, staring down at the body. "Something went wrong. I wonder what?"

"We don't have time to wonder about it. Dig a hole and dump him in it. We'll bury him."

"He doesn't deserve it," Josh said, "but I guess we can do that much for him."

The men made quick work of digging a shallow grave. They put Jack Fry's body in it, and Seth Donovan said a quick prayer for him. Then Fox said, "Let's go. We've lost time."

As darkness fell, Sequatchie finally called them to a halt, saying, "We can't go on. I can't read the signs."

"Can't we just continue on?" Sion asked, dreading the thought of stopping.

"If we missed them, it would be all over," Hawk said. "We'll rest, and we'll move on at first light."

Joshua started a fire, and they worked together to cook some of the venison they had brought along.

Fox sat down beside Sion and was quiet for a time. Finally Fox said, "I can't eat, Sion. I know Christians aren't supposed to worry, but I am worried."

"So am I. I don't see how anybody keeps from it. I've got faith, but still I keep thinking about Sabrina and Hannah in the hands of those savages."

Fox stared down at his hands and said, "I didn't know how much love I had for Hannah until I had to face up to losing her."

Sion did not answer, and Fox asked, "You think that's wrong, Sion, that a man can love a woman too much?"

Sion turned with surprise. "I don't know. I never thought of it like that. I know God has to come first, but after God a man should love his wife with all of his heart."

"Even more than children, do you think?"

"I think so. More than anything. It's hard to divide love like that."

Fox was quiet, and the two men listened as Hawk and Sequatchie spoke of their plans for the next day from across the fire.

After a time Sion said, "I found out something about myself."

"What's that?"

"I love Sabrina."

"You never told her that?"

"How could I do that, Fox? I'm her servant. She's a woman of property."

"That wouldn't matter if she cared for you."

"I think you're right." Sion dropped his head down on his arms, which were folded across his knees. "I wish I had told her," he whispered.

"You'll have a chance," Fox said. "Let's pray again. I've

been praying in my heart all the time, but I need to hear a pray-er's voice."

Fox prayed a short but fervent prayer, and then Sion prayed also. He had difficulty finding the words he wanted to say, but he cried out to God hoarsely, "Lord, I ask you to preserve their lives, keep them safe, lead us to them."

Others in the party became aware of what the two men were doing and soon all of the men were praying.

Finally, when the prayers died down, Hawk turned to his friend and said, "Sequatchie, I've never seen anything like that."

"These are praying men. Men of God. God's going to honor our prayers, friend."

They rose before dawn, ate a cold breakfast of meat left over from the night before, drank deeply from the stream, and then followed Sequatchie as he led them out again.

They traveled hard, and once Seth Donovan dropped back to say to Sion, "They're trying to lose our trail. Have you noticed how they've led us through creek beds?"

"Yes. They're clever."

"Not as clever as Sequatchie."

Sion found he put great faith in Sequatchie. The old Indian said little, and he looked like he was tired, but he sniffed out the trail as a hound would sniff out a deer or any other animal he was pursuing. Each time the trail disappeared into a creek, he made the whole party stop, and he traveled both sides of the creek until he figured out where they had come out.

"I don't see how he does it," Sion said in despair.

"It's something that's born in a man. You can learn a little tracking," Hawk answered as he joined the conversation, "but the good ones have a gift."

It was late afternoon that day when Sequatchie suddenly brought the party to a halt. They all hurried forward, and Sequatchie shook his head. "They have split up. Some went this way and some that."

"Can you tell which party the women are with?"

"No, the trail's too faint."

"We'll have to divide up. We can't take any chances on missing the right party," Hawk said. There was no uncertainty in his voice, and he looked over the group and said, "Andrew, you and Seth go with me. Fox, you, Sion, and Joshua go with Sequatchie. Just remember that we'll be outnumbered. I make out there's at least ten of them."

Sion knew it had to be done. He had counted on a full party to battle against the Indians, but now there was no hope of that.

Fox must have read his thoughts. "Don't worry," he said. "We'll find them, and we'll come on them by surprise."

The two groups went their separate ways, with Hawk leading his party.

Sequatchie looked at the faces of the men in his party. "Fox, you must help me track. I'm getting tired."

Fox immediately joined Sequatchie. The party moved forward, and when they crossed the stream it was Fox who ran quickly to his left. He returned after half an hour and went the other way. This time he was back in ten minutes. "They came out down this way."

They pressed the trail all day and finally, not long before sunset, Sequatchie called the men together. "Look."

The men gathered around to look at the definite footprint in the sandy soil.

"You see how fresh it is?" said Sequatchie, who could read a trail as a scholar could read a book. "You see the edges are not crumbled in yet. They're not more than an hour ahead. Maybe even less."

"What'll we do?" Sion asked.

"Someone must go locate them, and then we must creep in after darkness. We can't wait until dawn. We have to catch them by surprise. Their party is smaller than it was before, of course, but we don't know how many. I think at least five."

"Those aren't long odds," Josh said.

"I know. Fox, you must go," said his uncle. "But remember, if they see you, it's all up with us. You must go like the fox you were named after. Be as still as a mouse with your eyes like the eagle's."

"Yes, Uncle," Fox said. He turned and disappeared at once, his eyes down on the ground.

"He is a good man," Sequatchie said. "I'm very proud of Fox. Everyone check your weapons. Fox will come back soon, and then we must creep in on them. Not everyone is as quiet as Fox, but this time we must be."

"He's coming," Sequatchie said, and instantly the men all got to their feet. They had been tensely listening but had heard nothing until Sequatchie spoke.

Now Sion looked and saw nothing in the darkness, but finally he heard a voice say, "I'm here." Fox's dark form finally appeared only a few feet away. There was practically no moon overhead and only the light of a few stars broke the darkness.

"They're about a half a mile from here."

"How can we approach them, Nephew?" Sequatchie asked, and everyone noticed that Sequatchie had turned the command of the small force over to Fox.

"Most of them are drunk."

"Did you see Sabrina and Hannah?"

"Yes. They're there, and they're safe. I heard them speak to each other."

A rain of pure joy opened up in Sion. "Thank God!" he breathed.

"Yes," Fox said. "Thank God, indeed. We cannot wait until morning."

"How will we attack them, Nephew?"

"I listened to their conversation long enough to learn they have only one scout out. I think there are five of them at the camp. We will surprise the scout, and I will take him silently. As soon as he is dead, we'll all rush in."

Sequatchie said, "They may try to kill the women if we give them time, so we must be swift. Swifter than the striking snake."

"Just get me close enough," Sion said. "That's all I ask."

"Battle is a hard thing, but we must save our people," Sequatchie said. "Fox, is it time?"

"It is time," Fox said. "Stay close behind me."

Fire Cloud had been angry. He had split his forces to divide and confuse his pursuers, but he still somehow knew that the enemy was closing in on him. Bitterly he wished he had kept his whole band together so they could ambush those who came. They would have had a much better chance. Now he saw the folly of letting his men have whiskey. They were so drunk they could barely stand and would have been completely unconscious if he had not finally taken the whiskey away from them. Now the whiskey was in his own bag, and a murderous anger was boiling over in him.

His eyes fell on the two women, and he strode over to where they were seated on the ground. He grabbed Sabrina by the hair and twisted her head up. "I ought to take your scalp— as I was paid to do!" Fire Cloud began to curse her. He slapped her with his free hand, and when she looked back at him defiantly, this angered him even more. "You are proud! You won't be for long!" He grabbed her coat and ripped it as he pulled at it. "I'll have you now! I'll make a squaw out of you! You not be proud then!"

Sabrina knew there was no escaping this man, and she prayed a formless, wordless supplication, knowing that her life was in her Lord's hands. But still she was shocked that she knew so little fear.

Fire Cloud gave her hair another jerk as he threw her down and pulled at her clothing. Sabrina was fighting him off as well as she could when suddenly a shot broke the stillness of the night. Instantly Fire Cloud fell onto Sabrina with a grunt. He lay on her inertly for a moment before Sabrina realized he had been shot. She struggled to shove his body off, and by the light of the fire she saw the other Indians scrambling to their feet. Several shots rang out, and she saw two of the Indians fall at once and one run blindly into the darkness. Still more shots rang out, and a voice cried out in English.

Sabrina scrambled to huddle beside Hannah, trying to stay out of the path of the gunfire.

"They've come for us!" Hannah cried in a glad voice. "Look, there they are!"

Sabrina could see little, for her eyes were filled with tears, but then a man was before her, and she felt his hands take hers, and he lifted her to her feet. Before she knew what was happening, she felt herself enfolded in his arms. "Sion!"

"Are you all right?"

"Yes."

"I have to tell you, Sabrina. When I thought I'd lost you, it was as if the sun went out."

Sabrina was trembling. Now that she was safe, the weakness she had kept at bay since she had been captured was suddenly overwhelming her. She knew she would fall if he let go of her.

"I prayed you'd come," she whispered.

He kissed her cheek and then held her tightly. "God is good," he whispered.

"Yes, He is."

Hannah heard all of this, and then suddenly Fox was there sitting beside her.

He did not touch her for a moment, and then he traced the tears running down her face with a shaky hand. "You're all right," he said quietly. She moved closer and put her arms around him. She kissed him, and when he lifted his head, he said, "I need you, Hannah."

Hannah said as simply as she had ever spoken in her life, "And I need you, Fox."

A Wedding and a Proposal

Twenty-Four

*A*ndy Jackson was a man possessed of a violent temper. On most occasions he was able to keep it under control, for he knew the dangers of uncontrolled anger. Now, however, as he stood before Caleb Files on the street, the rage that had been just beneath the surface boiled over. He took a step toward Files, who suddenly turned pale and held up his hand as if to stop Jackson physically.

"You're a scoundrel, Files!" Jackson continued to reel off a string of derogatory names until finally, glaring at the smaller man, he declared, "I may not be able to prove it in court, but I know you're behind that Indian raid on my client!"

"I had nothing to do with it!"

"Shut your foul mouth!" Jackson said. "Your henchman, Jack Fry, did the dirty work, but everybody in the territory knows you give him his orders."

"I tell you, Jackson, I know nothing about it! Fry had a grudge against the Fairfax woman's servant. They had trouble earlier. You know that."

"The man—that Kenyon—wasn't convinced. It was the woman who was carried off. One of the Indians didn't die. With a little persuasion he told the whole story. They were supposed to kill the woman. That was Fry's order, and that's why Fry himself was killed. That Cherokee he hired—Fire Cloud—decided to keep the two women alive, and when Fry tried to kill them, he got an ax in his brain. The world won't miss him much. But as for you, I've had enough of you!" Jackson slapped Files across the face. "There! I'll let you choose weapons. Knives. Guns. Whatever you want."

"I won't fight you, Jackson."

"You won't! You sniveling coward! I'm gonna get my whip out of my buggy and use it on you!"

A crowd had gathered around the two men, hugely enjoying the scene. Files was not a popular man, and Andrew Jackson always provided good drama. One of the men in the back said, "He's going to cut Files to pieces with that whip. I wish my brother were here to see this."

Jackson glared at Files, his face pale with anger. "You're lower than a snake's belly. I'm going to cut you into ribbons, and when you get over it, I'm going to hunt you up and do it again. So either fight or get out of Tennessee Country!"

Files swallowed hard, and his face worked. Every man in the crowd saw that his hands were trembling uncontrollably.

Suddenly Files turned and ran down the street, and a great roar went up from the crowd. Jackson relaxed then. He laughed, and his eyes sparkled. "Well, folks, I rid you of at least one scoundrel."

One of the spectators said, "Come along, Andy. Let's have that poker game now. I intend to clean you out."

"Nope. I've got to go see a lady. I've got some good news for her!"

Hawk and Elizabeth sat on the front porch enjoying the warm March afternoon, sipping their hot tea. Hawk reached over and picked up Elizabeth's hand with his free one and said, "You know, I don't think I'll mind being a grandfather, but I'm sure going to hate being married to a grandma."

Elizabeth simply laughed at him. "Don't step on your beard, Grandpa."

"Well, we've been the finest-looking couple in the whole Territory South of the River Ohio. Now we'll be the finest-looking grandparents."

"You're pretty sure about all of this? Fox hasn't even asked for Hannah's hand in marriage yet."

"It's going to happen any day now."

"Yes, I imagine you're right. She and Fox are so in love. Isn't it sweet?"

"I remember it was pretty sweet when I was courting you."

"You! You weren't much of a courting man. I had to do most of the courting."

"But I made up for it. I've been studying up. I've been working on a poem for you. When I get it finished, I'm going to read it to you. Why, you'll cry your eyes out over it, it's so sweet."

"I don't think I'll hold my breath waiting for you to write a poem," Elizabeth said as Fox rode up on his fine bay stallion. He stepped out of the saddle and tied the horse up.

"Hello, sir. How are you, Mrs. Spencer?"

"We're fine. Have a seat, Fox."

"No, sir. I've got something to say to you."

"Well, you can't have her," Hawk said abruptly. He saw the distraught look on Fox's face, and then Elizabeth reached over and slapped at him.

"You shut your mouth, Hawk Spencer! This is serious."

Hawk stood up. "I'm too much of a joker, I guess. Of course Hannah's mother and I are pleased to give our daughter to you. That is what you were going to ask me, isn't it?"

Fox drew a hand that was not steady across his forehead. "Yes, sir. It took more nerve to come here and ask you than it did to attack those Indians."

"I don't know of any man who I'd rather have as a son-in-law. Well, go on in and see if you can convince her. It's not hard to handle a woman. Just cut yourself a switch. Use it on her every time she don't behave as you'd like."

Elizabeth laughed. "Yes, you've worn out quite a few switches on me."

Fox laughed with her. "I imagine I'd use about the same number on Hannah. Thank you, sir. Thank you, Ma," he said as he went into the cabin.

"He called me Ma," Elizabeth said. "Isn't that sweet?"

"He's hungry for a mother's love. He needs a ma and pa just like their kids will need a good, fine, handsome grandpa, and a grandma, too, of course."

Fox found Hannah washing dishes. She turned to him, and before she could speak he said, "Well, woman, it's time we started."

Hannah was startled at his abrupt beginning. "Started doing what?"

Fox drew her into his arms. "Building a cabin. Planting crops." He laughed and winked at her. "Starting a family."

Hannah put her hands against his chest. "Just a second. You haven't asked my parents yet."

"Yes I have. They were tickled to death to get such a fine son-in-law. What about you?"

Hannah could not resist his new mood. He was light-hearted and his eyes danced. She put her arms around him and said, "I'm ready, Fox."

Fox kissed her and whispered, "I've waited for you all my life, Hannah Spencer!"

────────

The church was packed for the wedding of Nathanael Carter and Hannah Spencer. Sabrina sat beside Sion in the row next to the front. Always before in church he had kept himself far back as befitted a servant, but she had taken his arm and said, "Come along."

Sion pressed her hand and led her down the aisle, and they took their seat. They sat there while Fox and Hannah came to stand before Rev. Paul Anderson. Sabrina glowed as the couple said their words firmly and with such obvious love that it touched her.

Finally the pastor said, "By the authority vested in me by the United States Territory South of the River Ohio, I now pronounce you man and wife. You can kiss your bride, Nathanael."

Fox turned and kissed Hannah soundly.

The church was small, and everyone took their turn at wishing the bride and groom and their parents the best, then they all gathered for the reception. Sabrina joined the other young women who served, and finally Hannah was free of well-wishers long enough to come over. "You look beautiful, Hannah. It was a lovely wedding."

"It was, wasn't it? I know I'll never forget it."

"You and Fox will be very happy together."

"What about you?"

"What about me?" Sabrina asked with surprise.

"When will you get married?"

Sabrina looked down and did not answer for a time. "I haven't been asked."

"Of course you haven't been asked. Sion's your servant. He can't ask you. You'll have to ask him."

Sabrina blinked with surprise. "I'd never ask a man to marry me."

"That's your pride speaking," Hannah said. "But pride isn't much of a bed partner on cold nights."

Sabrina stared at Hannah and then nodded. "I think you're right." She turned and watched Sion, who was talking with Sequatchie over to one side eating cake, and something changed in her face. It grew softer, gentler, and she tapped her chin thoughtfully. "You may be right, Hannah. You may be right."

Sion was outside splitting wood as Sabrina prepared their supper. He had been moody ever since the wedding two days ago, and Sabrina had kept to herself a great deal. She had been praying a lot, trying to find who she really was and what she wanted to do. She had also spent a good deal of time with Elizabeth Spencer, who had been a great comfort to her. So much had happened to Sabrina that at times she wondered if she was still the same woman she had been in England. She thought back to the selfishness that had marked her early life and could not believe some of the things she had done. She finally had confessed to Elizabeth that she was grieved over the selfishness and the sins of those times.

"They're all buried in the sea of God's forgiveness," Elizabeth had said firmly. "You are a new woman now starting all over again. God has given you a clean sheet, and what will be there will be what you put there."

Andrew Jackson had also paid a visit to triumphantly tell her that the land was now hers free and clear. "I've run Files out of the territory," he had said triumphantly as he handed her the deed. "You own this land. It's yours forever, Miss Fairfax."

Now a firmness and a resolve came to Sabrina. She straightened up, and a smile touched the corners of her lips. "All right, Mr. Sion Kenyon," she said aloud. "We'll see what's in you." Walking to the door, she called loudly, "Sion, that's enough wood! Come in. Supper's on the table."

Sion said little as the two ate. He listened as Sabrina talked about Fox and Hannah and their plans for a new life. "They're going to build a house. Not a cabin, but a real house out of boards, with glass windows in it."

"I know. Fox told me. I'm going to help him. I'm a pretty fair carpenter."

"Could you build a house by yourself?"

"I couldn't saw the boards up into lumber. A sawmill has to do that, or else you can do it in a saw pit."

"What's a saw pit?"

"You put a log on a high platform. You dig a hole, and one man gets in the hole and the other man gets on top. You start moving the saw up and down. It's not much fun being in the pit. Sawdust in your mouth, eyes, everywhere."

"But you could do it, couldn't you?"

"Why, of course I could, Sabrina. You know I can build anything I set my mind to."

Sion became more talkative and his good humor returned as he explained how he would build a house if he ever had the chance. Sabrina listened to him and asked him lots of questions. After the meal he bit into the huckleberry pie she had made and said, "You've become a good cook."

"Thank you. Not as good as Hannah or Elizabeth."

"Well, you've got time to learn. I'm not as good a woodsman as Hawk or Josh either."

"You've done wonderfully well, Sion."

His cloudy mood seemed to return and he looked to be filled with doubt. Sabrina turned to wash the dishes as Sion settled in the chair by the fire with his feet resting next to Ulysses, who was stretched out to soak up the warmth of the fire.

Sabrina glanced at Sion from time to time as she washed the dishes. It was clear that something was bothering him. He held a book in his hand, but it was unopened. He was staring into the fire, and while he was not looking she was admiring his profile. He had always been a strong man, and his wilderness experience had made him even stronger. Not just physically, but in his spirit.

Sabrina dried her hands and then went over to the table and opened the chest where she kept letters and papers. She took two documents out and stood holding them for a minute. She glanced at Sion and for a moment her nerve almost failed, but she straightened up and told herself, *Come along, Sabrina. You must do this.*

She walked over to stand by Sion. "I have two things to show you."

Sion stood up at once, as he always did in her presence. He took the paper Sabrina held out to him and stared at it. "This is the title to your land," he said, looking up.

"Yes, but it's a clear title now. Mr. Jackson says there's no question about it. The land is ours."

Her words caught at Sion. "Not ours. It's yours."

Sabrina did not answer. She hesitated and then handed him the second paper. "I want you to have this, Sion."

Sion looked at it. It was the paper he had signed agreeing to be her indentured servant for five years. He saw that she had written something at the bottom and held it up to the fire. He read the words aloud. " 'I do hereby set Sion Kenyon free from the articles described in this agreement. Sabrina Fairfax.' " He turned to her.

Sabrina knew that Hannah had been right. Sion would never ask for her hand as long as he was her servant. Now she felt fear run through her. What if he refused her? She didn't want to even consider that possibility. Instead, she very boldly put her arms around his neck. "You're not a servant now, Sion. You're just a man. You're free."

"I'm free to do what?" Sion said, conscious of her arms going around his neck and of her body so close to his.

"Free to do—anything you want."

Sion searched her eyes, and Sabrina looked at him with longing. He kissed her, and she clung to him with a sense of dependence. He held her for a long time and then said quietly,

"But I have nothing. People will say that I want you for your land."

"Do you want me?"

"You know I do."

"For my land?"

"Of course not."

"Then do what a man does when he loves a woman."

Suddenly Sion Kenyon saw a new life opening up before him, and he knew that he would share it with this woman. "I love you more than I love air or water or food."

"Tell me how beautiful I am and how much you love me. Say all the things that men say to women they love."

Sion held her tight, then kissed her again and said, "Will you have me then?"

"Yes, we'll have each other."

**The World Is Spiraling Toward Destruction,
and One Man Receives a Divine Mandate. . . .**

Young Noah has found life good and wholesome . . . until
he steps outside his village and discovers a world of tempta-
tion. Drawn by a beautiful woman yet repulsed by the pagan
practices of her tribe's dark worship, his inner struggle keeps
him in torment.

Noah strains to hear the voice of God—through the warn-
ings of a prophet, through the kind teachings of his grandfather Methuselah, through the loving concern of his family,
and ultimately through personal confrontation. The message
he receives is terrifying. Will he find the courage to obey?

Opposition intensifies to the call he has received, and a
precious medallion handed down from ancient times reminds
him of who he is—a man with a . . .

Heart of a Lion
Book 1 in the LIONS OF JUDAH series
ISBN: 0-7642-2681-9

Dear reader,

Many years ago, someone suggested: "Gil, why don't you write a series of biblically based novels tracing one family from the Flood to the birth of Jesus?" At the time I was too busy to consider such a thing, but the seed fell into the ground. Six years later, the LIONS OF JUDAH came to me in a rush, each story idea falling into place with seemingly little effort on my part. Naturally each novel has to be hammered out with all the skill I possess, but the first novel, *Heart of a Lion,* seemed almost to write itself.

One goal of every good novelist is to give pleasure, to entertain. The other is to edify, to give the reader more than pleasure. The Scripture says "He who prophesies speaks edification and exhortation and comfort." I am certainly no prophet, but I want every novel I write to accomplish these things.

Every story in the LIONS OF JUDAH series is intended to give pleasure, but I want readers to *learn* something, too. I stick as closely as I can to accurate history. I also try to paint a reasonable picture of how ancient people lived from day to day. I hope to offer readers an overview of the Old Testament, fixing in their minds the general history of the times and putting the heroes of the faith in the spotlight. Not as a *substitute* for the Scripture. Far from it! Indeed, my hope is that readers will turn to the Bible as a result of reading these books.

I want these novels to exhort, as well, to somehow give the reader a desire to become a more faithful servant of God. Most modern fiction does exactly the *opposite* of this—it urges the reader to indulge in the false values that have come to dominate our society. I spent many years teaching the so-called "great" novels at a Christian university. Many such novels stress the values of this world, not those of God. But I believe fine novels *can* dramatize godly values—without being "preachy."

Finally, great novels give comfort. I don't know how this works, but some books give me assurance and build my faith that dark times are not forever. God, of course, is the source of all comfort, but I know he uses poetry and fiction as well as people.

I pray that the LIONS OF JUDAH will give pleasure, enlightenment, motivation, and comfort to faithful readers.

Parents and teachers, here are books that will introduce young people in your charge to the most important history of all—how God brought the Messiah into the world to save us from our sins. I trust that the men and women of the Old Testament will come alive for readers young and old, so that they are not dim figures in a dusty history, but dynamic bearers of the seed that would redeem the human race.

Sincerely,

Gilbert Morris